1

ALSO BY BRAD BEALS…

Raising Ebenezer

The Road Parables

Blood Bound

The Book of Waters

CATASTROPOLIS

CATASTROPOLIS

A NOVEL

by Brad Beals

For my children,
And for theirs

PART I

Chapter 1

My neighbors see this endeavor as a chartered under-taking, a kind of public work sanctioned by the good people of New Alaiedon Township. They want to be a part of it, and I understand that, for the history I'm recording is theirs as much as it is mine. Word of this work has spread far and wide, so at all opportunities they present to me their offerings. I try to accept them with grace.

A funeral last week brought me this: Hank Gailey whispering in one ear that I must remember the corn blight of ten years prior, and his grandson in the other that I must not forget those awful tornadoes that took houses on three straight days. Three straight days! Noah Street, who boards our cow and delivers our milk in the morning, is a walking catalog of obituaries filed by year and cause of death. His wife, who accompanies him on alternate days, manages the births, and between them I have received a kind of local census at no fee.

Be it calamity or bounty, signs in the heavens or at our feet, all of it – if I am to take my neighbors' direction – all of it would have a place in this chronicle. And yet, as varied and as broadly cast as the scraps are, there is one memory that recurs in us, in all of us from that first generation. At the conclusion of an interview or following a re-lived bygone that simply must have its own chapter, my New Alaiedon neighbor will go wistful and nostalgic, or steely-eyed and amazed, and he will remember him. He may share a story, or he may go quiet for a time at the recollection. Sometimes a hand will rise of its own impulse and touch lightly, a spot on the forehead. But eventually, they will all say something like, "Tell them about Josiah. You must tell them all about Josiah Mench."

"Naturally," I reply. "We would have no story at all without Josiah Mench."

But for all the help, I can find no good starting point for this work. I search the space near me for inspiration. At my elbow a tallow wick burns a dirty light and blackens the stone of the wall behind it. Shelves on the wall hold pots and pans for winter cooking on the woodstove, crock jars of ball and cap for the muzzleloaders, traps oiled clean and

8

wrapped in linen. On the highest shelf, my gaze lingers. And then it is caught.

This one holds an odd-and-end assortment of books, but I see something else squeezed between Owen's *Mortification of Sin* and Malgainge's *Operative Surgery*. I unwedge it from its place. It is slim, rectangular, made of glass and plastic, and no bigger than my open hand. The engineering of it is a kind of awful mystery to us now, and it seems a dream as I think back on it, but I tell the truth, and there are plenty still living who can attest to this – there was a time when I could touch its surface and bring all the wonders of the world to me in sound and light and moving pictures.

It is a phone. I hold it under the shifting light and wipe the dust from the screen. As far as I know, the magical things – the music and visions, the messages from those long dead – are still locked inside. I run a fingertip over the glass, I press a button on the side, and I put it to my ear. It has not made a sound these many decades, and it's as dead as stone now, but as I hold it there, something does come. Memories. People, places, a happy parade of small days. I stare down the line of them, and though there is much – I am surprised at how much I remember – none of it is the starting point I'm looking for. There is no bridge between the ages as I had hoped.

But then I do see something. Beneath my own thumbnail is a line of black soot, a remnant of that day's work, and at the sight of it another memory comes. I think of Josiah Mench's father whose palm creases and fingernails were forever etched with engine oil, and I think of the trailer, the window, the shaking walls, and the bubbling blood on his lips. Then I remember that he was the first I'd ever seen, the first of thousands.

I knew it would end with Josiah, but only now does it make sense that it should start with him too. I should have thought of that. I should have just listened to my old friends from the beginning, that I must remember Josiah Mench.

Chapter 2

It's been cold these last weeks, but on this night a warm wind pushes the frost right out. Great clumps of damp snow are falling, hitting the drive and the porch roof like lobbed balls. I stand at the window and watch it, not thinking real hard, and half wondering at how strange the sight is. Just as I realize it's snow being blown from the pines that tower over our house, Josiah's face, white and surprised, is there in the window, and I let out a yell.

"What?" says Mom.

She is on the floor by the woodstove, her usual winter spot. She is reading a book.

"It's Jo. He scared me."

"Jo Mench? Outside?"

"Yep."

"Well let him in."

I open the door and stand aside to let him know he's invited in. He wears a heavy flannel jacket, and as he stands next to the stove the snow on his shoulders and sleeves begins to melt. The coat warms and gives off a stench of cigarettes and sour sweat. He was never clean, and wasn't encouraged in such things at home, but Mom always acted like she didn't notice, like he was just another neighbor to be welcomed in. Mom also thought Jo was some kind of genius.

"You're whiter than usual, Josiah," she says, and stands and takes up a spot next to him. "What's wrong?"

"Dad's sick," he answers and pushes a lock of slick, brown hair out of his eyes.

Though we were born just a week apart, he is shorter than I am by a head, and lighter even than Jack, my little brother. Mom looks him over for a moment and seems stuck for words.

"Sick how?" She asks, finally. "Sick like last year, maybe?"

"No. Worse this time. There's something ain't right, Miss Taylor. He don't talk right. And he's bleedin…"

"Bleeding where?" She takes a step from the stove and faces him. "Is he hurt?"

"Not hurt. Just sick. And bleeding all over."

She looks up at the ceiling like she's checking for cobwebs. She closes her eyes and rests her palm against her forehead.

"How much blood?" she says to the ceiling.

"All over, Miss Taylor. Blood comin out… from every…Not a lot though, it's thin, like…like…"

"Like sweat," says Mom, but she's not asking. She's finishing his thought.

"Yeah, like sweat."

Mom smiles quickly at us both and steps into the kitchen. I stand next to him, but I'm listening hard for what she might be doing. No sound comes, and I know then that she is crying or praying. I know now that she was also struggling with whether to go with Jo or to send him back alone with an armload of gauze and pain killer.

She goes of course. She tells me to stay back, to watch the littles, but I don't stay back either.

Jo lives with his dad in a trailer on Dobie Lake. It's not more than a quarter mile away, but there are only the deer trails to follow, so it's slow walking. I hold back just far enough to keep them in view, which isn't hard. I can see them against the snow, and the westerly wind covers the sound of my walking.

At the trailer, I stand on an empty dog house, just out of the window light. I can see into the bedroom but the window is small. I get glimpses of Mom and Jo worrying over the old man, moving from one part of the trailer back to the bedroom. Occasionally, I hear Mom give a command to Jo, who runs down the narrow hall, feet thumping like he's in a race.

It's warm for January but still pretty cold for standing stock still in the wind. I decide I want to see Mr. Mench, so I climb down from the dog house and move a five gallon pail to the window. I come at an angle so I can see the back corner of the room, and so Mom won't see me. His head is turned to the wall away from me, and Mom is just taking a wet rag from his head. I can see her arms.

He turns over. His face looks like someone has wiped wine over it, and his pillow is splotched with pink. His eyes are pointed at me, but they are unfixed, like they're not plugged into the seeing part of his brain. They go big for a moment, then close.

11

Just then, the lit eyes of a possum come around the front of the trailer, and I catch myself from yelling out. It waddles through the yard and sniffs at the dog house and is gone. I look into the window again and can now see blood on Mr. Mench's lips, dark, heavy blood, like engine oil. There are just bubbles of it at first. Then there is more. He opens his eyes wide, and the black blood rises up thick from his open mouth, and it falls like a solid thing to the floor.

His body goes stiff and jerks hard on the bed. I have a gloved hand against the trailer for balance against the wind. I can feel the vibration of his shaking, and I pull my hand away like I've touched a live wire. When he does finally go still, Mom's hands reach for his head, but I don't know what she does with it. I am off the bucket and running home by then, and I don't stop until I hit the back porch. The Dying is here now. It won't stay in the cities or pass us by as we thought it might, and there is nothing left to do but to watch it take whomever it will.

It will take us all, just about, and in its trail it will leave a fear. Not the fear of death or even the dying part of death, but a fear without shape or name, a fear as predominant as night.

Chapter 3

I find it hard now to reach back across that line. It's as if a gate has shut on my memories prior to it. There was a time before, I know that, but my mind doesn't keep it as though it belonged to me. Rather, it sits in my head the way photos belonging to someone else might sit in my hand. The images are still and isolated, and nothing in my memory gives them motion or puts bridges between them. They fade, but nothing new comes in, nothing is added.

So it's hard now to give an account of how we saw it coming. Mr. Mench wasn't the first I knew of the Dying. I remember an aunt and uncle passing on the same day. And I remember a time when we stopped going into Lansing, and there was a time when we stopped going anywhere. It's like the Dying was only a shadow before Mr. Mench. Then the thing itself came round a corner and I could see it plain, and I've long since forgotten what the shadow ever looked like.

Mom doesn't come home the next day, so I go back to the Menches. The trail winds close to the lake before turning west up to a higher spot where the trailer sits. Just off the path is a little arbor among a few small pines, and in it is a wide spot of earth scraped bare of snow. Jo has tried to dig a hole there, but the ground is frozen. In lieu of a hole, he's mounded up a pile of paving stones and broken cinder block. Next to the pile, his dad lies on the ground, rolled up in a blue tarp. I yell for Mom, and right off can hear the trailer rocking on its blocks. The door opens.

"Who's that?" a high voice comes from the door, but it's Jo's.

I wave my arms over my head, and he comes bounding through the littered yard and down the trail. We stand there for a moment, kicking at the ground, neither of us quite knowing what to say.

"Ground's hard," I say.

"Yeah."

"Maybe up higher in the woods it'd be softer."

He shakes his head at that.

"Here's the spot. You can see the lake from it. I'll cover him good to keep the coyotes off, and dig a little each day. Should have a hole before spring."

Josiah has a way of speaking, a resolution in his tone that invites no appeal. You can't argue with him because he leaves no crack to pry into.

"You can't just leave him here."

"Why not?"

"It's a . . . it's a body. They have places…They…"

Josiah looks at me. He is being patient with me.

"Things are different now," he says.

I don't yet have a sense of what he means by that, and I'm tired.

"I'll help you dig," I say.

"That'd be good."

The wind has died down over the night, and though it is early yet, I can tell it'll be a warm day, warm as winter goes. The sun is peaking through the trees and shining on the wet snow. I see Mr. Mench's socked toes sticking out from the tarp and have this thought: that it is a pretty morning. I am surprised then at thinking such a thing and at such a time.

"Is she still here?" I ask. "My mom? She never came home last night."

"She slept here in a chair till the sun came up, then left. Never made it back?"

"No."

"She should be easy to track.."

Jo runs up the trail and right away starts nosing off behind the trailer. I follow. Her tracks lead from the door, across the yard toward the trail and our house, but then veer left like she's changed her mind and rise up into the hardwoods. There, she has walked along another trail, wide enough for people, but marked here and there with deer droppings. She had stopped to sit on a downed log, had sat there long enough for her feet to melt a patch of snow. Then her tracks go on in longer strides as though she has rested up or, as I've thought since, made herself determined.

"Where's she going?" I ask Jo, who is moving fast enough to keep me winded. "Why didn't she just walk up the drive?"

Jo stops, and I see his eyes flash back to the trailer, up the trail we're on, and beyond us in the direction the tracks are leading. His eyes go narrow – it is a look I will soon come to know well.

"She didn't want to go home, but she didn't want the road either. The Gellises and Tripps live back here. She knows them, right?"

Jean Tripp is one of her best friends. Mom had been on the phone with her just two days before, talking her through some crisis. She is probably checking up on her.

We step from the woods into the Gellises' backyard and follow her tracks straight across it, through a hedge, and then up to the next house, the Tripps. I knock hard on the sunporch door, then wait. I am just turning to go around the house to look into windows when I hear a banging on glass. Mom's face is on the other side of the porch,

14

behind the inner door. I go to open my door, but she shakes her head hard and yells a no through the window. I crack the door open anyway.

"You didn't come home."

She smiles, "I can't come home. Not yet."

"Because why?"

"Just not yet."

"Because of what happened to Mr. Mench?"

She nods.

I look over the woods to the east, toward the lake and Mr. Mench's frozen body. I turn back to Mom.

"I'm just as likely to have it as you. I've been with Jo and…and I touched him . . . Mr. Mench."

"You touched him?"

"The tarp blew off" – I say too quickly – "so I wrapped it tight around him and my chin rubbed against his bloody hair."

"Then you can't go home either."

She looks at me with knowing eyes, and that closes the distance just fine. She can see me lying a mile off.

"What about the Tripps? Won't they catch it now?"

She glances into the house, and when she looks back at me her face is pained.

"Mr. Tripp is dead. And Jean won't be long behind him."

"She's dying?"

"She needs my help."

"Like Mr. Mench?"

"Like Mr. Mench."

"We need you too."

I feel like the air around me is too thin to breathe.

"The littles need you."

"And I need you to look after them, Liam. Just for a day or two."

"A day or two?"

"Till your dad comes back."

"What about you comin back?"

"As soon as I'm well, I'll come back. Just as soon as I know it, I'll come."

15

"What if you're not well?"

"Liam, you need to run on home now. The littles will be getting up. They'll need breakfast. Can you do that for me? Watch them today and tomorrow, and by Saturday, one of us will be home."

There is a shriek deep in the house. She turns her face away from me.

"Mom, what's happening to us. What is this – "

" – One of us will be home soon."

She is smiling again, and nodding as she says it. Her cheeks are wet.

"We'll all be home soon. And you'll take care of them until then, ok? . . . Until we're all home?"

On the word home her eyes take hold of mine and hold them there for a long few breaths. Then she lets go and looks past me.

"And Josiah?"

He moves forward, between me and the door.

"Yes, ma'am?"

"You have food enough for a few days?"

"Yes, ma'am," said Jo.

"I'll check on you when I'm done here, ok?"

I push him aside to make another appeal, but Mom speaks first.

"You have to trust me, Charles."

She never used my first name except to put a point on something.

"Get along now, both of you."

She shuts the door, but I can see her lips say goodbye.

Walking back, Jo asks me about my dad, where he is. I tell him what I know, that he's gone into Lansing with a few other dads in the neighborhood. I'm not exactly sure then why they left, but I know now the Dying had hit the city hard. I suspect they'd gone in to help or find other family or friends to bring them out here where things seemed to be safer. I can't say for sure because they never came back. None of the dads ever came back. And that day, through a screen door at the Tripps, was the last time I saw Mom alive.

Jo stops and throws himself down on a dead log. He too is having trouble breathing, but it's worse, and for a moment I think he is asthmatic like Ben Carter from church. But then his breath comes in

16

deep, and he lets out a long sob. It is mournful, but it has anger in it too.

Without thinking, I take one big step toward him, take aim at his nose, and swing my fist down. It is gloved so I don't hurt him bad, and I miss so his nose doesn't even bleed, but I put a good shock into him. He falls off the log onto his back and his crying stops. He blinks hard and then looks at me.

"Whatdya do that for?" he asks in perfect self-possession.

I don't answer him right off. I just stand there waiting to pop him again if he should start crying.

"I don't know," I say, and I really don't. "Just felt like I should do it."

All of a sudden I feel silly. I let my arms hang loose, and I help him up.

"It's not my fault, Liam," he says, checking his nose for blood with the back of a glove.

The words hit quickly, just beneath my thinking and leave me confounded, like I've just had my pocket picked. I can only answer him with a blank and stupid stare.

"Never mind," he says, shaking his head and plodding off through the wet snow.

As I watch him walk away, I realize I am angry, and that I was blaming him. I can only stand there in the convergence of thoughts and begin to think back over the events of the past day. As I do, each gets sanitized by the light of my own narration. Jo had chosen us and had come to ask for help. And Mom chose to go. She had to go. So of course, neither Jo nor Mom had any real part in any of it. I see that clearly. I see that I am an idiot.

As I hurry my steps to catch him, I am remorseful, but I don't know how to act on it. I do catch him, and as we walk back to his place together, I am looking so hard for an act of penitence that I don't even think to say I'm sorry. We pile the stone and cinder block over his dad, then share an hour of digging. It is some time during this work that it occurs to me that Jo's insight came as he was grieving for his father. I don't know what to make of such an ability, so I put away

17

my thoughts about it. I would do that often over the coming years with Josiah Mench.

When I go back to the Tripps' house two days later, I find Mom's body on the living room couch. I may have cried then, but if so I don't remember it. Mrs. Tripp is dead too and lies with her husband in the garage where Mom must have dragged her. We decide to leave the couple there in case family come by and want them. They never do, and over the years they both dry up like mummies.

We lash my mom's body to an old toboggan and drag it home. We follow just about the same route our house had taken a hundred years earlier. Up Dobie Road, through the winding woods and a half mile east up Stillman. We go right past Leek Cemetery and never even think of stopping. We don't know yet that things will never come back to normal, that we could dig a hole right there and borrow a proper marker and not a word would ever be said about it. Instead, we bury her in Mr. Quinn's big yard right behind our house. A piece of cedar decking stands there still as headstone, alongside many others.

It isn't long that the dead will only be buried in yards and gardens and nearby places. It is only children left to do the burying, and they tend to take the simplest way with such work. But most of the dead have no children to bury them, so they lie where they fall and when the spring thaw comes, they foul up the air for months. Eventually we'll come to refer to that winter and spring as The Dying. It puts most of us in the ground, but it leaves a child here and there to fend off a thousand other killers.

Chapter 4

It's not long after my mom dies that the rest of the neighborhood takes ill and follows, and by the end of February there is not another soul to be found as far as we can wander.

Jack and I survive it, though I suspect we get a lesser version of it as we both spend a few days fevered, sore in the guts, and peeing red.

The littles do not survive. They go fast, thankfully, and die just minutes apart. Jack takes that hard. He is closer to them in age and feels he's let Mom and Dad down. For months after, maybe for years for all he would tell me such things, Jack fears Dad coming home and him having to explain where his daughters are.

There is Jo too, which makes three of us. But the houses around us, whether there'd been kids in them or not, are empty, and many weeks go by before we come by others.

We eat well these first weeks. When our stock of canned and dried food runs out, we just break open the next house. It's staying warm that proves troublesome. As the dying runs its course, we lose one-by-one those systems that make a house work. The power goes first, which means we have to find another water source as our well runs on electricity. Part of the house is propane heat, but the furnace is electric, so six-hundred gallons of propane sits for some years before we figure out how to make use of it.

We have a woodstove by the back door. It worked well enough that Dad would shut off the heat on the ground floor. Now we depend on it utterly, even going so far as walling off the upstairs and the newer part of the house for the winter so that the stove becomes the house's new center. And firewood becomes the center of activity. Like our three meals, it stabilizes the day in a rhythm.

Dad would burn until the end of March, then switch to propane, and he would usually cut it close. I recall more than once in a winter having to cut wood and haul it in heavy snow. So it's not a surprise when we find ourselves woodless in the middle of March. There are longer bolts behind the garage, and I do manage to get some of them cut up into rounds, but I don't know the first thing about running a chainsaw, so it's not long before I dip the bar into the frozen soil a few too many times and dull the blades. Not that it matters much, because we can't split even the few rounds we have. None of us is strong enough yet to swing an axe with splitting effect.

"We need to find wood," I say to Jo and Jack, who are cleaning Dad's guns on the kitchen table.

"We got plenty," says Jack. "I was just back there this morning."

"It's not split, and we got no way to split it."

19

"The Minnaars have a log splitter," says Jo as he reams out the barrel of an old .38 revolver that had once belonged to my great grandpa.

"Thought about that," I say, "and we should probably go get it, but I doubt we could get it started. I say we go looking for wood that's already split. There's a house over on Lynn Road that always has rows and rows."

They both stop their work and look up.

"That's almost Williamston," says Jack.

"We ain't been that far," says Jo, "and that's a long walk for hauling wood."

"I don't mean walk there."

I let the words hang for good effect, and Jack gives Jo a look.

"What do you mean then?" says Jack.

"You know what I mean."

But Jo says it first.

"We drive."

It might not seem like much, three boys driving a car when there's not a chance of running into another, but this is one of those lines we've chosen not to cross without ever pointing it out. To get behind a wheel and direct a car down a public road is as adult an activity as any of us can imagine. It takes some warming up to the idea, so I sell it as an adventure.

"It'd be just like riding the four-wheelers up north," I say. "Throttle, brake, steering wheel. Simple. We'll take Mr. Quinn's pickup. It's like Grandpa's, the one I drove in the hayfield loading square bales. It's got a big bed. It'll save us trips if we load it up high. I'll drive real slow, and we can look for deer."

I turn to the door and slip my coat on.

"I'll go get it now, so put your winter stuff on and bring the rifle."

I walk out without waiting for an answer. Truth is, I could probably start that log splitter, and it sits just four or five houses down the road. Truth is I want to drive that truck.

We get to the house just fine, and it's as I remembered. Twenty or thirty face-cord of hardwood, stacked in long, neat rows. We load the truck high – too high, it turns out.

We've just come through a thaw, so there is no snow on the roads. But the night before has been cold, so the wet roads have turned to ice. As we come up the first of two hills near our house, I'm too slow; the tires have to grip the road to push us up. But there's nothing to grip so the back end goes right when the tires spin. In a breath, we're in the ditch and tilted at such an angle that we throw half the load into the neighbor's yard.

"Nice work, brother," says Jack, who is already climbing out the passenger window.

I feel the truck want to roll further and yell a NO, but Jack keeps going. Quicker than I can move to grab hold of him, he slithers out and is kneeling safely next to the window looking in.

"What's wrong?"

Jo and I must have looks of relief or fright or both.

"No problem. Let's go."

Then he laughs and reaches his hand in for the rifle on the seat next to Jo. That's when the wood that is still in the bed shifts and the truck finishes its roll. Jack yanks his arm back, but his sleeve catches a piece of split oak on the ground, and the top of the truck's window settles on his hand against the wood.

Even above the noise of shifting wood and groaning metal, I hear the tiny snap of breaking finger bones, then Jack gasping. It takes a minute or two to get enough wood clear so Jo and I can stand next to the truck and rock it, but at the first push Jack pulls his hand out and rolls groaning into the frosty grass.

Back in the house we peel his work glove away and find three fingers – middle, ring, and pinky – broken at their base ends. The bone of his little finger is pushed through, the bottom end pointing up through the tear, the other pressed down into flesh. But the other fingers seem to have broken clean, though the bruising makes it hard to know for sure.

"What are you gonna do?" asks Jo.

I can see only one answer clearly, so it's the one I give.

"Cut em off."

Jack moans at that and begins to tear up.

21

"Well, at least that little one. The truck's done most of the work." Jack is going white, so we lay him down on the couch. I think it over for a minute. "Though I suppose we should find a book on it or something."

"There's two doctors that live right next to each other over on Dobie," says Jo.

"Just cause you're a doctor doesn't mean you got doctor books lying around."

"The library…" says Jack in a hiss.

"That's a better idea."

"We gonna drive there too?" asks Jo.

"It'd be a long walk," I answer. I see that Jo looks unsure about it. "Besides," I add, "I think I learned a lot on that last drive."

Chapter 5

I leave Jo home with Jack and take the van into town. It isn't a town, really, just the businesses that grew up around that exit off I-96. It is the first time I've been there since before Dad left, and it doesn't match up at all to my memory of it. The buildings are the same, though being unlit they look corpse-like now. What strikes me hardest is the stillness. The intersection at Jolly and Okemos roads had been as busy as any I'd ever seen, and all the time. I stop the car right under the light and look west, then north, then east. The wide, straight roads are empty as far as my eyes can see. There is a car here and there in the parking lots. A white SUV is still parked next to a pump at the Marathon station. The driver's door is open and a booted leg hangs beneath. But the roads are desolate, and the sight makes me feel that way too.

I drive the two miles down Okemos road to the library. The doors are locked, so I walk around the building pushing at windows and the big garage doors in back. It is thoroughly locked.

I'd seen a show once on tv about what would happen to our cities if humans were wiped out. I remember being amazed at how quick the wild would take things over. A broken window lets seed and a few critters in, and before long you've got a jungle where once was a living room. We believe most of what we heard on tv, so we're careful to keep houses buttoned up. We look for keys or push open windows, and when neither works we go on to the next house. There will come a time when we need to break in, but we haven't arrived there yet.

There is no next library here, so I pick up a landscape stone and pitch it through one of the tall, narrow front windows. It is darker than dark, but that's no matter. We've explored a lot of houses and have gotten into the habit of carrying lights or glow sticks. I carry a small mag light. At the front I grab a basket, then go straight to the non-fiction section. I walk the aisles quickly, scanning titles until I find something medical sounding. I'm not sure which books I left behind or most of what I took, but I can give the title of one of them because I can see it now on a shelf near me. *Where There Is No Doctor.* Next to it sits *Weed Garden: A Field Guide to Edible Plants.* Taken together the two books have been for us as Squanto to the pilgrims. I slip back out through the window, then place one of the bigger shards of glass in the opening. I'll come back when I can board it over. Of all the places in town, the library seems the one to preserve as long as possible.

On the way back I'm sidetracked when I see a girl running down the sidewalk in front of 7-11. I have the same feeling of adrenalin that I'd get spotting a deer in our yard, or a raccoon on the back porch. She sees me too and is angling off the walk and into the road, her arms waving wild. I stop and roll down the window.

"Hi?" I say.

She is younger than me by a couple years, Jack's age probably. And though she's dressed in nice clothes, they're dirty. Her hair hangs down in flat, greasy strips that frame a dark-skinned face, almond-shaped brown eyes. I think to myself she was once pretty.

"Are you nice?" she asks, breathless.

Just then I hear a bang from behind her. She doesn't look back, and I don't answer, just stare past her to the 7-11.

"Am I what?"

"I asked if you were nice," she says.

Another bang.

"What is that?" I ask.

"Boys shootin bottles," she answers.

I catch the sight of something small rising up in the air behind the store. There is another bang and I watch it fall back to earth unharmed.

"What do you mean am I nice?"

"Some kids ain't nice around here, and I want a ride home."

"Like those kids?" I nod toward the store.

"Them?" she laughs. "Bunch of kindergartners."

"Shooting guns?"

She shrugs.

"So are you nice, and will you drive me home?"

"Where do you live?"

"Just down Jolly." She turns and faces east as she says it.

"Not far? My brother's hurt and I need to get back."

"Not far," she says then runs to the passenger side.

We head east down Jolly. As we pass the 7-11, I can see four or five kids looking up at another thrown bottle. But when they hear me, they all swing around, including the shooter. He takes aim at me then raises his gun and fires over the van. The rest erupt in laughter and shouts of some kind of triumph. I roll the window up.

"That can't end good," I say.

"They're harmless," she says.

"You're the first person I've seen since…since everything. Other than Jack and Jo I mean."

"You ain't been far then," she says "I can't get far enough away from the people around here. See 'em too much."

I notice the office buildings along both sides of the road have most of the windows broken out.

"The boys back there do that? Break those windows?"

"Not them. They wouldn't be caught dead there. You see the paint?"

She points through my window. On the brick wall of a bank, a white circle with a crude bird at its center is spray painted between two broken windows.

"What is it?"

"The Westgates. It's their sign. All the buildings along this stretch, both sides, belong to the Westgates."

"What do you mean belongs? It's nobody's now."

"It's nobody's, so it's whoever takes it – first find, right? – and the Westgates have taken everything in this part of Okemos."

"Why are they called that?"

"It's where they live. Westgate subdivision."

"And what happens if someone else goes in? If someone goes into that pharmacy looking for medicine, what will the… Westgates do to stop them?"

She doesn't answer for a moment then turns to me and says, "They might shoot em."

She pulls the sleeve of her coat up then holds her arm out. She has a tattoo on her wrist, the same symbol as on the bank.

"Or they might just take em, like they do the buildings."

"Take them?" I ask.

"Here's my house."

She goes for the door before I am stopped, so I have to slam on the brakes. She says thanks, jumps out, and runs to the side of the road, but there is no house here, only a stubbled corn field and woods beyond that. I roll down her window to yell, but she stops and looks back at me. I listen instead.

"I hope your brother's ok," she yells through cupped hands and then takes off running through the field. I look past her and search out the point she is aiming at. There is nothing there but a deer blind up on stilts at the field's edge.

The thought of Jack and what I'll have to do when I get home nags at me, so I don't see where she ends up. Not right then anyway.

Chapter 6

When I get home I drive Jo up to the first doctor's house, Dr. Minnaar's. While he rummages through it looking for instruments, I study my manual. There is little about amputating fingers, but I do find a few good hints from a chapter on cutting off arms and legs. I may need a tourniquet, for example, and I should make sure there aren't nerves right next to the sutures. The nerves are drawn a bright blue in the illustration, but I doubt they'll present themselves that way in our kitchen.

Jo finds nothing, so we go to the next house, Dr. Spedoske's. While Jo searches I read some more, this time about infection and how important it is to keep everything clean. Alcohol will work for that, and I have plenty in the linen closet. We'll also need to change the dressing often, so I add gauze to our grocery list.

We have better luck here. In a bedroom closet, Jo finds an old-fashioned, black doctor's bag. It has in it the two things we need most: surgical scissors still in their sterilized shrink wrap, and a suture kit. We find gauze but no Lidocaine. This will have to be an old-school amputation like they did in the Civil War. A shot of brandy and something to bite down on.

Back home, we get a pot of water hot over the wood stove and let a few towels simmer in it. I clean the big kitchen table with the alcohol then lay Jack down. Jo stands across from me, polished clean now and in an old MSU sweatshirt. I've convinced him that he is a necessary part of the sterile environment, so he agrees to shower under a 5-gallon bucket that hangs from the ceiling over the old hot-tub. He stands next to Jack's head and holds in front of him another big stock pot. I explain to Jack when he looks at it with some wonder that the pot has extra gauze in hot water.

He doesn't seem to care much for explanations, so I start. I open his hand. Until now it's been cradled closely to him and wrapped tight. The wad of gauze under the towel is red all the way through, but the bleeding has slowed to an ooze. The white end of the bone sits up above the torn flesh. It is not splintered but broken clean through like a pruned twig. That's good news. If it had split lengthwise I would have to take the finger at the joint, which gets a lot more complicated.

I need to clean the wound and inspect the skin and flesh around it to make sure there is enough to cover over the bone's end. I set his arm along his side and turn the hand up. Earlier I'd drilled four holes through the table top and fed leather shoe laces through. Now I use these to cinch down his wrist. I'd thought of all his limbs that way but didn't want to ruin the table completely.

The cleaning is painful for him. I douse the open wound with the alcohol and Jack hisses through closed teeth. When he's settled down, and I think I am as ready as I can be, I take hold of the end of the pinky and pull it gently away from his hand. The angle of it is unnatural and makes my throat twitch. I pray silently for steady hands. Then I give Jo a look, and slip the scissors up from under the table.

"Do it quick!" shouts Jack. He is sweating terribly, his face the color of old snow. And he is starting to cry.

"You got it, brother," I answer, then I give a nod to Jo.

In a flash, Jo grabs the stock pot, sets it over Jack's face, and begins banging it with a big spoon, all the while screaming at the top of his lungs. Jack's whole body clenches up like a jolt of lightning is striking him. After a few seconds of this, Jo pulls the pot away, leans down gently and says, "Sorry, man."

Jack is breathing heavy, but says nothing, only turns his astonished face back and forth between us. Finally, he says, "What the...*why*..." Then he trains his eyes on the ceiling and says, "Just do it."

"It's done," I say. "Lookee." I hold up the finger, but he squeezes his eyes tight. Then he turns his head the other way and retches onto the table.

The rest of the work goes more slowly, and there is no tricking him out of the pain as the sutures go in and out. But within an hour I have his stub sewn up tight and the others splinted up well. I give him a big shot of Nyquil and another of the port wine Dad used to like (there's no brandy in the house), then lay him down on the couch. He will catch a fever and moan through the next two days.

27

I clean the table and take the trash to the back porch. When I come back in, I sit on the coffee table by Jack. Then I say as matter-of-factly as I can, "Saw some people today."

They both stop what they are doing – Jack moaning, Jo piecing together the muzzle-loader he's taken apart.

"Up by the 7-11. A girl and a bunch of little boys shooting bottles."

"Did you talk to the em?" asks Jo.

"The girl," I answer, "not the boys."

"What'd she say? Who is she? Did you know her?"

"Just a girl. Never seen her before."

"What was she doing?"

"Wanted a ride home."

"Where does she live?"

"Don't know. On Jolly somewhere."

"You gave her a ride home but you don't know where she lives?"

I explain what happened, and they are both silent for a while. Talking about other people, real living people, is almost as strange as seeing them. We've begun to think we are the only ones, that there is something unique about where we live and how the dying has moved through the world in such a way that it hits us with a lighter touch. It seems now that isn't the case, and that opens a whole new category of thinking.

"Maybe we should go get her," says Jack dreamily.

"Go get her? For what?"

"Maybe go get all of 'em. So they can live here with us." His voice trails off. His eyes are slits. "Take care of 'em…"

"We're gettin by fine," I say, "and we don't need more mouths to feed." I put a blanket over him. "That's it, Sunshine, go to sleep."

I sit down on the floor and help Jo get the trigger and guard screwed in under the breach. It's tricky. You have to pull the striker back part way before the guard will sit flush against the barrel. Then you have to hold the striker back with one hand and work an allen wrench with the other. But I only have to show him once. I only ever have to show Jo something one time.

"I've been thinkin we should go back to the library," I say, "get all the books we might need."

28

"Need for what?"

"For anything we don't know how to do. The cars won't run forever. We need to know how to change oil and coolant and other stuff. I want to know how long gasoline lasts. Does it go bad? A tractor will run a long time but you have to know how to take care of it. Grandpa told me that."

"I can change oil, plugs, filters, all that stuff."

I look at him funny.

"I'm serious, I can." He is running a patch of Hoppes over the metal parts like he's done it before. I cringe a little. Mom always had a fit when Dad cleaned a gun inside the house.

"Dad did all that stuff," Jo is saying, "and taught me how. I could change the oil since I was 6."

"Ok," I say. "Good. We could get more books on medicine too, on hunting and trapping, and cooking. I've wanted baked bread so bad I've had dreams about it."

"Bread would be good," says Jo and he looks at Jack. His moans have turned to shallow snoring. "That's a good sign," he says.

My mind is running fast on its own track.

"We don't know how to grow a garden either, and the canned food won't last forever. We need to know how to grow and can our own. How to dry it maybe. British ships would store meat in salt. Sucks the water right out. Pack it in salt and eat it five years later."

"I'm sick of canned food. Dad used to grow tomatoes and cucumbers. We'd eat the little tomatoes, the cherry ones, right off the vine."

"We should go as soon as Jack is better."

"Where else are you thinkin?"

"Meijer, see what's left, and Home Depot. They're not far from the library."

"Your dad didn't have much ammunition except for the .22, but you can't shoot deer with a .22."

"Why don't you write down what we need?"

"I can tell you right now. We got twenty shells for the .243, two and a half boxes of 12 gauge bird shot, and 2 buck. No slugs. A couple hundred fifty-caliber balls and a half pound of pyrodex – "

"What's pyradex?"

"Like black powder. For the muzzleloader."

"Ok. Why don't you just be in charge of the guns. We still need to start a list of things we need."

"You start it, and I'll let you know what to put on it. I'll lose it if I do it."

"Fine," I say.

Jo gives the guns another rub and puts them back in their places. It is a blessing on the house, like hands on the heads of children – shotgun behind the back door, rifle over the big front picture window, the .38 in the kitchen junk drawer. He leaves the muzzle loader in its case and slides it under the couch. But the .22 he slings over his shoulder.

"I'm goin to the trailer," he says. "Be back in a couple hours."

"Don't forget to look for that star-shaped screwdriver."

"I won't," he says as he steps out. I know he won't. He doesn't forget things.

I look at Jack now. He's white and sweaty but sleeping hard. I think again of infection. I don't know anything about it except that in Civil War hospitals more men died of it than from their wounds. We learned that from Mom. She loved teaching the Civil War. We spent almost a whole year on it when I was nine or ten. Took a trip to Gettysburg. We were homeschooled. I don't think I've mentioned that yet.

I think of the story of a boy soldier who'd had a foot amputated, but the stump doesn't heal, so the doctors take another chunk, and then another, and so on right to the hip. But they never do catch up to the infection. It goes too deep, and he dies in some agony.

But another thought comes to me, that most of the operations on soldiers are big amputations – arms and legs, so I tell myself that there will be less infection in something small like a finger. That's the way we think now. We draw conclusions from our few years of memories and paint the whole new world with them. But even now I second guess every thought, and itch to ask an adult. Soon the itch spreads to wanting a book to open, to finding the truth or the falseness of a thing in the printed word.

I look at Jack's bandaged hand on his chest. There is no one to ask now and no book to open to tell me what's going on inside his body, only the manual that says to keep the wound clean. To keep everything around it clean. I've done that as well as I know how. Now I wait. If infection does set in and spread up the arm, will I be able to take off the hand? The forearm? At what point will my courage dry up?

I think that over hard. It seems an important thing to think through, like I need to make the decision now because if I wait until the time comes, my legs will go weak, and I'll just choose the easiest thing. So I determine right then that I will do whatever I have to to keep him alive. I will steel myself against fear and pain, mine and Jack's both. I go further than that even. Cutting off an arm might turn out to be one of the simpler things we do to survive. There's bound to be worse things, so I include them in my oath.

Dad's Bible sits on the window sill over the couch. I reach for it, and as I pull it up from among the other books it rests with, it opens to 2nd Kings, chapter 5. I sit down on the floor and read it. This is where Elisha tells a guy called Naaman to dip in the river Jordan seven times to heal his leprosy. Everyone in this story is hot-headed, and the whole deal almost falls apart, but in the end the man is healed. Dad had always cautioned us against reading God's word in such a random way, but still, I take the story as encouragement.

I open up to the Psalms too and read the first one my eyes meet. I don't remember which, particularly, but it speaks of God doing violence to my enemies. I think to myself that it doesn't apply much to me as I have no enemies. Turns out I am dead wrong about that.

Chapter 7

The finger is all I take from Jack. Three days later the fever runs itself out, and the wound is fully scabbed. The other fingers, the broken ones, look angry for some time, weeks as I recall, but they don't go rotten like we fear they might.

So a week after the trimming, as we come to call it, the three of us hitch the wood trailer to Mom's van and drive into town. It's warmed up over the last days, and the roads are clear and dry. The yards are still snow covered, but some of the wide, open fields have streaks of brown showing through.

We pass the intersection at Jolly Road, and I point out the paint markings on the 7-11 and the little strip mall next to it. There is a pharmacy there, and I am tempted to see what it still has but think a better plan will be to get a book at the library that describes all the drugs, then find a pharmacy unclaimed. We can stock everything we might need at home. There is a Rite Aid near the Home Depot, and Meijer has its own. The visions of the boys shooting bottles and of the girl running off into field have fueled my thinking over the last week. I conclude that the kids here, at least that group, are wild. Thinking our way around them will give us the advantage should we ever need one.

The library is as I'd left it. It hasn't been marked, and the glass shard is still there in the knocked-out window. We load the back seats of the van with a couple hundred or so books we think might someday be useful. We pretty well clear out the gardening and medical sections, and take much in the way of cooking, craft, and home repair. There is a half shelf of survival books, five or six of which look readable.

We leave through a back door this time, leaving it locked, and board up the broken window with a few pieces of plywood and trim that I'd brought from the house. I take a careful measurement of the window and write the dimensions down on the inside cover of a book on alternative home construction. On the front cover is a big house – a modern-looking two story with attached garage – made entirely out of straw bales and mud. The idea of it intrigues me, makes me think there might be other ways to look at the things around us.

"Why are you so worried about this window," asks Jo, "when we've broke plenty of others and left em that way?"

I tell him that our future depends on what's in this building. I tell him to think about our food. There's plenty to eat now, but unless we learn how to grow and keep our own, we'll be in trouble when our stock is gone or spoiled. That should make us think not just beyond this week or this season but years into the future.

And that should open up all kinds of other thoughts, including this: that there's no one to hand down to us any kind of knowledge. No parents or teachers to train us. No internet to go to for new information. I tell him that if we're to survive we'll have to re-learn everything. And that's why my thoughts keep returning to the library and the books inside.

When I am done, Jo just smiles, points to his head and says, "All we need's right up here."

We drive to Meijer next. I have in mind some kind of adventure here, a shopping spree. We'll race down the aisles with our carts, laughing, and we'll take whatever our van and trailer will carry. It's not like that. Even from the parking lot, as we roll the windows down, we smell the decay inside. We learn later that it is the meat in the freezers that take longest to rot. A year later, in a different store in a different town, we find the meat left out at a deli counter dried up like old leather, but the packaged meat in the freezers still smell like death.

Inside the store it's like a battle has been fought. The aisle floors are so thick with whatever the shelves had held that we can't get our carts down some of them. We avoid the produce and deli sections and start in canned goods, picking up anything edible. There isn't much in the way of variety, but we take a bounty in canned artichokes, olives, okra, sardines, and such, things we would have held our noses at just months before. When we have half a cart full we move to the dry goods, hoping to find beans, rice, and pasta, but that aisle is empty of all but a few boxed meals like scalloped potatoes and Rice-aroni. The hardware section too has been pretty well cleaned out, which is fine as we'll hit the Home Depot next.

We do better in the garden section. It'd been winter still when the dying came, so stores hadn't opened their outdoor garden centers yet.

Still, there are enough seed packets left that we can plant most of the acre in our backyard in corn, tomatoes, cucumbers, squash of all kinds, beans, and peas. In years past, I'd seen our garden full of these things, so it is an easy thing to pick those seeds from the racks. I can picture us plucking the fruits because I've done it. I don't know what to expect from eggplant, kale, beets, or turnips , but I grab these too.

I am reaching for kohlrabi seeds when I hear a funny yelp from the next aisle, like someone has stepped on a tack. Then, "Liam!" It's Jack. Something has scared him. "Liam!" he yells again.

I run around the end cap, turn into the next aisle and slip on spilled fertilizer. I get up on my hands and knees and looking down, find myself face to face with a dead woman. But she's laughing. Jack's flashlight is trained on her, and the moving, jittery shadows make her dried lips play up and down against her teeth. I jump back and scoot away on my butt.

Her hair is gray, but her face is the color of jerky. White teeth and black gums shine out from a grinning oval. Her eyes are sunken and empty. It is a familiar sight now, but as often as we look on one, an old corpse still works into our nerves.

"Look there," says Jo, who'd heard Jack's cries too. She lies next to an empty shopping cart. Jo's light is on her leg. She has somehow kicked through the metal bars at the back of the cart, the little shelf where we used to put our milk jugs. Her leg has gone in at one angle but under the cart it turns at quite another. It's broken just above the ankle.

"Got stuck there and probably starved to death," says Jack.

"Or died of shock," says Jo.

"There's nothing in the cart though," says Jack. "She could've pulled it to the door at least, yelled for help."

"The cart was too heavy," says Jo, figuring it out as he speaks. "It was full when it happened. Looters emptied it after."

"But how'd she do it?" asks Jack. He holds one foot up and makes like he's losing balance. He is mimicking her, not in a cruel way but as a way of thinking it through. "Maybe she slipped and – "

" – Never mind," I say. "Let's go."

We don't linger over such scenes like we once did. Early on there is an honest fascination with the blank look of a corpse. It is so other-worldly, so suggestive of the novel – an untold story, a thing out of place, a private death. But by now we've learned to step past such things quickly and, in a very deliberate way, not think about dying.

We go to Home Depot next. The destruction here is of a different quality. In Meijer, the aisles and shelves have the look of something ravaged by desperation, and it's complete, throughout the whole store. Here the damage seems to have sprung from anger or something close to it, and it is random. Some aisles or sections are untouched, some are wrecked. And where there is more to break – the lighting and paint aisles – the damage is spectacular.

There is an air of menace in the building still and we move through it quickly, sticking closely to my list. We find tools for firewood – axes, mauls, sledges, an arm load of extra handles, no chainsaws, but a few chains and files to keep them sharp. I don't know the size of Dad's, don't even know there are different sizes until now, so we take a wide collection. We find two sturdy wheel burrows for moving water buckets up from the creek. These we fill with bags of cement and hardware: hammers, saws, drivers, any hand tool whether we know its use or not; nails, screws, bolts and nuts, hinges of all sizes and descriptions.

Once my list is checked and everything is loaded, we go back in and grab up whatever our hands go for. It is now that we give in to the imperative lust for things. Each of us takes one of the rolling trash bins we find in the warehouse, and we go at the shelves like kids set loose in a toy store. At first, I find that if I am considering an item and I recognize it, then my brain can justify it as having potential use. And that is the signal to take it. But at some point in the ransacking, I stop thinking at all. If I can hold it, it goes in the bin.

Everything goes in the bin, until it will hold no more.

It is a haphazard mess we try to stow away in the van and trailer, and much of it won't fit. We decide to take what we can and hide the rest for later. I recall a story that Dad had read to us about a magical, evil book that the main character wants to hide. He tells himself that the best place to hide a leaf is in a forest, so he hides a book in a huge library of books. We put the carts back inside and leave them in plain sight in three of the most destroyed parts of the store.

Loaded with our plunder, we head home. We decide to go the long way around – a few miles east down Grand River, south on Meridian another few to where Stillman T's into it. We know the route well because Dad was always claiming it to be quicker than taking Okemos Road. He was always trying to prove it, though if he ever did we never heard of it.

We will prove nothing that day either. At the corner of Van Atta and Grand River, a small army of boys on quads crosses our path, spots us and turns an arsenal of guns in our direction. This is our introduction to Ricky and the Westgates.

Chapter 8

"What do we do?" asks Jack.

"I don't know," I say.

"You better stop," says Jo. He is squeezed up between us. "But don't let them know how many of us there are."

"They can see."

"I mean at home."

"Why?" asks Jack.

"Cuz if they think there's more of us at home, they'll be careful."

"How do you know that?" I ask.

He shrugs and says, "Just people."

I stop in the road, and the quads begin to circle. We can hear the boys hooting even through the noise and closed windows. On their backs are spray-painted the bird sign.

One of them stops a few feet from my door. He looks about my age, but even sitting on the quad, he is taller. His eyes are pale blue. Long blonde hair spills out from under a tight blue ski hat. There is something strange about his lips and tongue, but I don't catch then what it is. He has on an expensive-looking ski jacket. I look around. Most of the boys wear something like it. Expensive, but dirty. He pulls a pistol, a big revolver, from inside his coat and sets it on his lap, then motions for me to roll the window down.

When I do, the noise of the quads and the smell of gas fumes fill the van. He says something I can't hear, and seems annoyed. He looks around and raises a hand, but the noise goes on. When he fires the gun into the air, the quads stop. Then he gives a cutting motion across his neck and the riders turn off their machines. This seems to be their chief.

The quiet is instant, everyone listening for the boy chief to say something. Then someone laughs and the silence breaks, fills up again with hoots and coyote-like cries.

"What's the matter with them?" asks Jack.

"Nothing," says Jo. "Just trying to scare us."

The boy chief raises his hand again and the noise stops. When he speaks this time, I hear him clearly.

"Get out."

"You want us to leave?" I ask, and motion in the other direction.

"Get out of the car," he answers.

"I don't think so," I say.

"He doesn't want the car," whispers Jo. "It's a minivan. I think he wants the trailer."

"Why?" asks Jack. "He can get the same stuff where we got it." I listen to their conservation but keep my eyes locked with Chief's.

"He doesn't need it," says Jo.

"Then why does he want it?" asks Jack.

"Cuz he doesn't want us to have it," says Jo. "Taking is just what he does."

He fires again, this time into the bumper, and points the gun right at me. "We're comin," I say, trying as hard as I can to sound indifferent. We climb out, and the three of us stand shoulder to shoulder.

"You armed?" he asks.

"No," I answer honestly. I'd been too worried over the list and had forgotten the deer rifle.

"Is that right?" He nods to two boys behind the van and each jumps into a side door. They begin a search.

"Nobody goes around without a gun," says Chief.

"We do. How's it your business anyway?"

"Oh it's my business."

"How's that?"

"Cuz I see what you got in that trailer, and it belongs to me. My business is right there in that piece-of-crap trailer."

"You own the Home Depot now? And Meijer too?"

"First find."

"What's that?"

"The law of first find. Nothin belongs to no one till somebody finds it, finds it first."

"And you *found* Home Depot?"

"No, not me. We." He holds his arms out and turns right and left as if to say behold. The other boys, in affirmation, shift or nod or curse.

"We found it, now we own it. The Westgates. That's the law, man." He looks at Jack now. "What happened to your friend?" Chief points the gun at Jack's hand.

"Broke a finger," says Jack.

"That's a lot of bandage for a broke finger," says Chief.

"Broke it and cut if off," says Jo proudly.

Chief looks at Jo, then at Jack, then me. He purses his lips a little like he's just heard something he approves of. Hmmm was all he says to it, and his eyes go to the trailer.

"Let's see what you got," he says.

He puts his pistol away and hops off his quad. Then he walks behind the van, and steps onto the tongue. He moves his weight nimbly. A few of the other boys take his cue, leave their machines, and stand close. They are all armed, but I can't shake the sense that their guns are just toys.

"You guys building something?" asks a little blond kid in a nascar jacket.

"What's that?" I say.

"He means you got a lot of cement here," says Chief. "You building a swimming pool?" He laughs loud at that and few of the others join him.

"Fixin a wall," I say.

He grabs a splitting axe. "Looks like you're gonna take down a forest too," he says. Then he stops for the shortest of moments and I see that an idea had flashed behind his eyes. He drops it and snatches a different one, not a splitting axe this time but a bit axe, sharp as a razor. He pulls the rubber guard off it and runs a thumb across the blade. Then he takes the gun from his coat and puts it to Jo's head.

"Get down on your faces," he says to Jack and me. Jo starts to lower himself. "Not you!"

Jack and I lay down on the road.

"What are you doing?" I yell up. "Take the trailer. Take the van too. You can drive it off right now."

"Of course I can. I don't need you to tell me that, and do I look like I'd be seen dead driving a minivan?"

The boys snicker.

"Then what?"

He motions to the boys closest to him and whispers something to each. Then to the whole lot of us he says, "Let's see how sharp this axe is." And at the words, two of the boys grab Jo at the legs and neck, and the third pulls his hand away from his body. Then they press him down to his knees so that his arm is stretched out, his forearm resting against the long steel tongue of the trailer.

What Chief has in mind to do strikes Jack and me at the same time, and we both start struggling, or yelling out for him to stop. But boots on our backs and gun barrels at our ears shut us up.

I turn my head enough so I can see Jo's face in a headlock. He's white and wide-eyed, but there is a fighting anger there too. Behind him I can see the axe go part way up and down, up and down, like Chief is getting used to its weight.

"What good will that do you?" I spit out as loud as I can.

"I don't know yet," says Chief. "I'm waiting to see."

"Am I supposed to offer you something?"

39

"No. We figured that out already. Everything you have here is mine."

"Then what?"

"This is more about – curiosity." He lowers the axe, and takes a step to me so our eyes meet. "If I were to cut off your friend's arm, what would you do?"

"What do you mean?"

"I mean what I said. What would you do? Would you save him? Could you? You took this one's finger off and he seems just fine. Could you do that for your friend here?"

"No! I mean yes, I'd try to save him, but I can't fix a cut-off arm."

Now a thought comes to me – Jo's words from earlier about not giving them a full picture.

"I'd...I'd take him back home...as quick as I could..."

Now the words come as quick as the thoughts, one atop the other.

" – take him home and have my sister do it like she took Jack's finger off. Maybe she could fix an arm."

I am yelling this, crying almost. The boys around us jump in on it and start up their own shouts and jeering, some calling for blood, others screaming just to make noise.

I try to make myself heard above it.

"If she couldn't do it, I'd let one of the Quinn brothers do it."

I want him to think there are many of us, a whole, deadly clan of us.

"They're all hunters and know how to gut animals. Is that what you want? Just to know what I would do? That's what I'd do!"

"It wasn't you took his finger off?"

My story has come so quick I'm starting to forget it already.

"No! It wasn't me. It was my sister. It doesn't matter, though, cuz he'd die. Nobody could fix it. You'd kill him!"

Chief's face goes flush and his eyes narrow. Then he raises the axe high over Jo's arm, and the voices of the others, instead of pitching higher, go quiet.

"Not good enough," he says as he lifts it the rest of the way.

40

And in that heavy silence where even breathing has stopped, as the axe hangs in the air, he smiles, gives out a grunt, and brings it down hard onto the road.

He thinks this is hilarious and laughs out loud until every one of his little imps is laughing with him. But it isn't a right laughing. As I get to my knees, I look around and can see that more than one of the laughing boys are also on the edge of crying.

When they settle down again, Chief says, "Let him go."

Jo stands up. His face is tear-stained, but his eyes are fiery. He is angry, not scared. This is not the same crying boy I'd hit on the nose months ago.

"We're just messin with ya," says Chief. "Just havin fun."

"You done then?" I ask. "With your fun?"

He considers me longer than the question requires, and I feel I'm being read.

"Yeah," he says finally. "I'm done."

He steps over the tongue, walks straight to the quad, and starts it up. The ax is still in his hand and for an awkward moment, he can't figure how to hold it and work the throttle, so he tosses it to the road. Then he takes off north, up Van Atta. The others scramble to catch up, and in less than a minute they are gone.

"You ok?" Jack asks Jo.

Jo spits hard and sets his teeth as he eyes the now-empty road. A spot of blood under his eye runs down his cheek like a red tear.

"You're cut," says Jack.

Jo dabs at it and looks at his hand. "Chip from the road. The ax."

"Were you scared?" asks Jack.

Jo looks at him like he's stupid and says, "He wasn't ever gonna do it. Couldn't you see that?"

Jack says nothing. Neither do I.

"His clothes are from – from Abercrombie. His mouth is stained purple from eating candy." That's what it was. "He's a punk from the suburbs. Probably never even hooked a worm."

"Then why'd he do it?" asks Jack.

Neither of us answers.

"You're saying he's not dangerous then?" asks Jack.

"I never said that," says Jo.

"Why didn't he take our stuff?" asks Jack. "You said he didn't want us to have it."

"Why do people do anything?" says Jo.

"Doesn't matter now," I say. "Let's get back before they change their minds."

At home, we unload the van and trailer and put most of it in the solarium, a narrow, windowed room attached to the back of the house. Our thought is it will be safer there than in the garage. Until now we haven't thought to lock the doors, much less that someone might come with a mind to steal.

We've just finished dinner – Dinty Moore, mandarin orange slices, and popcorn. I am reading *Watership Down* by candlelight when two thoughts keep interrupting me. I wrestle with them for a minute, make them quiet, then read some more, but they're as fitful as rabbits. Finally I set the book down.

"Jo?" I say. He's trying to fix an old camp stove he found in the garage. It is the size of a briefcase and unfolds into a little cooktop.

"Yeah?" he says, without looking up.

"Remember that time I hit you?" I ask.

"What time?"

"The time out by the Tripps' house, when I knocked you off that log."

He has to think about it for a moment, then it comes to him. "Oh yeah. I forgot." He goes back to his stove.

"Well, I'm sorry about it. Sorry I hit you."

He looks up again, then gives a nod.

"And I'm sorry I thought it was your fault, my mom dying I mean. You were right about me thinking that, and I should have said so because I knew it right away, but for some reason I – I didn't. I don't know why."

"Thought you did say you were sorry," says Jo.

"I don't think so."

"You helped me bury my dad. I guess I took that for a sorry."

"Maybe that's what I meant by it. You see some things better than I do, and that would make sense."

42

Without looking up he gives the same nod but with a wry smile this time.

The other thought is that I haven't prayed. I wonder often about that. Once, in the good time, when our van went spinning in circles down an icy expressway, Mom had started praying right in her fear. Lord help us, she had said out loud, over and over until we were settled safe in the median.

I hadn't said or thought anything like that when Jack's fingers were crushed or when I thought Chief would chop Jo's arm off, and I don't know why. I did thank God after the fact, but I wonder what has to happen to a body before prayer comes up out of it as instinct. I used to suppose it was simply animal survival that kept me from praying like Mom did. Turns out it's not survival at all, but a fever that would throw its host into the fire.

Chapter 9

The next morning I wake to Jo shaking me gently.

"There's somethin you gotta see," he says.

I follow him down to the back deck. Jack is already standing there and staring out toward the southeast where the sun is an arm-length's fist above the treetops. Between us and it is a thick, black plume of smoke rising up and up. There is no wind that day, so it stands in a column. The winter sun behind it gives the smoke its own light, like it too is on fire.

"You think it's the Reeders' place?" I ask them both. The Reeders owned a big house and barn at the end of a long cul-de-sac just east of us.

"No," says Jo. That's the direction, but the smoke's farther off."

"Let's take a look," says Jack.

We walk this time, cutting through Mr. Joseph's 40 acres, something we never dared to do before the dying. We are armed. Jack found a book on preserving food and now Jo has it in mind that we need to shoot a deer and start experimenting. So we take the shotgun loaded with buck, and the .243. Jo carries the .22 in case we flush rabbit or run a squirrel up a tree.

He is right about the smoke being farther off. We pass by the Reeders' place and into a field of last year's corn stubble. Across the field, about a quarter mile off, is a big stand of hardwood, five acres maybe. It is surrounded on all sides by farm fields, and right from its center the smoke column rises. At the tree tops we can see yellow tongues of flame.

"What would be burning that hot?" asks Jack. "Can't be more than a deer blind or two."

"There's a house in there," says Jo.

"Really?" asks Jack. "Never seen it."

"There's no drive. The guy who owns it doesn't come out much. Didn't come out much, I guess. But when he did, he'd drive his four-wheeler to Mr. Reeder's barn where he had a truck, go into town to shop or whatever, and take the quad back."

"How do you know?"

"Seen his lights at night and asked Dad about it. He walked out there one day to ask if he could bow hunt the wood stand. He wouldn't let him though."

The day is bright, full of spring promise. Overnight the brown streaks in the fields have caught up with the snow, so there is about equal parts of both. As we go over a tree line in the middle of the field, a pheasant goes up at my feet. The sound of it stops my heart. Jo swings the .22 around and fires off 3 quick shots, but the bird keeps flying. I start to head across the rest of the field, but Jo begins talking.

"My dad had one of those crazy .22 shotguns. Two barrels. One for .22 and the other a twelve gauge. One day he's hunting with it – nothing particular, just whatever shows up. It was a good gun for that kind of hunting – and a lone duck comes dropping into a pond just off the two track he's on."

Jack and I let our gun butts rest, and for a moment we forget about the burning house in the woods.

"So he puts the gun up and bang! pulls the wrong trigger, fires the .22 instead. It spooks the duck and before he can fire again, it's gone. So he spends the day in the woods. Just him and Petey, our old Labrador, and whatever they can shoot. I don't know if he gets anything, but on the way back to his truck, he stops at an irrigation ditch, crouches down in the reeds, and waits out the last few minutes of day light. Well, just as he's about to call it quits, he sees a duck coming in, wings set like a plane about to touch down. He waits, he waits, then he jumps up and fires, shoots the right barrel this time, and down it goes. Splash! Petey dives in and brings back a big drake mallard. They head back to the truck and go home for the night."

"That's not much of a story," says Jack.

"He's right," I say. "That's a lame story."

"I'm not done," says Jo. "Dad gets home and goes to clean that duck and what does he find? A bunch of little holes and one big one, .22 caliber sized, right through the breast." Jo shoulders his gun and starts into the field. "I've been trying to hit a flying bird with a .22 ever since."

Jack and I share a grin and follow him.

The house in the woods barely qualifies as one. It is a log cabin, set low to the ground, something from another age. And it burns like dry kindle. Flames shoot out from the few small windows with the roar of a gale wind. We stand at the woods' edge behind a chicken-wire fence that surrounds a little garden of last year's bean stalks and squash vines. Beyond it is a small yard. Even from this distance the heat of the blaze hurts on the bare skin of my face.

"Wonder what started it," says Jo. "No one's been here for months."

"Lightning maybe. Was there a storm last night?"

"Not that I heard," says Jack.

We move back into the woods and watch the fire for some minutes, saying nothing. In the years before the dying, we'd sit in our backyard with my dad and his friends around a camp fire, and it would always strike me that just staring into it was a kind of entertainment. It is the same here, but there is a more urgent fascination to it. I'd never watched a house burn down; it has the feeling of spectacle. It holds the eyes.

I pull my mine away and look around the space carved out from these tall maples and cherry trees. It is a rectangle, about a quarter acre. Behind the house is a shed. Opposite the front is a wide area that I would otherwise say is a driveway, but there is no drive there. The trees crowd right in, all the way around, without break except for a few trails wide enough for a quad.

I am just wondering how they had managed to build a house without pulling a truck up close to it, when I notice that at the east end of the yard some of the trees there are quite a bit smaller, none bigger through the trunk than my forearm. There'd been a drive cut through at that spot years ago, so I figure to myself, and whoever lived here let the woods take it over again like he'd just borrowed the space for a time.

There is a garage at that end too.

"Let's see what's in there," I say and start walking towards it. Jack and Jo stare at the fire for a moment longer, then the spell breaks and they follow me.

I tug on the garage door, and up it goes. There in the dust is an old 3-wheeled atv and a quad. The rest is typical garage – cup-boards, workbenches, tools on the walls, junk. We go through it all piece by piece, as we do any new space we are looting. And looting it is, though we know by this time that no owners will ever return to begrudge us our loot.

We walk through slowly, opening the closed spaces one by one, turning over every item, exploring every dark corner. We wander back to the door and watch the house burn, then get back to our rummaging. But now the house is starting to fold in on itself, so we all three stand in the door and watch it go. The north end goes first, real slow, just like a camp fire settling down on its embers. In five minutes the whole structure is almost at ground level.

"Must be a basement it's falling into," says Jack.

"No. It's just dug out low," says Jo. "Easier to keep it warm in the winter and cool in the summer."

"Like a sod house," says Jack, pleased at the connection.

"Right."

When it seems the fire will do nothing more than simmer, I turn back into the garage. That's when I see a sprinkle of dust fall from the plank ceiling above us. I haven't thought about it before, but the garage is oddly made. Most have nothing but tresses up above, a crisscross of two-by-fours. But this one has a ceiling, which means there's a closed space above it.

I take Jo and Jack by the shoulders, point up, and put my finger across my lips. They nod and look up. Then I go about just like before, opening cupboards and poking at the junk, but I am looking now for the way into the attic space. The garage has two narrow bays with a set of wood shelves between them. Above the top shelf is a trapdoor, the shelves themselves acting as ladder to it.

"Probly a coon," whispers Jack. "Remember the time Dad shot one living under the deck?"

The door in the ceiling has no handle that we can see and seems to be just a frame that lifts out. I take a length of oak trim that stands in the corner and use it to push hard against the door. It lifts up, but falls right back into place.

"It's not hinged," says Jo. "Hit it good on one end and it'll flip over."

Jo has called it right, for that's just what it does.

"Hello?" I yell toward the opening. "Anyone up there?"

We don't expect a voice to answer back, but we listen for movement. The house behind us isn't roaring anymore, just crackling and popping like a bonfire. No sound comes from the attic.

"Hey!" I yell again. "We're gonna light this garage up! You better climb down from there if you don't want to get roasted." Jack looks at me strange, but I shake my head.

Then Jo yells out, "Let me put a few holes up there first, then we'll burn it!" He points the .22 toward the house and begins firing slowly, a second or two between each shot. At four we hear a scrabbling from above, and dropping dust marks something moving from one corner of the attic toward the hole. But not quite to it. I put up a hand to stop Jo, then we each aim our gun at the hole.

47

"I bet it's a cat," says Jack.

"It's a coon," says Jo.

"Bet ya a dollar it's a cat."

"You're on."

It wasn't a cat.

Four small, white fingers appear from out of the black and slip over the frame's edge. Then another four. They pull at the edge of the opening, and a white face, squinting against the light shows itself between the hands. Wisps of long hair fall down and hang there. It is entirely human, this thing we're looking at. It is a girl.

We put our guns down, and Jo whispers to Jack, "You owe me a dollar."

Chapter 10

She is younger than any of us – seven or eight maybe. When we do finally talk her into coming down, she won't go farther than to sit on the quad. She takes our questions in turn and with little in the way of elaboration. At each question she eyes the attic door like she would fly there.

"What's your name?"

"Becka."

"How old are you?"

"Seven and a half."

"This your house?"

A nod.

"How'd it burn down?"

She looks past Jo toward the burning house.

"You do it?"

Another nod.

"How?"

"Left the stove open."

"Wood stove?"

A nod.

"How long you been alone here?"

Becka looks at her hands like she wants to count days or weeks or months on her fingers. She looks up and shrugs.

"Your mom and dad die?"

Another nod.

"You here by yourself?"

Her eyes go to Jack, to the house, then the attic. She nods again.

"No brothers or sisters?"

Another nod.

"Oh."

"You want to come home with us?" asks Jack.

"Hold on," I say.

"She's seven," he says. "We can't leave her here."

"She's gotten by so far," I say, "Besides – "

But before I can finish my argument she is up the shelves and into the attic again. The door slides over the opening and drops into place with a thud.

"She's quick as a cat anyway," says Jo.

"I don't think she wants to come home with you," I say.

"Maybe she doesn't want to go," says Jack, looking at me, "with someone who doesn't want her."

"She's gotten by so far."

"You said that."

"Musta meant it."

"So we just let her live out here in a garage? No food, no water, no bed. She's seven."

"I know how old she is."

"A seven-year old will die out here without a house."

"She's kept herself alive this long. She musta found water, kept warm all winter. Maybe she knows more than most seven-year-olds."

49

"She burned her own house down, and probably her food with it. Why are you arguing? You know I'm right."

"We can't pick up every stray we find is all. There's lots of strays. And every one is another one to feed."

"I'm not talking about every stray, just this one, and she can't eat much."

"She's gotten by so far," I say again as I wander to the door. The house is not a house anymore but a wide bed of orange embers planted here and there with water pipes and conduit. It glows and pulses like something living. Jo and Jack join me.

"The wind's picking up," says Jo, who always has an eye out for weather.

"The garage could catch fire if it blows this way," says Jack.

"It's not," I say, wanting to contradict. "It's blowing west."

"It's an east wind," says Jo.

"No," I say. "That way's west."

"It comes from the east, so it's an east wind."

"Whatever."

Jack points at the house. "Look. Those trees."

The trees along that edge of the yard are smoking. Then one lights up near its bottom. We watch the fire slither up its trunk until the whole thing is alight. A smaller one behind it catches fire too.

"Just the dead ash trees will burn," says Jo. "The rest will be fine."

We've come to take his pronouncements on natural things as book truth, so we don't even offer up comment to this one.

Jack goes back into the garage and picks up the piece of oak. He pushes it against the door, but it doesn't budge.

"She's sitting on it," he says. "Help me."

Like everything of wood around me, my arguments against this are turning to ash. The three of us together push up on one end until we hear the little crash of her body thump against the floor. Jack jumps up the shelves and stops the door from sliding back into place. He climbs into the attic. Jo pulls out a flashlight and climbs up too.

I decide to let the two of them wrestle her out of there and walk to the garage door. Three or four other trees are burning now. I am trying to make out how many are ash when I hear a scream, then my

50

name being shouted. The tone of it makes me spring up the shelves and into the opening without a thought. My flashlight is out and in my hand.

"What's wrong?" I shout. The sudden darkness, the flashing light through the dusty air, and strange shrill sounds make my head spin.

"There," says Jo. His light is on the far wall. With her back against it sits Becka. Her face is hiding between her drawn up knees. And on either side of her, under each arm, are two small, crying children, a boy and a girl.

"Where's Jack," I ask. Jo's beam goes to the right a little. He sits Indian-style on a stack of ceiling panels and is holding his hand.

"She bit me," he says.

"Serves you right," I say. "Bringin home strays is dangerous."

With some coaxing and some creative description of what it might be like to die in a fire, we manage to get the three out of the garage. Jack picks up one of the twins and begins walking out of the yard back through the trees toward our house. Becka flies at him in a rage, but Jack seems ready for it. He switches the child to his left hand and with his right strikes Becka on the forehead, an open-handed slap that sends her to the ground stunned.

He stands over her.

"You can come home with us, with your brother and sister, or you can stay here alone and die. Make up your mind."

He walks away. Jo has the other twin and follows Jack. I carry the guns and walk past Becka without looking at her. I can hear her crying. We get to the tree line where Jo just told the duck story, and they set the twins down to rest.

"There she is," says Jack. "Don't look at her." I glance back and get just a glimpse of the girl standing behind a tree watching us. Jo and Jack pick the kids up and set off across the field. We are just to the Reeders' backyard when I turn and see Becka slowly picking her way through the stubble behind us.

"Should we wait for her?" asks Jack.

"Just so she can see where we're going," says Jo.

We move that way back to our house, a hundred yards at a time, with Becka always in sight. At the house, we don't go in but sit on the back deck. It is like drawing in a wary animal – no quickness, no gestures, every movement calculated for trust and friendliness.

She seems stuck at the back gate and will come no closer. Finally, Jack yells out, "We're not gonna eat ya! Come over here and tell us how to feed the little ones! They look hungry!"

"Ignore her," says Jo. "She'll come when she's ready."

We look the twins over carefully now. They are somewhere between one and two. They can walk fine, but have few words to say. Both are diapered in old t-shirts, which we promptly burn. When we go to scrub them clean in snow, they both let out a howl and Becka comes running the rest of the way through the yard. We don't intend to move her by torturing the little ones, but that's how she takes it. We've been using snow on our own bodies the whole winter.

They'd been fed ok, but that is about all. Their nails are too long, though she's tried to clip them some time back. They are dirty in places that a seven-year-old would probably never think to clean.

"Go get em some food," I say to Jack.

"What kind?"

"Fruit maybe? Canned peaches."

When we put it in front of them, they go at it like hungry pups.

Jo asks, "Where we gonna put em?"

"Hadn't thought about it."

"We could take the walls down," says Jo.

"Too much winter left for that."

"What about the basement on this side?"

"No windows."

As he often does, Jo is doing his thinking as he stares out toward the lake and his home.

"I been thinking," he says.

"About what?"

"I been thinking about moving my trailer over here, maybe putting it up in Quinn's yard, or...or closer if you don't care. And how maybe I am thinking about it not for me but for them, like God knew we'd need it so he put those thoughts in my head early."

He pulls his eyes away from the horizon and begins picking at the dirt under his nails.

"That make any sense? God talk that way to us?"

"My dad says...said...that he talks to us through the Bible."

"I wouldn't know about that," says Jo.

"You never read it?"

"Nope."

"We should read it. Out loud, I mean. We used to do that at night. We could take turns or something."

"But he could talk to us that way, right? If he wanted to, he could put thoughts in somebody's head?"

"He's God. He can do whatever he wants, but...I don't know. I figure if it's not in the Bible, it's not God talking, and if it is in the Bible already then why do you need any other way? Just read the Bible."

"The Bible says somethin about trailers?"

"Not exactly. You have to read a lot of it to know what it says about the stuff it doesn't talk about. That's not exactly what I mean. What I mean is – "

Jo stands up and begins walking in long strides through the yard. At first I think he's getting something out of the shed, but he just keeps walking.

"Where you going?" I yell after him.

"Home," says Jo.

"For what?"

"Just home," he says, not looking back.

"Moving the trailer's a good idea!" I yell after him. "We could use Mr. Quinn's tractor and pull it over tomorrow!"

Jack comes out from the house then. "Where's he goin?"

"Home," I answer.

"For what?"

"No idea."

"You make him mad?"

"I don't think so. Maybe. I don't know."

"He left his gun." It stands against the house by the back door. "He musta been thinking hard about something to forget it. He never forgets it." Jack picks up the gun and slings it over his shoulder. "I'll go see what he's doing."

"You're leaving me? With them?"

"If she could look after them, you can too."

He steps off the porch, but instead of heading south, across the yard, on Jo's trail, he goes west.

"Why you goin that way?" I ask.

"Thought I saw a broken window at the Steimers'. Wanted to look. Watch, I'll catch him before he even hits the pines." He begins running.

"I'll go with you," I say.

"Don't leave them," he yells, running backward. "Stay here. There's a fire in the stove. She might burn our house down too!" He turns and is sprinting now, almost through the Steimers' yard already.

I tell myself I should go with him, and I don't know where the thought comes from or why it's so insistent. Watching him run, I feel a funny knock in my ribs that makes me want to yell out, to stop him, to grab hold of him and keep him there, with me, in our house. But I don't.

Chapter 11

That night I get out canned chili and fruit cocktail and warm them both on the wood stove. Becka still isn't talking, but she isn't shy about sharing our food. And for all her ignorance about keeping the little kids clean, she does have a knack for mothering. She feeds herself and the twins at the same time, like she's been doing it that way for a while.

I dig up some of dad's old t-shirts for diapers. She seems grateful. She doesn't say so, but she does turn them over and over in her hands and smell every one like she's sniffing flowers. Then she looks up at me and whispers, "Where do you potty?"

"Next door. There's an old barn foundation with a tree growing in it. You kind of sit…and…hang there…if you can reach the…never mind. You can use the bathroom, but you'll have to go get another bucket for the flushing."

She looks at me like I'm talking backward, so I show her where the bathroom is and tell her to come get me when she's done. We've learned a lot just figuring out how to go to the bathroom in this new world. At first we'd fill the toilet, then get a pail of water from the creek that runs through the Park's corn field, haul it back and flush the day's collection. That didn't work well. If we were lazy about it for just one day, the house would smell up so bad you could hardly sleep. We knew there must be a better method. We struck on the outhouse idea, but found the frozen ground too much for us. The barn foundation in the lot next to us will prove a good fix until the soil thaws out.

But for emergencies – though this was not one we've anticipated – we keep a full bucket handy. When Becka finishes, I show her how to dump the bucket into the bowl, but I realize as I'm doing it that it will be too heavy for her. Tomorrow I'll go to the creek for a refill and show her how to use the arrangement next door.

I hear the back door open, and when I step out of the bathroom, I am greeted by Jo.

"Where's my gun?" he asks. "I left it on the deck."

"Jack had it," I say. "He brought it to you."

"When was that?"

"He was right behind you," I say, and there is a quick pull on my insides like I've fallen through air. "Just a minute or two behind you. He was going to the Steimers then through their back yard to catch you at the pines. You never saw him?"

He shakes his head. "Why the Steimers?"

"Thought he saw a broken window." I put my shoes on, grab the shotgun, and hand Jo the .243.

We walk to the Steimers and find that a small kitchen window has been pried out from its casement. This is new. We'd been through the house months before and cleaned their pantry out pretty well. Other than that, we'd left it as we found it. But now the place is up-ended. Every cupboard door and drawer is open, the insides flung everywhere.

"Makes no sense," says Jo.

"Maybe he walked in on something," I say.

Outside we can find nothing. It is dark now, and the snow on the lawns is so patchy that we could walk miles without leaving a footprint.

"We'll have to wait till morning," says Jo. "Maybe we'll pick up something in the grass."

"I knew something would happen."

"What do you mean?"

"I mean I knew. I could feel something wrong when he walked off. It was weird."

"Nothing's wrong yet. Maybe he just found something to do. He would have walked by the Quinns' and the Flemings'. Maybe he found something there to interest him. Let's check it out."

"You can. That's fine. I don't think he's here."

I let him walk off alone at first, but I decide against it and catch up to him before he reaches the Quinns'. We circle it slow, peaking into the windows and looking for light, but there's nothing. The next house over, the Flemings', is the same. We go by the Campbell's, Smiths, and Parks; then cross the road and look into the three houses on that side on our way back. I guess the road had set our limits on familiarity because at the time of the dying I knew none of the family names on that side.

When we do finish the circuit and are back at the house, Jo says, "We'll see more in the morning. I'm sure of it."

But it isn't the morning light that tells us where Jack has gone. It is a big white pickup truck that pulls into our drive as we're getting Becka and the twins fixed up for breakfast. We tell the kids to stay put by the fire and not to come out, that we need to talk to some friends.

It's Chief and some of his tribe. There are a dozen or so packed into the cab and bed. As soon as the truck stops they spill out, open the gate and begin pulling out a piece of plywood loaded with something heavy. Jo and I stand on the deck and watch. No one says anything, not even Chief. He gets out of the car and stands next to me and watches.

There are too many in the way for me to see what's on the board, but when they have it out of the truck and begin walking it toward us, they turn, and I can see that it's a body. My heart makes a stumbling thump, and the next breath comes in a gasp. I think it is Jack coming home to us as a corpse. We'd seen that in the early days of the dying, while there were still a few adults around to bring the bodies. But the boys are being too careful with this one. Whoever is on it — and somehow I know now it's not Jack — is alive.

I can't tell if it's a boy or a girl. A winter hat is pulled down over his or her head, and it nearly covers the eyes. The body is wrapped up tight and in so many blankets that it looks cocooned.

They step onto the deck. Chief pushes some things off the picnic table and says, "put him here." The boys obey, then step back.

"What is this?" I say.

"My cousin," says Chief. "Marcus."

He nods at the boy. His words are plain, none of the bravado of our last meeting.

"Why are you bringing him here?" I ask.

"For you to fix him," says Chief.

"What do you mean?"

He looks to one of the boys and says, "Show him." A little blond kid in a Detroit Lions jacket steps forward and begins pulling away the blankets around his legs. He does it quickly but gently, like maybe he's been the one to do the wrapping too. The last is a bloody towel. When he pulls this one off, a smell like old cheese hits my nose. The foot looks like something has nearly pinched it off through the middle. Most of it below the crushed part is black, green around the toe nails. Above the break, the skin is gray to the ankle and swollen like it might burst if I breath on it.

"What happened?"

"He was changing a tire and the jack broke. Wheel rim landed on his foot." It Chief talking, and he says it quick, like he wants to get his answer out first. None of the others adds to his story, and most are suddenly interested in other things — my backyard, their own shoes.

"What do you want me to do?" I ask.

"I want you to take his foot off before he dies of poisoned blood."

"Poisoned blood?"

"Yeah. You get infection, step on a nail, get a finger cut off, you get poisoned blood. He'll die if we don't cut it off. Where is she?"

"Where's who?"

"Your sister, who do you think?" He goes for the door, but Jo steps in front of him.

"She's not here," he says.

Chief looks down his big nose, sucks in his gut and sets his considerable chest against Jo's. "Not here?"

Jo shakes his head. Chief looks past him, through the door glass. Then he looks back at the boy on the table.

"That's fine," he says, grinning now. He steps back. "Here's how we're gonna do it."

He walks back to his cousin and begins folding the blankets back over him.

"I'm gonna leave Marcus here. Someone here knows how to cut off fingers and put in stitches. Whoever that someone is can do it for Marcus too. And because I'm a man of my word, I promise to take care of your friend the same way."

"What friend?" I ask.

He turns right and left with arms out, and says, "You lose more than one friend last night?"

I say nothing. I wait for the story.

"We trailed you that day in Okemos. Two of my boys been in that house watching ever since. Funny. They never saw the sister or the hunter boys you mentioned. Just you three. We decided last night that we were done sneakin around, that we'd just come over and tell you plain that you fix up Marcus or we burn your house down. Then your friend comes peekin in our windows and made the whole thing easier."

Chief starts toward the truck, and Jo says, "You coulda just asked."

"What's that?" Chief says.

"You coulda just asked for our help and we'd a done it."

This strikes him as funny. He grins like he's just proven himself clever and dodged a prank aimed at a him.

"No. You mighta tried, but now you'll do more than try."

He gets into the truck and rolls the window down. The rest of the boys climb on, pushing, jostling each other like brothers for the best places.

"If he lives, you can ask him how to find us. His head's not working too good right now. You find us and we'll trade back."

"And if he doesn't live?" I ask.

"Then don't bother." He puts the truck in reverse and begins backing out. "Eye for eye, tooth for tooth, blood for blood."

I follow him down the drive until he backs into the road and points west.

"But it's not our blood," I say.

"It's yours now," says Chief, and he puts it in drive. "Yours to lose, yours to save."

"How long then?"

"One week." He tears away. The boys in back brace themselves like they know it's coming.

"I could follow him," says Jo. We watch them speed west down the hill, lean into the curve at the Parks', and disappear .

"What's the point? He knows where we live. If we found Jack and we did manage to get him out, they'd just come back. He might not a cut your arm off, but I think he would burn a house down."

Jo is quiet, which means he agrees with me. We walk back to the deck. Then he says, "That ain't a finger you'd have to cut off."

"I know it."

"The bone would have to be sawed."

"Right."

"There's other things in there too. Veins and nerves and stuff."

"Tendons," I say. "Or ligaments. I forget the difference."

"You think that's all in those books?"

"I'm hoping," I say.

We stand over the boy. He is fevered. His breathing is quick and shallow. Every few seconds he opens his eyes, but they are opaque, independent of the brain.

Jo looks off to the south and says again, "That ain't a finger you'll be cuttin off."

"I know it."

Chapter 12

I spend the next hours combing through the books we've taken from the library. I try to get Jo to help me with this, but he seems pretty upset about the dying boy — it's clear he's dying though we say nothing of it — and wants no more than to watch over him and the little ones. I leave him alone.

Most of the books are useless for this task, but not all — I still have the copy of *The Illustrated Manual of Operative Surgery and Surgical Anatomy* by Bernard and Huette. Not only does it lay out all the steps for taking off an arm or a leg, it also has illustrations of every instrument an operation might need. So I don't have to guess at what forceps, retractor, or bistoury is. I can see it. I can also try to approximate it with a hand tool from the garage. Forceps are pliers. A retractor works like a clamp but in reverse, keeping things apart instead of holding them together. And a bistoury is just a sharp knife, though I think we'd call it a scalpel.

Once I think I know the whole procedure, I call in Jo to hear me rehearse it. I make him lie down on the table, cinch his leg down like I had done with Jack's hand (I only get one more pair of holes drilled before the battery dies), and give Jo the book to hold.

"What do I do with this?"

"I may need you to read it to me if both my hands are busy. Just check and see if I've got the order right. Elevate the limb. Make a cut on the anterior side half way around. Then the posterior side a ways below the dissection line. That'll give us a big flap to work with. Posterior means back side. Dad used to say 'get goin before I swat your posterior.'"

"Shouldn't you wash it first?"

"Well, yeah. I'll wrap the foot up in plastic wrap, wash the leg with alcohol, and use a sharpie to mark the cut lines."

Jo scrunches up his eyes at the page he holds open above him.

"There's nothing about a sharpie there," I say. "It's a civil war book."

"Right."

"Then clamp and divide – that means cut – the saphenous vein." I point out the vein in the illustration. "I'll need you to hold the vein shut with the needle-nose pliers and maybe sponge up the blood."

"While I'm holdin the book too?"

"Yeah. Then I cut the fibula at a 45-degree angle and trim the sharp end with bone nibblers. Side-cutters will work for that." I forget what comes next. "What's next?"

Jo runs his finger down the page like he's lost his place. "Next is . . . hang on . . . the next step – "

" – I remember. Finish the posterior flap. Cut back along the edge of the bones, keeping the fat and most of the muscle. Though it sounds like the more muscle we keep the higher chance of inflection."

We'd found a stack of orthopedic surgery magazines at Dr. Spedoske's. One of them has an article on amputating the foot of a diabetic. I can't follow most of it, but I do find a long discussion on risks of infection.

"Let's just keep the skin. Next we pull out the sciatic nerve and divide it. I'll use the small needle-nose for that. Once it's cut, it should pull back up into the muscle. Cut the tibia at a 45 degree, then straight down to take the sharp end off."

Jo has the book on his chest now, and his face is the color of skim milk.

"You ok?" I ask.

"Yeah. Just need to lay here a minute."

"Ok. We're done." I take the book and read silently the last steps on sewing up the skin. I will need to leave it loose since it will tighten up over the next weeks. I go through the steps once again in pantomime over Jo's leg. Incise from the anterior to the posterior, divide the saphenous vein, finish posterior flap, extract and divide the sciatic.

Incise to the posterior, divide saphenous, extract the sciatic. The words are other-worldly and nearly trick me into thinking I am doing something other than cutting off a foot. Incise. Divide. Extract. Suture. They sound like terms from math class, and there's no blood in math class.

"Will he be awake for it?" Jo asks. His color is back, mostly.

"I hope not," I say. "He's delirious now. I think he'll stay that way, though I don't know what the pain will do to him."

"Might kill him," says Jo.

"It might."

Jo sits up. "When you wanna do it?"

"Soon. Before the sun gets too low."

It is the middle of the afternoon now. I've spent half the day reading and getting tools and supplies together. I have Jo keep an eye on Marcus, which amounts to dribbling water and children's Tylenol into his mouth.

Jo has me worried. I'll need him to be steady through this. I don't think there is much of a chance that the boy will survive it, but what chance there is lies in doing everything right and quick. He nearly passed out just hearing me describe it. What will happen when the blood starts to flow or the boy wakes up screaming? He will need to be focused, to always have something to do. Jo is good with any task that requires his hands to be moving. I need to keep his hands occupied.

But I have myself to worry about too. I have to be quick. If I do it quick, there'll be less blood, less pain, less stress on his already weak body. If I do it quick, there is more of a chance we'll get Jack back. So I rehearse the operation in my head, over and over.

Incise, divide, extract, suture.

But I am starting to find that the more I go over it, the more I imagine it going wrong. The adrenalin I've been running on all day is thinning and agitates only the smaller parts of me, the motors of nervous worry.

I walk Becka, Nate and the twins to the Johnson house next door and start a fire in the hearth. I've loaded Becka with canned fruit, crayons, and coloring books and present the excursion as a picnic. The

62

walk and shift in activity is good for me, and I feel a rising acuity in my eyes as I step back into the house.

"We do it now," I say to Jo. "I'll get the table ready. You get him cleaned up." I give Jo a roll of Saran Wrap and a bottle of rubbing alcohol. We'd taken the lower floor wall down and put Marcus and his plywood stretcher in the living room on two saw horses. We'd thought about doing the operation right there, but the blankets are so dirty we'd have to move him anyway. And the kitchen table will be steadier.

My dad taught me that no matter how small the job, you always underestimate the number of tools you'll need, so a wise man starts with the whole tool box. I load up a TV tray with every kind of plier and cutting tool I can find. I put a new edge on a small lockblade and two paring knives. These will be my scalpels. I have chisels, serrated knives, hacksaw blades, hammers, and screwdrivers. On a paper plate I have laid out a dozen little O's of silk thread, each one the first half of a square knot. These will tie off whatever veins we run into. But I also have a ball of twine, a real of fishing line, and rolls of masking, electrical, and duct tapes. Behind me on the floor is my dad's tool box filled with every hand tool he owned. I can't imagine why we might find use for a crescent wrench, but I have one.

We lay out clean towels and move Marcus to the table. The foot is covered, but I can still smell it. The area I'll be cutting on – about half-way between knee and ankle – is clean. I lift the leg and realize we haven't got anything to hold it up. I've been focused too much on the surgery, not enough on the nursing. "Can I use a pillow or should it be something hard?" I ask Jo.

"How would I know that?" he says.

"Look in the book. Read it. It's in that first paragraph."

Jo seems annoyed. He hands the book my way and says, "I forgot something in the living room."

Before I can stop him, he's gone. I don't want to keep moving Marcus's leg up and down, so I let the book lie on Marcus and wait. He comes back with a mantle clock.

"Thought we should know how long this takes," he says. It seems a strange idea to have at this point, but it makes some sense.

"OK," I say, "now read that paragraph to me, and hurry up, my arms are getting tired."

Slowly, Jo picks up the book and holds it in front of him. He squints his eyes and begins reading. The words come slow. "When lifting the patient's leg, it is important to have something under it to hold it up. Use a . . . a box or a big book . . . or . ."

Jo closes the book quickly and looks around for something. He picks up a plastic crate that holds art supplies. "This should work." He tries to shove it under the wrapped foot.

"That's not what the book says."

"What do you mean?"

"I read that part today. That's not what it says. You made it up."

"Why would I make it up?"

"I don't know, but you did."

It occurs to me then that I've never seen Jo read anything. He is always working on things, but never does he have a manual or instructions nearby. He can't read. I don't say anything, because it also occurs to me that he's been trying to hide it all along. There was the list he wouldn't start because he'd just lose it. Truth is he never loses or forgets anything. There was the time he stormed off the porch when I mentioned reading the Bible in turns.

He can't read, and I'm sure of it, but the fact creates a kind of dissonance that I have to wave away. I don't have time to consider this, and I let the matter go.

I set the book, open to the pages I need, on Marcus's belly and put the crescent wrench on it to hold it open. I hand the sharpie to Jo and point to where I need a line drawn.

"Start here, come over the top and half way around to here."

I look at the book again and re-read the instructions for the cut that will shape the posterior flap.

"From the end of that line along the middle, back to here, then down under and back to the beginning."

Jo says nothing, but draws the lines perfectly.

My heart is beating drum-like. I hand Jo the hacksaw.

"I'll need that next."

Then I pick up the lock-blade. I set the point of the blade on the black mark where it begins at the side of the calf muscle.

"Wait," says Jo.

I look up at him.

"Wait for what?"

"We're forgetting something," says Jo.

I hold the blade there and wait. I can hear the blood beat inside my ears. Jo is staring hard into the distance between us. His eyes are pinched almost closed.

"I can't wait anymore. We have to do this now."

The point of the blade goes in and Jo shouts, "Tourniquet!"

I pull the blade away. A tiny drop of blood slides down Marcus's calf. We spend the next ten minutes getting a tourniquet on – a skinny leather belt of mom's, a piece of broom stick for twisting it tight, and twine for tying it in place.

I pray this time, start the blade up from the same spot, up, towards me. The blade slips right into the skin and fat, touches the shin bone and slips up and over to the other side. There is very little blood. I bring the blade down to where the line stops and turns toward the foot when Jo says, "He didn't feel it."

"That's good. Maybe he won't wake up."

I begin the ninety-degree turn down the leg toward the foot.

"No, Liam, I mean he didn't feel nothin. I am looking right at his face. I couldn't watch, so I looked right at his face, and he didn't flinch."

Jo puts a finger under his nose, then feels at his neck for a pulse, but I can tell he doesn't really know where to look.

"Liam, I think he's dead."

"Let me try."

I don't know where to look either, so I grip his neck with both hands, my fingers pressing in everywhere for the thump of a beating heart. I wait a few seconds, listening with my fingers. I wait a minute. I feel nothing.

"We check deer. . ." Jo has a funny look on his face, like he doesn't want to finish.

"What? How do you check deer?"

"You know a deer is dead if you . . . put a stick in his eye and he doesn't blink."

I pull back on one of Marcus's eyelids, hold out a sharpie, and say, "Go ahead."

Jo takes the other end and touches it gently at the corner of the eye. There is no blinking. He does it again, this time harder and right on the green part. Nothing. I let go, but the eyelid stays open. One eye open, one closed. It doesn't look funny at all, and I make them both closed.

I look up at Jo for something, a word, a look.

"Did I wait too long?"

Jo shakes his head.

"I think if you'd a done it earlier, and he was this close to dying, you'd a killed him with the knife. Better this way. He didn't feel nothin at all this way."

I think Jo is right in this, but still, I am bothered by dreams of it for many nights.

Chapter 13

It doesn't occur to me until after that we let Jack's whereabouts die on that table.

"We could write a note on one of their buildings," says Jo. I look at him to see if he's joking, but he keeps at his chore – sharpening knives – with a straight face. Does he know that I know?

"Maybe they don't look at the buildings anymore. I mean if there's no one around to challenge them, why bother?"

"So they do own everything," Jo says.

"They think they do."

Then I remember the girl with the tattoo.

66

Jo says, "We could go back to where we ran into them last time."

"We could do that."

"Then if we didn't find em, we could get the stuff we hid at Home Depot."

"Right."

He sets down a big Swiss Army and picks up a skinning knife.

"So what do you think we should do?"

"I think I know someone that can help."

"Who do you know who's not in this house and still alive?"

As we gather our stuff, I explain to him what the girl had said to me before I dropped her off by the corn field. She knows the Westgate Eagles, knows them well enough to be tattooed with their logo. She'll know where they live.

We hook the trailer up again and head out by Okemos Road. Where the businesses are closed, we drive slow, looking for signs of life. There are no boys shooting bottles by the 7-11 this time, and apart from a few more broken windows, it all looks just as it did two months earlier.

I stop the car where I'd dropped her off. The cut corn field is bare now, and the frozen furrows are muddied and criss-crossed with deer track. Across the field where the woods begin, the deer blind is still there, sitting high up on its stilts.

"I don't see anything," says Jo. "Is there a house in those woods?"

"Nope. The woods only go a little ways, then it's I-96."

"You really think she's in that blind?"

"I don't see where else she could have gone."

As we drive the width of the field, the blind sharpens into focus. It is not empty. A movement obscures the light between the windows. There is apparatus on the roof that is not the usual deer-blind paraphernalia. The structure is bigger, more sturdily built than we can see from the road. It stands on four big posts, 6x6's rough sawn, maybe out of trees from these woods. The bottom must be 15 feet off the ground. An iron ladder goes straight up to a trap door beneath. When I cut the engine, I hear a distinct knock from above, like a boot heel on a wood floor.

"Anybody home?" I yell. "Hello!"

Jo joins me for a good, long round of yelling, but no one opens or answers back. We decide to knock. Jo goes up first and I follow. Just as he is about to rap his knuckles on the wood, the door flies up and in its place appear the twin barrels of a side-by-side shotgun. One barrel for each of us. Jo puts an arm over his head like he is fending off a hard rain.

"It's me!" I shout. "I drove you home a few weeks ago. You asked if I was nice."

"I don't remember your answer," comes a girl's voice from the space above, "and you're trespassing now, so I think your answer doesn't matter too much."

"We came for your help. Can we climb up?"

"You may not. Climb down and talk to me from there."

"Can you at least not point the gun at us?" says Jo.

"You'll just have to get used to that," she answers.

At the bottom we watch her climb down with one hand, like she's done it many times before. The other holds the gun.

"Sit," she says when she steps off the ladder. The posts are anchored in concrete forms just big enough to keep our butts off the muddy ground. "What do you want?"

She looks like the same girl, but there is something different about her. I feel I am looking at a much older version.

"I told you about my brother, that he was hurt."

"I remember," she says.

I explain to her what we did with Jack's hand, how we ran into the Eagles, how they'd followed us home and taken Jack in exchange for our fixing one of theirs who'd gotten a foot crushed under a car.

"Marcus?" she asks.

"Uh huh."

"How is he?"

"He's dead. He died before we could do anything for him."

The girl seems moved by this, but whatever sign of it she might have shown is cut off, and she gives us that same flinty look.

"Did you know him?" asks Jo.

Her eyes go to some point behind me and beyond this encounter. For a moment, she is somewhere else.

"You told me before that you knew these guys," I say.

"I did?" says Maya.

"You said you belonged to them and showed me a tattoo."

She pulls herself back and looks down at her arm.

"Yeah," she says. "I did."

"You did what?" asks Jo.

"I did know em. And I did belong to em. But I don't now, don't belong to em I mean."

"Could you help us find them?"

"Sure. I could."

"Would you?"

"Sure." She settles down on her haunches and shifts the gun to her lap. "If the price is right."

Jo and I exchange looks.

"Nothing's free," she says, "and everything's for sale. I'll tell you where Ricky lives for ten tanks of propane and thirty cans of meat."

"What do you mean meat?" I ask.

"Canned meat. Canned chicken. Canned ham, turkey, chili, whatever. I got nothing left but canned vegetables and fruit."

I am about to agree to her terms when Jo says, "Five tanks and 10 cans."

"You think he's just gonna keep your brother around till you find him? He'll kill him as soon as he's tired of feeding him. Or he'll just stop feeding him. 8 tanks, 20 cans, and I'll draw you a map."

"We've got a week," says Jo. "We can find him by ourselves if we have to. Five tanks. 15 cans. And you come with us."

"No deal," she says, and slings the gun over her shoulder. "I ain't never goin back there." She starts up the ladder. "You're on your own."

I watch her climb, but Jo turns to go and says, "Come on."

She is at the top, pushing up on the trap door. I shout up at her. "Eight tanks, 20 cans, and a map!" As soon as I say it, I hear a groan behind me.

The girl takes her hand from the door, turns her head, and looks down at me with a grin. "Let's start over," she says. "And I'll be bargaining with you this time."

Chapter 14

"Twelve," says Jo under his breath, "when she'd a done it for three." We are unhooking another tank from a gas grill. We've spent the last two hours working our way through a neighbor-hood off Dell, and this will be the last of 12 tanks. We have the 40 cans of meat in our own pantry, but this deal has cut our supply in half. Jo complains indirectly – mutterings, body language. I don't argue with him. He's right, and I am still appeasing him over the reading thing, so I leave it alone.

We are in Quinn's pickup. It's four-wheel drive and the only thing we have that will get us through the muddy field. We follow the map she's drawn on the back of an envelope. It leads us to an area a couple miles northeast of the girl's deer blind. Here are several old, wealthy developments with wide walks and proud oaks. As we wind our way deeper into one of these neighborhoods, the deal I'd struck for the map seems not quite so lopsided. It'd have taken us a year to stumble onto the little cul-de-sac where Ricky lives. I mention that to Jo, but he just shakes his head.

As we turn onto this street, we catch sight, about three doors down, of a boy hitting a golf ball at a house. Most of the windows are broken out, but there is still a big one on the second floor. I can see a ball hit just above it and bounce back into the front yard where a hundred other balls are scattered.

He is standing on a landscaped island in the middle of the concrete circle. There are others nearby, younger ones holding clubs and watching at first the boy doing the swinging, then us as we drive closer. One of them drops his club and runs for a house on the opposite side.

I drive up the road slowly, but when the little group begins to walk warily toward the house, I punch the gas and put the truck between them and it. They scatter. Jo is out even before I stop, the shotgun at his shoulder. I am swinging the door open when I hear him yell Hey! Stop! He fires one shot. A boy goes down to his knees at the bottom of the drive.

70

"Stay there!" I yell. I have the .38 aimed at him. He is crying. I yank him up by the arm and drag him to the truck. "Get in," I say, and put the barrel of the gun against his neck as a prod.

The other boys have made it to the porch of the house. As I circle around the island, the door opens and an older boy steps out with a rifle in hand. It isn't Chief. I drive to the end of the road, a hundred yards or so, and turn the truck sideways. I drag the boy out and the two of us stand behind the truck. Jo is in the bed sitting cross-legged on a bag of rock salt. He has the .243 now and is eyeing the boy with the gun through the scope. The boy walks down the drive and onto the street.

"That's far enough!" I yell, but he keeps walking. "Put one close to him." Jo fires. A talcum-like puff erupts between the boy's feet. He stops now.

"That was close alright," I say to Jo.

"He's bow-legged."

"Where's my brother?" I say. "Where's Jack?"

"I don't see Marcus in that truck. We're supposed to be trading, remember?"

After we'd delivered the tanks and food to the girl, Jo and I sat in the truck and talked over two things. One was to hatch a couple of plans. We'd catch one of the boys if we could. This plan was simple in its parts: scare them, shoot if we have to, throw one of them in the truck. How that would work itself out we would just wait and see. The other plan was to watch the house until dark and then break Jack out, or catch one the boys, whichever opportunity presented itself as least likely to get us killed.

The other thing we talked about was what to say – should we find ourselves in a position to bargain – about Marcus. My thought was to say nothing about him being dead and to wait for a chance to spring Jack. Then if things didn't go as we wanted we could explain how Marcus had died the very day they brought him. In fact, I pointed out, our being there suggested that Marcus did survive. How else would we have found them except that he'd told us?

Jo's thought was to be more direct. Tell them he died, that he was half way to dying when they left him, and that Jack had nothing to do with it. He thought we should appeal to something brighter in their natures, propose a truce, propose that we cooperate and see some advantage to our mutual survival. As bright as he is in other ways, he had no idea that there was nothing good in our natures. We would tell them nothing.

I ask the boy next to me, "Where's Chief?"

He is shaking. "Who – who's chief?"

"Ricky I mean."

"Ricky is gone."

"What do you mean?"

"He's gone."

"Gone where? Gone like he left or gone dead?"

"He left. He left yesterday."

I say to the boy standing in the street, "I want to talk to Ricky." I point to the porch. "Have one of those guys go get him."

The boy in the street seems hesitant, like he is thinking hard. He looks toward the porch.

"Go get Ricky."

No one moves at first and then a stocky kid with glasses steps into the house. A minute later he steps out again and says too loud, "He's busy. He'll be out in a minute."

I shove the boy back into the car just as Jo says, "He's not here."

I catch a glimpse of someone moving between two trees behind one of the houses on our right.

"They're trying to get behind us. Don't shoot if you don't have to."

I climb in. The boy is scrunched up against the other door, crying hard now. We take off. The mirror on my side explodes, then I hear the shot.

We fly through the neighborhood until we find ourselves on Hatch Road. I stop the truck and Jo scrambles in, pushing the boy to the middle.

"We need to get home and get out of there."

"Outa where?" I ask.

"Out of your house. They know where we live. There's no reason they wouldn't come for Marcus. We need to find another house. You

72

know of any with a woodstove? And what do we do with this one?" Jo nods at the kid.

The boy has pulled himself down to his bones, trying to thin himself out of our vision. He is still crying, but quietly now. His face is pressed into his knees, his arched back shivers with the rhythm of sobbing . He is thin and mangy, much like Becka but without that stray-cat look of knowing how to survive.

"Have you seen my brother?" I say sternly.

His back goes still. He lifts his head an inch and nods it.

"Is he in the house back there?"

He gives his head a shake, but I don't want to have to look at him while I drive. "What? Say yes or no."

"No," he says hopelessly and drops his head again.

"Is he alive?"

The boy doesn't answer, so Jo takes hold of his jacket collar and unfolds him.

"Alive?" I ask again.

"Yes. I mean, I think yes."

"What do you mean I think?"

"He was there yesterday. He left with Ricky."

"You mean Ricky took him somewhere?"

"Right. He took him."

"Where'd he take him?"

"I don't know. He didn't tell us. Just says to Sage – that was the one with the gun in the street – he says to him he had to do something, and he'll be gone a few days."

Jo says, "Who went with him? Was it just the two? Him and Jack?"

"No. There were others. Little ones I hadn't seen before. Littler than me."

I cross a set of railroad tracks and the truck feels like it's leaving the ground. There is nothing yet in my rearview mirror, but I want every second I can buy to pack up things at the house.

"We won't be helpin anyone if you kill us," says Jo.

"I'm not gonna kill anyone. You said little ones? Like how little?"

"Four years old, Five, a couple are six or seven maybe. No one was older than your brother. But with girls you can't tell always."

73

"There were girls?"

"A few."

We take a left onto Dobie, heading south.

"Has Ricky ever gone somewhere like this?"

"He goes lots of places."

"Somewhere for a few days? Where he doesn't tell anyone what he's doing?"

The boy nods slowly as though he is just realizing it.

"Yeah he has. More than once."

He looks at me. "I saw you before. By the 7-11. You gave Maya a ride."

"So that's her name."

"Her name's Maya. She was nice to us."

"When?"

"Before Ricky tried to kill her."

"He did that?"

"Well...he sort of did. I saw 'em behind the garage wrestling, and he was chokin' her like he was gonna. I yelled for some bigs to come and he stopped."

"Why'd he choke her?"

"I don't know. They were like that all the time, even before the dying came. Their dad was mean. He yelled a lot . . ."

"They're brother and sister?"

"Yeah. But Marcus and Maya got along ok. Marcus liked everybody."

"He was her brother too?" I ask.

"Yeah. There was seven. Two big kids and two little ones, and Marcus and Ricky and Maya, but they're all gone."

The boy goes quiet now and dreamy, chasing his own thoughts back through the months. I know the look. We all know it.

We take the corner onto Jolly Road hard and he slides into me. This shakes him out of his dreaming, and he says, "We had four." Then he looks around at the truck, at Jo, and at me, and starts crying again.

We pass Maya's field when Jo says, "We could stop here and ask if she knows where he went."

74

"We will. I want to get the food, guns, as many tools as we can loaded and out of there first. I think I know a house we can try."

The boy cries through this, but pitches out words between passing sobs: "You . . . gonna . . . hurt me?"

"Maybe," says Jo.

"We might," I say, then add, "but probably not today."

Chapter 15

The summer prior, my dad looked into buying an outdoor wood boiler. It's a woodstove that sits out in the yard but heats the inside of the house. Whenever he saw one he would point it out and more often than not stop to ask questions and watch it work. I didn't know at the time the mechanics behind it, but I did know every house within five miles that had a wood boiler.

One of them was a small log house over on Walline, two miles south of us. We won't be able to use the boiler, since the pump and well both run on electricity, but the house will have a wood supply.

"Best of all," I say to Jo as we pull up the long driveway, "it's got a woodstove on the inside too."

"How do you know?"

"See the stack?" I point to the shiny stove pipe sticking up from the center of the house.

The front door is unlocked, and as I push it open I am met by the familiar smells of decayed flesh and must. I go to the stairs and head up, leaving the lower floor for Jo.

There is a kind of protocol we follow when breaking into a new house. We look for bodies first, and while we find them in almost every conceivable place – bathtubs, closets, garages, even one on a kitchen table – the most likely places are still the beds.

This house is built to keep in heat so the windows are small, the light meager and diffused. The stairs end at a short hall with closed doors on both sides, another at the end. I push open the left one first. It's a small room, a child's. The walls are painted brightly – light blue, pale green. A model of our solar system hangs in one corner. Bunk beds take up the rest. The top bunk has only a sheet, but the bottom is mounded high with stuffed animals. I pick through them carefully, tossing them onto the floor, expecting each time to uncover a foot, a hand, a face. But there is nothing under the pile.

The door at the end of the hall is a bathroom, empty. I push open the third door. The smell here is stronger. The shades are pulled, but even in the darkness I can make out three forms on the bed. Two lay under a thin white sheet. A third, a child's, lay on top near the edge of the bed, as though he'd crawled in after a bad dream. I yell for Jo that I've found them.

We pull a tarp off an old boat in the back yard and lay it next to the bed. Then taking one side of the sheet, we slide all three off the bed and onto the tarp. We bind it up tight, tying both ends closed with the electrical cords from a lamp and a fan. The dryness and decay have made the bodies light, and the tarp slides easily on the carpet, so it is not too hard getting them down the stairs, through the kitchen and out the back door. We pull them deep into the woods behind the house.

"Should we bury them?" asks Jo. Before I can answer he says, "Yeah, we should. If we're gonna stay here, I mean."

"But not now," I say.

"No. Not now. But later. After we get Jack."

"Right," I say.

We stand there, just looking at the rolled up tarp.

"It'd be hard," I say, "to dig a hole here with all the tree roots."

"Yeah."

"But if we wait too long there won't be anything left to bury. The animals will find it."

Jo is quiet, and his eyes are narrowed and focused. I've seen him look this way when he is stumped trying to plumb the hidden workings of some device. He is trying now to work out the puzzle of corporeal existence.

"You think it matters," he says finally, "if they're buried or not? If worms get em or coyotes?"

"Matter to who?"

"Well…I guess that's my question. Does it matter to them or to God or anyone?"

I don't have a ready answer.

"I mean there's not gonna be relatives coming to visit their graves so I'm thinking it doesn't matter much now what happens. It's just their rotten bodies, right? And they'll rot buried in the ground just like they'd rot on top of it."

I say, "I guess." But I am thinking about all the bodies we did bury, and thinking that at the time I liked the idea that we were somehow helping, doing right. Then I remember something Dad had read to us, and I say it aloud.

"The sea will give up its dead."

"What?" asks Jo.

"That's from the Bible. At the end of things, the dead will rise again, even the dead in the sea. And a body would decay in the sea just like it would lying out here. It'd just be different animals doing the eating."

Whether or not that satisfies Jo, I can't tell. He turns and walks back to the house, his eyes still narrowed. I look at the tarp and wonder if it satisfies me. Would I be doing these folks wrong by not putting them in the ground, letting the woods subsume them instead?

I am also trying to think ahead. If we are still here in the summer, we'll start taking trees out of these woods, and I don't like the thought of having to walk around this spot every time. I reach down, untie the cords on the tarp, and open it up like a wrapping on a gift. And then it comes clear to me, the reason we bury the bodies. We bury them for ourselves, so we can walk where we want to.

By the time I get back to the house, Jo has moved down the protocol and gotten the mattress out of the bedroom to the top of the stairs. With some effort, we get it out of the house and drag it onto a pile of brush waiting to be burned.

Though the bodies are gone, the smell lingers, so I get a good, hot fire going in the stove while Jo opens up all the upstairs windows. The kids sit around the fire and eat noisily – tuna, canned peas, peaches. Jo and I sit at the kitchen table and talk through what to do next.

"Maya might know where he goes," I say.

"And it might cost us a lot if she does," says Jo.

A blush passes over his face like the shade of a scudding cloud, and he shakes his head.

"But that don't matter."

"He took little ones with him," I say. "That's weird…Hey, kid, come over here."

He obeys.

"What's your name?"

"Nathaniel."

"I'm gonna call you Nate."

"That's what everyone calls me."

"So you never saw the littles before? The ones with Ricky?"

He shakes his head.

"I don't know where they came from. They aren't from our neighborhood, I don't think."

"Did Maya know where Ricky went?"

Nate looks up at the ceiling and blinks hard.

"She went with him once. That was right before they got in their fight. She left after that and lives in the woods now."

He looks at the empty coffee mug in his hand and says, "Is there any more?"

"Go look in that cupboard there," says Jo. "I'll open one more."

I stand up and walk to the sliding door that overlooks the deck and backyard. The sky is gray as slate and the woods lightless. Matching shades to my own moods.

"What if Maya won't help?" I ask the window.

"Why wouldn't she?" says Jo.

"Why would she live in a deer blind by herself when there's a whole world of empty houses?"

From the corner of my eye I catch movement in the woods.

"She'll help."

"But what if she doesn't?"

"I don't know," I say, and in my head I think *she'll help whether she wants to or not.*

I expect to see deer and have to think where I've packed the .243. But it isn't deer. From the south, a long and lean dog, a hound of some kind, comes loping in between the trees. It sniffs at the air every few steps. Then I see another behind it, a skinny Rottweiler. Further back still are three smaller dogs, two light-colored mutts, bone thin – I can see their ribs – and a small black and white one, the kind that herd sheep.

"Keep the kids inside," I say.

"Why?" asks Jo.

"Look."

Jo stands next to me and watches as the hound moves quicker to the scent. The other dogs follow, and soon they are bunched up. We hear a growl and a yelp, but can't see any more than their hind parts tugging and dragging.

"Where's the deer rifle?" I ask.

The hound has dragged something off at distance to devour it in private.

"You think they're dangerous?" asks Jo.

"I don't know, but they're hungry, and dogs act different when they're together."

"Maybe they're turnin into wolves."

"Huh?"

"Wolves turned into dogs – over time, I mean – now maybe the dogs are turnin back into wolves."

"I hope it takes a long time, then. I hate wolves."

Jo goes to the front door and grabs the rifle and shotgun, unpacked as soon as we got here. He racks the first into the rifle and hands it to me.

"Won't chewin on em make the dogs sick?" Jo asks.

"I don't know."

I crack the screen door and set a kitchen chair against the opening for a rest. I take aim at a tree that is just behind the Rottweiler's head, and squeeze. The dog skips backward one big leap, looks my way,

79

then goes right back to eating. The others, untroubled by the noise, only turn their eyes to the house. Their jaws keep working.

"They're hungry," I say to Jo in a way that suggests I am building an argument, "and they've been wild for months. They're probably more wolf than dog by now."

I remember a show my dad and I had watched about pigs getting loose from farms in the South and how quickly they'd turn wild. I am sure I am looking at feral dogs now.

"We can't risk them jumping at one of the littles," I say. "They might have rabies. Plus they'll scare off the deer."

But where I think I might have to work to convince him, it takes no more than that. He reaches into this pocket, pulls out another round, and hands it to me. "You might need all five shots."

I decide to take them big to small. They are arranged like that anyway: the hound at my left, the Rottweiler straight on, and the three smaller ones close together to the right. The deck rail will be in the way for all but the hound, so I step out quietly, sit on the bench of the picnic table, and use the deck rail as a rest. I squint into the scope and blink till my eyes are focused. But when I can see the crosshairs and the gray-green bark of the maples clearly, there is no hound in view. I pivot the rifle to where I think the Rottweiler should be, but the woods are empty there too.

I first hear the sound of paw pads hitting the earth, then the deep drawing of breath through the big muzzle and lungs of the hound as it nears the deck. Jo yells something from behind me. I push the gun up and over the deck rail to shoot down into the yard but the angle is all guesswork and I miss. The silent dog hits the steps and turns as I am racking in the next round. I don't get it racked in time to aim and have to shoot from my hip as the dog skids a sharp turn. The bullet cuts through him and hits the corner of the house.

Still more deep breaths, but of a different note. The Rottweiler has come over the rail behind me. I swing the gun around just as the dog's chest opens up and a ringing tone explodes in my head.

I turn as Jo steps onto the deck, the 12 gauge shouldered. He is firing into the woods now, but the report of the gun is muffled. I can feel each shot in my chest, but hear nothing but a far-away whump, like I'm under water.

I look into the woods. In the distance I can just make out the bushy tails of the sheep dog and one of the mutts. I fire once in their direction as a way of saying don't come back. Still no sound but the ringing, and Jo is smiling and talking words I can't hear.

"What?" I yell.

He waits until I'm done tugging at my left ear.

"Wolves. I said I wonder how long it'd take wolves to get here from the U.P."

"I don't know. I thought you hated wolves."

"I do. I was just curious. I can picture em trotting right across the Mighty Mac, can't you."

"Sure," I say. The ringing has settled to a level just below the sound of his voice. And it will stay there for some days.

Chapter 16

Maya gives us a friendlier welcome this time. She invites us up into the blind. It is about the size of a garden shed and just as crammed full with things. The walls are entirely shelved, the dominant motif being canned goods. The space above our heads is cleverly filled with cargo nets stuffed with clothes. Two small chairs, the kind we used in kindergarten, and a propane stove the size of a big toaster take up most of the floor space.

I must have a wondering look on my face because she says, "Bathroom's down there," and points through the Plexiglas window to a port-a-john in the woods. "Except when it's just pee, then I open the trap door. And I get drinking water from the pond." She reaches behind her and turns a plastic spigot screwed into a wall stud. Water shoots from it into a coffee mug. She hands it to Jo.

"Is it filtered?"

"Of course," she says, her words making the short shift from indignance to pride. "Ten inches of sand, ten of charcoal."

"Your tank on the roof?" he asks.

"It's gravity fed. Where else could it be?"

"Don't it freeze?"

"Just on top when it's real cold."

"How do you get up there?"

She points to a corner of the ceiling where another trapdoor is cut. Jo looks at the arrangement of hose running from the spigot, up the wall and through the ceiling. He takes a sip and nods his approval.

I have only the sense of what they are talking about. Jo takes care of our water supply and I know he will sometimes douse embers from the stove in water, then use it as filter material, and that he's spent hours amounting to days putting together a tank-hose-spigot system that we keep in our breezeway. Here he is sizing up another craftsman's work and finding some quality in it.

I am picking my way carefully through this. We need her help. We know that last time her help came at a price. I don't have time to go scavenging for a hundred tanks of propane, so I'll let Jo do the negotiating this time. But in case he's not direct enough, I do have the .38.

"Where does Ricky go?" I ask Maya. "When he leaves by himself?"

She weighs the question while she looks at me. "Why do you wanna know?"

"Jack wasn't there. Neither was Ricky."

"Are there others missing too?"

"From Ricky's house?"

"Did he take more than just Jack?"

"He took some littles. They aren't from that house though."

"How do you know?"

"We just know."

"You must know the house real good if you know who belongs there or not."

"Someone else knows the house."

"Who?"

82

"Nate."

"How do you know Nate?"

"He's with us now."

"With you. What's that mean? How's he with you now?"

"He just is. He's fine and he's with us."

Maya shifts in her seat like she's squaring up to come harder with questions, but then she goes still. Her eyes move between me and Jo, then skip out the window like a bird flying for day-light. She stares out at nothing for a long minute, her eyes blinking as though with the arrival of old thoughts. Then she stands.

"I'll show you where he is," she says, "but you have to promise me something."

"Ok."

"Will you promise?"

"Let's hear it first," I say.

"Promise that when I say I'm goin no farther, you'll listen and take me home."

I began thinking through other conditions I might add, but I realize we haven't offered her anything yet in the bargain. Jo says it before I can.

"We promise."

The three of us drive into Lansing that afternoon. It is the first time I've driven any of the big expressways around Lansing, and they're growing over with weeds. It's waist-high at the shoulders, but weeds and grass are taking root in the seams too so that the roads are segmented by thin walls of green. It is the starkest image of abandonment we've yet seen, and we are silent for much of the drive. Abandonment. It stains the memories deeper than anything else. There's fear too, and desolation and hunger. But the sense of being forgotten and left behind, even years later, is still strongest.

We drive slowly through one of the big neighborhoods, Maya directing me with lefts and rights. Then she says to stop.

"His house is on the next block."

"Whose house?" I ask.

"My cousin's. It's probably where he took the kids and your brother."

"Why? What's he need kids for?"

"Kids'll do what you tell em, specially the littles. They want to be told what to do now."

"Jack ain't that little," says Jo.

"He's littler than Ricky," says Maya.

She gets out of the truck and sits down under a big oak tree.

"Is this as far as you're goin then?" I ask through the window.

"I'll wait here" she says. "Have you thought about what you'll do when you find em?"

"I'll tell him that Marcus died and I came to take Jack home."

She looks doubtful but says nothing, then she gives me directions to the house.

"I'll wait here," she says again.

We drive slowly down the street looking for movement, for signs of life, but there are none. The house itself looks like all the rest — mournful, empty.

I leave the shotgun in the truck and have only the .38 in the back of my pants. I knock on the door. Jo looks through a front window while we wait.

"It's a mess in there," he says. "Just like the others. No one's livin here."

The side door is open, but we knock again and wait a minute before going in. Jo is right. It's a mess, but of a different kind.

"Someone's been livin here," I say.

The smell is bad, but it isn't the death smell of most other houses. It is just dirt and old food.

"Sure this is the right place?"

As soon as he says the words my eyes fall on a picture of Ricky and two other boys. They are wet and smiling big in some sunny backyard. Ricky holds a garden hose.

"It's the right place," I say. "How long do you think they've been out of here?"

Jo is looking at a pile of trash in the kitchen sink. "A while, I'd say. A few weeks maybe. There's nothing fresh here, and there's cobwebs."

We drive back to Maya who is sitting in the branches of the tree now.

"What now?" I ask her. "No one's there."

Maya shrugs her shoulders, then lowers herself to the ground.

"I guess we go lookin."

"Lookin where?" asks Jo. "Lansing's pretty big to just go lookin around."

"What do you do at night?" she asks. "Before you go to sleep, I mean."

She looks at both of us, then cocks her head and says, "What do you do just about every night it ain't rainin before you go to sleep?"

Jo looks at me like it's a trick question.

"Build a fire," I say.

"There you go," says Maya. "That's what I do too, except it's tiny so no one sees it. It's what everyone does at night instead of watching TV. We build fires. Tonight as soon as it's dark, we go for a long drive around town and look for fire light."

It seems like a good idea, so that's what we do. We drive up and down neighborhood streets, one block after another, with no more plan than that of kids let loose at night. We get lost and stay lost but we keep driving, looking for sparks in the sky or light dancing on trees in some small backyard. But we see nothing, no sign at all that humans still have a place in the city.

I drive until the other two are sleeping, until I can keep my eyes open no longer. Then I park in a random driveway and sleep until the rising sun in my side-view mirror hits my eye.

I wake to the sight of a big raccoon and four little ones sniffing around a trash pile at the side of the garage I am parked in front of. As I watch I think about the night before and how big the city really is when you try to see it one house at a time. One of the raccoons, disappointed with what the trash offers, jumps up into a tree and begins climbing. It puts in mind Maya in the oak tree yesterday and then tree climbing in general. Soon I am back home with Jack, high in our own maple tree, seeing all the way to Dobie Lake, seeing the Reeders' house on Cherithbrook and the Spedoskes' lights on Dobie.

And then I see what we need to do.

"Wake up," I say to Jo next to me. Maya is in back so I say it again and loud. "Wake up! I got an idea."

We spend the next hour looking at the Lansing skyrise. It's not much of one, but there are a few high points: the three smoke stacks at the old powerplant, the Boji Tower in downtown – to this day its clock is stuck at 2:40 – and a few radio and cell phone towers.

The plan is simple. Climb as high as we can, wait until the sun goes down, and look for campfires.

"But unless it's out in the open, a field or something," says Jo, "we'll never see it. They're probably in a house with a backyard and trees. We'd have to be in a plane right over head to see the fire."

"I know that," I say. "We won't be looking for fire but for smoke. Right before dark we should be able to see smoke rising up if there's not too much wind."

"I'm afraid of heights," says Maya.

"You live in a deer blind on stilts," says Jo.

"It's not that high, and I got used to it."

"What do we do till then?" asks Jo.

"I'm hungry," I say.

"So am I," says Maya.

"Let's go shoppin," says Jo.

We choose an old neighborhood off Michigan Avenue. The houses have been well kept and there are few with broken windows. Houses tended to be looted in clumps, and we would often find entire streets and blocks untouched.

We start at an old Spanish looking house with stucco walls and tile roof shingles. It is set a little further from the street and nearly hidden by trees, overgrown shrubs, and high grasses. It is a small jungle in downtown Lansing.

A sliding door on the back patio is unlocked. We step through it. The usual smell is there, a body in the house, probably in an upstairs room.

We find the pantry well stocked and pick out a few cans of Chunky soup and fruit cocktail. By now, eating cold food right from a can seems almost normal.

Jo is in a thoughtful mood. "What will we do," he asks as he slurps syrup from a spoon, "when the canned food goes bad?"

"It doesn't go bad," I say. "It's good forever."

"No it ain't," says Jo, and with such conviction I don't argue with him. "Dad got sick from old tuna once. Made me clean out the cupboards and throw everything away that was a year or more past the date. That's why they put dates on the cans. It'll go bad, and then what?"

His question brings back an old thought and gives it greater force as I consider it.

"When we get back, we'll put in a garden. I hadn't thought about food going bad before we ate it. We need a garden. We'll grow a whole garden of food."

Maya is just listening, eating pineapple, then she walks out of the kitchen and down a hall. Her scream makes me jump. Jo and I run to her. She stands in the doorway of a small sitting room and points. The look on her face is not of fear; she looks like she's bitten down on something rotten. In the room is a reclining chair, and in the chair is a very old woman.

I am about to pull her away, back into the kitchen, when she says, "Hold on."

She steps into the room.

"Look at her."

I'd read of dead people that they seemed always to have a peaceful look. We never saw those dead people. An old corpse looked always to me to be a soul in agony – pained and hungry. This one looked that way, like she was running from something and thirsting at the same time.

But there is something unusual about her face.

"What is that?" asks Jo.

Maya reaches out and touches a lower lip that has retreated below the gums. It is red. A thick line of red borders the open hole that is her mouth.

"Lipstick," says Maya. "And there's mascara on her eyes." Except it isn't on her eyes or eyelids because she has none. The black paste has been brushed carelessly onto the top of her orbital bones so that they look like extra eye brows.

"Why would someone put make-up on a dead body?" asks Maya.

"Why would someone try to feed a dead body?" asks Jo. He points to a crust of dry bread wedged between two fingers of her right hand, but not in a way that any person would really hold it.

"Let's get out of here," says Maya.

We agree and head back down the hall and through the kitchen. I grab my clam chowder and reach for the sliding door when Maya screams again. On the other side of the glass a blond boy stands looking in at us. He is naked and wild-haired, and in his right hand he holds a knife.

He is not more than 3 years old.

Chapter 17

I look down at the boy through the glass. As I reach out to push the door open, he springs backward and squats on the patio, looking the three of us over.

Maya speaks first.

"Hi there. What's your name?"

The boy looks quickly right and left and then jumps further back, into the green wall of weeds and ornamental trees. And then he runs. He is a shadow racing through the thick cover, but we can follow his movements through the yard and around the side of the house.

"Go to the front!" says Jo.

We run through the house and fling the front door open in time to see him sprinting down the sidewalk deeper into the neighborhood.

"Let's follow him," says Maya.

"What for?" I ask.

"What do you mean what for? He's a baby."

"He's gotten along fine so far, and there's gonna be kids like him all over the world growin up like animals. You can't help every one."

My conviction in this is half-hearted, and Maya senses it. She starts down the sidewalk.

"Come on."

He isn't hard to follow, though for a scrawny three-year-old he covers a lot of ground. He runs for three blocks then ducks through a window into a little cape cod. We knock, then try the door.

"He probably couldn't figure out the deadbolt," says Jo.

I put my head into the window, and pull it right back out.

"Stink's worse than anything yet."

I take a deep breath and climb in. The thick air that hits me makes my throat clench, then convulse. I tighten my gut against it and quickly unlatch the locks. I throw the door open and run out into the yard.

"Can't be worse than a dead body," says Jo.

But then the air reaches him there on the porch and his face goes sour.

"What *is* that?"

We open the back door and break out most of the windows on the ground floor. After a half hour of yelling in for the boy, we get our courage up and step in. It turns out the smell is a little of everything. There are four bodies – two in an upstairs room and two in a dank basement. It's the downstairs corpses that have rotted the worst. But that's not all of it. The boy has filled two toilets with feces, then the bathtubs and bathroom sinks. Then it seems he doesn't bother aiming at anything and drops wherever he happens to be. The refrigerator is wide open, its contents emptied onto the kitchen floor long ago.

"Found him!"

It's Jo yelling from upstairs. He is in a back bedroom. High up in a loft, the boy is buried in stuffed animals. His wide, blinking eyes are visible in the gloom by their whites.

"He won't come out, and I ain't goin in there. He's still got the knife."

"Here," says Maya, and she hands Jo a Dumdum sucker.

Jo opens it and gives it a long sniff.

"Mmmm, good. You want some? Come on out and have some candy. Mmmm."

We take that approach for a few minutes, until none of us can stand it in there any longer. I suggest we go to the yard and wait for him to come to a window. A few minutes later, as we stand in the breathable air, we see a curtain move and a face appear.

"Now walk real slow," says Maya, "see what he does."

We walk down the sidewalk, back toward the other house. Four or five houses down, we stop and wait.

Jo doesn't wait well. He gets fidgety quick, and where normally that would show itself in talking too much, now he is silent. I think Maya is making him nervous. Instead of talking, he runs to the closest garage and looks in through a side door.

"Can't see nothin," he says.

He comes back to the front, pulls up on the garage door, and finds it unlocked. Inside is a car, big and very old.

Jo appreciates it for a while, then says, "I've been thinkin about what do we do when cars quit working."

"Yeah?" I say. Maya doesn't seem to be listening. Her eyes are on the sidewalk behind us.

"Horses," says Jo. "We find horses, start growing hay. In fact we should try and find a few before the next winter comes."

He'd been thinking about it.

"You think there are horses still alive?" I ask.

"There has to be some. The dying didn't come hard till March. Some would have gotten through that winter. Some folks must have let em go, knowing what was coming, don't you think?"

"I suppose," I say. "Wouldn't a horse break free if it was starving?"

"Not if it's locked in a stall. Remember when the Demmer's barn burned down and there were a bunch of horses that died? They didn't break free with fire comin at em, though they could've as strong as they are."

It occurs to me then that there is a whole world of knowing that is closed off to me. I don't know a thing about horses, not much more about gardens, but if Jo is right about expiration dates and gas engines, I might be depending on both someday soon.

"We'll get more books from the library when we get back."

That is the only solution to being boxed in by my own ignorance. Books on gardening and horses.

Jo is about to speak, but he stops. I'd forgotten about the reading. I wanted to say something, to ask him about it, but Maya is there.

"See him yet?" I ask her.

"Nope. Maybe we should go back."

Jo is just starting to pull down on the garage door when he stops.

"There he is."

Behind the big car is a window that looks out on a back yard. The boy's face, not so wild-eyed this time, is on the other side.

"He followed us through the backyards," says Jo, amazed. "He musta hopped every fence. Let's keep walking."

As we walk, Maya says, "He was going into that house when we first saw him. He was gonna come right through that door like he knew the place. Maybe he put the make-up on the old lady."

We go back into the other house and leave the sliding door wide open. It isn't long before the boy creeps onto the patio, cautious as a rabbit, and sits down cross-legged between two big planter boxes.

"We could just grab him," says Jo.

"No," says Maya. "If we miss, he'll never come back. We can just wait."

"I can't just wait," I say. "I came here for Jack. If the boy doesn't want to come, he won't – "

" – he wants to, it'll just take time."

"I don't have time," I say and stand up like I am leaving.

"Then leave me here," says Maya. "Pick me up tomorrow."

"If I find where Jack is tonight, we go get him tonight. I'll need you with me."

"If the boy trusts me by tonight, then I'll come too. Otherwise I'm staying."

The lump of the .38 under my sweatshirt calls me to it. I feel the pull. I could just point it at her, and she'd do what I wanted. It'd be simple, and there is nothing to stop me. The thought comes as any mundane set of options might – like what shoes to put on – and it surprises me. I can use the gun or not use it. It surprises me enough that my fingers relax, and I walk out of the house.

Jo follows me, and we get into the truck without a word. It seems we are both itching to get something done. I head down Michigan Avenue first, toward Boji Tower. The weeds make the road to the capitol building a long green fairway. I punch the gas, and soon there is only the sound of the winding engine and the whack whack of long grass hitting the grill.

Chapter 18

Our plan is to spend the rest of that day scouting out high places. We almost give up the idea since rising smoke can be seen from any height above the trees, but Jo points out that smoke can be scattered by the lightest wind and that a high perch may be our best chance to see fire light.

Boji Tower is the highest of the downtown buildings, so we start there. We find a stairwell door propped open in the lobby and begin the long, dark climb to the top. Jo is in front of me. I keep running into the back of him, so I stop and wait until I can hear the pat of his feet hitting the steps about a half flight ahead, then try to keep him there, slowing as he slows or speeding if he gets too far up.

His footfalls stop so I slow my climb.

"Where are you?" I whisper. There is no need to whisper, but whenever we'd break into a place, and especially if it's dark, the sense of trespass is strong. We all whispered like conspirators in those days.

Jo doesn't answer. He has a small light out and is moving up the steps again.

"Looking for a door?" I ask.

"Yeah."

"We can't be half way even."

"I know. I want to see how many flights are between each floor so we can count."

We come to a door with a 7 painted on it. White letters on a dark paint. After 3 more flights we come to an 8, and from then on Jo says out loud as he hits the landings, "One . . . two . . . three, 9_{th} floor . . . one . . . two . . . three, 10" And on we go, our lungs working hard, and our legs burning. At what should be the 34_{th} floor is a steel door with the word *roof* in white paint. It's locked.

"Dang," says Jo.

We had wanted to get to the spire on top. From the street it seemed to have ladder rungs running up its side. It would get us another five stories higher, maybe more.

"Let's go down to the 33_{rd}," I say, "see if there's another way up."

We hadn't tried any of the doors coming up, and so we both exhale some relief when the bar handle moves and the door swings into the stale air of a long hallway. To our left is a bank of elevators, to our right another hall that runs along the south side of the building. Jo props a little trash can to keep the door open, and we head into the heart of the building.

The office doors in this hall are mostly glass and many of the walls have windows so that enough late afternoon sun sifts in that we don't need Jo's pen light. The hall runs clear to the other side where there is a mirror image of the door we'd just come through. More elevators, more halls to right and left.

"If we can get into the offices," says Jo, "we'll be able to see in all directions. Maybe we don't need to go higher."

"We've got some time. May as well look around."

We find another stairwell in the middle of the building – we had run right by it – but it's locked too. We stand near it, looking through the windows into the offices opposite.

"This one looks good," I say. After months of breaking windows and jimmying doors, we are still reluctant at the first strike of a hammer or throw of a rock. We'd get over it in time, but I remember, as I held a fire extinguisher poised to thrust through a fancy beveled-glass door, I remember glancing over my shoulder in a quick flush of fear that some adult interloper would catch me in the act.

No adult comes, and I hit the glass hard. It shatters but not clean through. The pane, which makes up most of the door's center, spider webs in pieces so small that I can't see through. The clear glass has changed to the color of frost. I throw it harder, and this time the glass bursts and falls into the little waiting room on the other side. We stand there a moment, exulting nervously in the violent sound and the surmounting of an obstacle placed there by the old world. In the silence that comes after, we both jump when we hear a clank of metal down the hall.

"The door," says Jo.

We run to it. The trash can is gone and the door is closed over it. Jo pulls on the handle but it won't budge.

"Can musta slipped," he says. "The door pushin against it, it musta slipped real slow and just took this long to...to..."

He pulls again at the handle and shakes it hard.

"We're locked in," I say.

Jo looks around for another opinion but arrives at the same one.

"Yeah. What now?"

"Let's keep doing what we're doing. Worry about how to get out of here later. The sun will be down soon and if we can get into the offices on the east side too that'll be four directions we can look. Then we'll find Jack."

"Then we'll get out of here."

"We'll find a way."

"I mean out of Lansing. There's something different here. I don't know what, but it's different. The air, the streets, something makes it feel more broken than back home."

I know what Jo means, but it is getting dark and I don't want to draw out more things we'd have to fight, so I say nothing. I tell myself it's to protect him, but I am protecting myself too. I'm not quite letting myself think about the predicament we are in but certain knowledge is pressing in on me, and it has everything to do with that brokenness Jo has mentioned. There is the fact of sheer walls and ledge-less windows 33 stories over concrete. And there is that deep, metallic finality of the closing door. In the country, a window escape or a locked door are annoyances to shrug off. Here they block all

94

retreat and demand to be grappled with. I know what Josiah means about the city, but I don't see things as broken. I see them as working just exactly as they'd been meant to, like machines given their assigned programs and set free to cut and crush. The city is just moving along as it's been made to, as it's always done.

We have no trouble breaking into the offices on the east side. Interior spaces will always give way to the brute argument. So we sit in a comfortable room and watch the blocks of city before us fall into the tower's shadow, then into the earth's.

In the hour of dusky light before full sunset we move about the compass points – lobby to office to lobby – looking for smoke whisping up into the windless air. We end our circuit back in the same big chairs of the conference room, everything in front of us swallowed up in darkness. Then we spend the next hours moving to and from our four stations around the building, straining our eyes for light. But in all the blackness of night there is not a pinprick of it.

The morning dawns red and hazy, the promise of nasty weather. Jo is awake, sitting cross-legged on the big table and staring out at the rising blush of color. His brow is pinched and his eyes intent, like he is seeing something a long way off. But when I stir, he breaks from his spell, looks at me.

"I'm hungry."

Then he jumps down and walks out of the room toward the shattered glass door.

"Where ya goin?"

"Lookin for food,"

"Bring some back!"

I watch the sun go higher and diffuse itself through the heavy air. It is a sloppy sunrise, and I see nothing of promise in it.

Maya is east of us too, somewhere between the sun and the tower we're locked in. It's a fairy tale in reverse. I wonder about the wild boy and how she's gotten along with him. Then I wonder on a whole line of thoughts that pass before me like the cars of a slow train. Maya. The boy. Becka and the twins. The dogs. The dying foot. Horses. Gardens.

I let the thoughts come, and keep myself from holding on to any one of them for long. It is like thumbing through an album of pictures I know. A part of me can think on other things while my eyes see and remember, so as the images click past, I think of time, of how long we could live up here before we too die and dry out. The last thought pictures are of books and libraries and buildings, and then I think through all the spaces we've seen on this 33rd floor, and then I am back in the glass room. There is no meaning to the thoughts beyond that, and I hear myself sigh.

"Found this," says Jo behind me.

"Ouch," I say as I jerk in my chair.

"What's wrong with you?"

"Stiff. Shoulda slept on the floor."

He sets down a cardboard display box about the size of a laundry basket. It is half filled with little wrapped snacks like cheese and crackers and pretzels and a few candy bars. On the top of it is a little box for dropping in coins. We spend the next minutes quiet while we tear through our breakfast.

"I'm thirsty now," I say.

"There's a water cooler in the next office. We should bring the whole thing over. I'm pretty sure it just runs on gravity."

We do that next. It would have been easier to just bring the snacks to the next office, but having spent the night in the big room is enough for us to call it home. We don't talk about it, we just both assume it.

The sun is higher now and shining right into the east windows, so we go to work. At some recent point, we've both arrived at similar conclusions: one, that unless someone comes along and opens the fire door, we'll die here. Death has found its way out of our dreams and lives with us. And two, we don't like that conclusion so we'll try hard to stay alive long enough to come up with something else.

So we go to work making the 33rd floor livable for now. We spend that day and much of the next going through desk drawers, closets, and cupboards looking for anything edible. We've learned long ago to avoid refrigerators, no matter how promising, and there are several. We find a few more water cooler jugs still full, and a lot of pop. We figure to have a month of water and a couple weeks of food if we stretch it.

It turns out we figure poorly.

Chapter 19

"*Then… Joseph… says… to them… do not… intep… inter…* what's that word?"

"Interpretations."

"*Do not interpretations…bel…belong…to God?*"

"Good."

I am teaching Jo to read. We'd found a Bible in a desk drawer, and my thought is that familiar passages might be helpful, but he doesn't know who Joseph was. He doesn't know who Moses was. He knows that Jesus did some wild things and then got himself killed. And that is the sum of all religion for Jo Mench.

We've been in the tower a few days, maybe a week – the days got lost and we never did find a way of setting them right – when I suggest it.

"I can't," replies Jo.

"I know. That's why I want to teach you."

"No, I mean I can't learn it. You can't teach it."

"Why do you say that?"

"Just know it is all."

"But what makes you know it? Did someone tell you you can't learn to read?"

He says nothing to this, but his look makes me think I've gotten close.

"Your teachers tell you that?"

He shakes his head.

"Never had teachers."

"Your dad? Did he tell you you couldn't learn?"

His eyes dart at me now, and then away to the gray, rain-streaked window where they stayed fixed. I don't press him further.

I wonder now what kind of man Mr. Mench had been. He'd never said much to me except to nod hello and mumble my name. That he should believe his son unable to learn something that came as easy to me as breathing was a hard thing to square up in my mind. I find myself feeling sorry for the man, then disliking him some, then being out-and-out angry.

"He had no right keeping that from you, you know. I don't mean to speak bad of him, especially now, after he's…you know… but he had no right to do that. And how'd he know that anyway? You learn things faster than anybody I ever knew. How'd he know?"

Jo looks at me like I've missed something.

"He never said *that.*"

"Never said what?"

"That I'm not able to learn."

"That's what you just said, he said you couldn't – "

"He never said I can't learn, that I'm not able to. He just told me I couldn't."

Now it's my eyes that tell Jo to keep going.

"He wouldn't let me learn. He knew I could and that I wanted to, but he wouldn't let me because he couldn't read either. He couldn't read a thing, and he got to the point where he was stubborn against it. I remember asking him once about a stop sign, how the first letter was the same as the first letter in speed. I asked him if that was how reading worked, but he don't answer. The thought of it got me excited, and so I don't notice he's getting mad and I just kept asking questions. Like how many letters there are and do they make different sounds or was there a different letter for every sound because I could make hundreds of sounds. He wasn't answering but I didn't notice it, the questions were coming too quick. Then I said something like 'I bet you could learn to read if you just tried' and I am going to say we should try together, but he hit me before I could – "

Jo stops talking, and the abrupt silence makes me think he's said too much.

98

"That was the only time though," he says, not so much as a retraction but as if he is reminding himself of the fact. "He never hit me other than that, and he was real sorry for days after."

We talk more about his dad, the things he was good at — cars, hunting and fishing, fixing anything. When it seems that Jo's desire to talk has run itself out, I say what must have been obvious to us both.

"He's not here now. What's stopping you from learning it then?"

He thinks about it for a while then shakes his head.

"He's still my dad."

"You think he'd wish that on you? Maybe he doesn't want you to learn because he didn't want to be reminded all the time that he can't read."

"Of course I know that. I'm not stupid."

"So what then?"

"He's just still with me, that's all. It's still hard to go against him."

"Nothing wrong with that," I say. "Nothing wrong with not wanting to go against your dad, I mean. But I think maybe you're not being fair to him."

"How do you mean?"

"Well, don't you think he's got a better view of things now?"

"I'd like to think it, but who's to say?"

"The Bible says we've got a soul that lasts forever, so maybe he's able to see some things now that he couldn't before. And maybe now, you *not* learning to read is going against him."

"You say 'maybe' a lot."

"Yeah."

He must not have held that against me because the next day, after spending a couple of hours trying to pick the lock on the stairwell door, he comes to me.

"Ok then. Let's try it."

We try the Gospel of Matthew first, but the genealogy makes for tough pronunciation. I can hardly teach him words if I can't say them myself. The Gospel of Mark is easier, but Jo keeps asking questions that has me going to the Old Testament for answers. I try the Psalms, but even those assume too much prior knowledge. So we end up at the beginning, in Genesis where God creates the heavens and the earth, calls Abraham, and saves his people through Joseph.

"How do you think Joseph kept from going crazy?" asks Jo. "In prison for something he didn't do. No way to get himself out except to wait for a miracle – that'd make me crazy."

"I don't know," I say, "but he must have stayed busy. It says that he gained favor in sight of the guy running the prison, and then the guy put him in charge over it, so he must have been doing some kind of work."

"Right," says Jo. "Maybe we should stay busier up here."

"Why? You going crazy?" I say it as a joke, and he smiles at it, but it isn't the kind of smile I usually see on Jo's face.

"Not yet, I don't think, but…" He shakes his head and says, "nothin' it's nothin'"

"What's nothin?"

I don't think he's going to tell me, and I've learned not to push him on certain things, so I pull the Bible to me to continue the lesson. Then Jo says, "Well, it's like this. I worked over that lock today for a couple of hours, and I did the same thing yesterday."

He stops like he's waiting for a response from me, but just as I am going to say so what, I can see that he's thinking. His eyes are just starting to squint and his body is stone still. He goes on.

"And both times in the middle of it, when my butt was numb and my fingers were starting to bleed, I felt like I could do that exact thing, poking at that lock and feeling the metal pieces inside of it forever. Like I could just lose myself in that work. And I don't mean picking locks forever, I mean that lock on that door forever and ever. Like I could tumble right into it and just go spinning on and on. And both times it was something outside of me that made me break away from it, from the spell or whatever it was. The first time I slipped and put the end of a paper clip under my nail. The other time was you making me come and eat something. It was weird. I felt like I was at the edge of some part of me for the first time, like I could have stepped over it somehow, and…and…then what?"

"Maybe we should leave the doors alone for now."

"What else would we do?"

"We can keep making the rope." I've been tearing out wiring wherever I can get at it, but it's mostly short runs of computer wire that I tie together at their ends. The longer pieces are buried in steel conduit. We figure four or five of these braided together would be strong enough to hold our weight. It's the 33-story length that makes Jo give up on it.

"We could try the elevators again."

"Why? You think they've come down since last time?"

"No, but we could climb down to the bottom and pry the basement doors open."

"And if we can't open em? Even if we were healthy, we couldn't climb up steel cables. We'd die down there, there in that black hole. No, we save that for the very end. But even then I'm not sure I'd want to do it. I'd rather starve up here in the light."

"Maybe we could – "

" – We've checked the vents. There's no tools to take the door out. We've busted out a window and screamed our throats bloody for two days. I know the lock on this door. I can see it now plain like it was drawn in a picture. I just haven't got the pins worked right yet, but I'm getting closer."

"Sounds like you're getting closer to goin nuts, and I need you here, all of you."

"What for?"

"For one, I've spent a lot of hours teaching you to read. It'd be all wasted if you went crackers."

"If I went nutso?"

"Right. It'd be a waste if you went psycho now."

"Bonkers?"

"Cuckoo."

Jo's mouth flattens into a near smile, and this time it's the familiar one. But there is still a strain behind his eyes.

The next morning I sit with Jo while he works the lock. I'd found an old squirrel-cage fan in a utility closet. The bracket that would have held it to a wall has a narrow flange that runs around three sides of it. I am working it off by bending it back and forth with a set of cheap pliers I'd found in a receptionist's desk. It's our hope to have two strips of steel a few inches in length and a quarter of an inch wide. Jo thinks that if he can slip two into the lock together he might be able to work the tumblers or pins or whatever with both hands. It seems to me that the way he's described it is true — he can actually see the inner workings of the lock, at least what can be explored with straightened out paper clips.

"How close are you?" he asks. His eyes are closed and with one hand he works a piece of wire into the keyhole. The other hand turns gently at the knob.

"Got one done."

He lets go of the knob and takes the thin strip of steel from me. "It's rough. We'll need to file this side down. There's slate tile in two of the bathrooms. Can you bust a piece out?"

I bring back a piece of slate and work the strip against it until my hands are cramped. Then I finish bending off the other piece. An hour later we have two strips, smoothed and nearly identical in size. The steel is thin, and except for a point or two where I'd had to bend it, much stronger than a paper clip.

Jo takes both and slips them into the lock together, but after a few minutes says, "I need one to be narrower."

"You mean shorter."

"No, narrower."

"How are we gonna do that? It took me an hour just to get the rough edges off. How much is narrower?"

"Needs to be an eighth of an inch."

"We'd be better off starting over." I grab the squirrel cage and begin bending the flange back and forth again, weakening the metal a little bit with each motion, except this time I don't grip where it meets the frame but half-way down, an eighth of an inch into the metal.

"It's not bending straight," says Jo.

He's right. The first two had bent easily and on a line since the metal had already been bent on a 90-degree angle, but this time the bend wanders. When I break the metal at the third spot, the tear begins to move and makes the strip at that point even narrower.

"It's not gonna work," says Jo. He's right again, and he's not going crazy this time, though he is getting to be annoying. "We need to work one of the other two down."

So that's what we do. For the next two days we run one of the strips, wedged firmly into the edge of a broken piece of wood flooring, against the slate wall of a bathroom. It is a windowless, interior room, and except for a couple of glow sticks, which we are saving for an emergency, we've been long out of candles and pen lights, so we take half-hour turns in the darkness.

I stay close when Jo is at it, for the work is hypnotizing and the blackness makes you forget what up and down means. I fear he might fall off that edge he'd spoken of, but he doesn't. And when he sits in front of that lock and slips those strips in, all fears – mine and his – of going nuts seem childish and far away.

"I'm moving it. I can just feel the last pin." He pulls the smaller strip out and gives it a few sharp drags along a piece of slate, working off a corner burr, then slips it back in.

"It wants to rise, I can feel it. Here. Take the knob." He shifts to let me hold the knob while he works both strips. "Turn it real soft, clockwise. Now hold it there."

He is still for a long time, though I can see the small tendons in his hands go taut and loose in coordination.

"It's lifted."

"What do I do?"

"Turn it clockwise, but I'll tell you when."

Jo gets himself up onto his feet so that he can turn while still holding the strips.

"On three, nice and easy, like this." Jo swings his head in a smooth motion to show me the tempo. "Ready?"

"Ready."

"One…two…three."

We move together. I turn the knob and Jo holds the strips in place as the cylinder turns with it. But there is something not right in the action of the metal in my hand. I can feel a catch, a quick gathering of tension, then a release. It happens so quick that my hand passes right through it and I feel it only as a memory. I say nothing.

After I've turned it fully, I hold it there. Jo takes a deep breath, puts his hands behind mine and pulls. The door doesn't budge.

"No…" he says in a groan. He yanks the knob again. "I thought it was…thought for sure I had it…"

Jo kneels down again at the knob. He begins to work the strips, probing the lock, but he stops suddenly. He pulls them out. The narrower strip is shorter now, broken off half way, the broken piece still inside. Neither of us says anything. We just stare at the keyhole.

The sun is low now and the light is draining away. Jo's stomach begins to growl, and it is strangely loud, for I've gotten used to a world without sound.

"You hungry?" I ask.

"No," says Jo. "I'm sick."

Chapter 20

I'm having trouble thinking. The task in front of me is a simple one – glue a cd to a cardboard box. The only decision to make is which side to put the glue on. It should be easy. I glue the printed side so that the mirrored side is outward. But the simple train of thinking is stuck in a tight circle. I tell myself to put the glue on the side with writing. I look at both sides, then I set the cd down, and in that second I forget. So I have a talk with myself about what I am doing.

"We need a big mirror," I say. "Lots of little mirrors to make a big mirror."

"A big mirror for what?" I ask.

"A big mirror to catch the sun light."

"Why do we want to catch sunlight?"

And here's where I have to will myself to think, to remember. "We need sunlight to…to…sunlight as a…a light…a signal light. We need a signal. A lot of mirrors to make one big mirror to catch the light and signal someone down there, out there. So mirrored side out."

Then I put glue on the printed side and press it to the box, and pick up another cd, and just manage to get that one glued right. And then I stop and look at the next one and wonder, "which side should I glue?"

I jump away from the table and walk out of the office as deliberately as my legs will let me. I need to clear my head. It's happening often now, sometimes two or three times a day. I am losing hold of things. The food has been gone for some days, and I can feel my body feeding off itself.

I turn the corner into the lobby and nearly run over Jo. He sits cross-legged in front of the open elevator shaft. We found the parts to a steel bed frame in one of the offices. One of the pieces works well as both a pry bar and a way of holding the door open. It's wedged in diagonally, and Jo is tapping it mindlessly with a yardstick.

"Hey," I say.

"Hey."

I am surprised to see him there. He's been working for days with another door – the maintenance room's. We're hoping to find a tool box, or anything else that will let us move to some new scheme for escape. This morning he said he was almost there, but now he is here doing nothing.

"What happened? Did you get it open?"

"Yep."

"Really? You picked the lock?"

"Of course."

"And?"

"And nothing. There's nothing in it except cleaning stuff."

"Cleaning stuff?"

"Brooms, mops, Pine sol. Stuff to clean with."

I sit down next to him, and for a second I can't remember what we had hoped to find there.

"I am thinking we might build something to stand on and hang down there."

"Down where?"

"Just down there, at the next floor. Like a tree stand but attached to the cables. Then maybe we could pry open the door on the floor

105

under us. I was thinking about that as I was working on that lock and how we really needed there to be a toolbox in that room."

Tools. That's what we were hoping for.

"But there aren't any. We have no tools for this."

"For what?"

"For this. For being here. We have to get out, go back to the woods. It's no good here."

Jo stands up and walks to the elevator. He seems unsteady, not quite over his feet.

"What are you doing?" I ask.

"I don't know. We need to get back."

He doesn't seem to see the open shaft, so I reach out to pull him back from the edge, but he jerks away from me. His balance is gone now, and without a sound he steps through the opening.

I don't move for some seconds as the conflicting weights of seeing and disbelief hold me in place. Then I drop to my knees and crawl to the edge. I say his name, but my voice is fearful, and it cowers in my throat and then comes out like a cough. Then I take a deep breath to yell. That's when I hear him.

"I'm here," he says back to me. I can hear his struggling now. There is physical effort in his voice too. He isn't but a few feet down, but the shaft is an utter blackness and he's swallowed in it.

"What happened? Are you on the elevator?"

"I'm on the cables, but I'm slipping. Help me, Liam!"

I find my voice now as the weights are gone. "Slide down, Jo!"

"I don't want to!" He is further away, slipping down. "Oh God, Liam, help me! I didn't know what I was doing. I didn't want to do this. I don't want to die!"

He was slipping. His voice is being swallowed up in its own echo.

"Don't fall, Jo! Let yourself down slow! Don't let go!"

"I don't want to go down there!"

His voice comes up from some floors lower. A deep vibration fills the shaft as Jo slides along the steel cable. It is lower than sound, like the deepest note from some monsterish instrument. I keep yelling down at him, encouraging him to not let go, to let himself down to the very bottom, that I won't leave him there.

He says no more, and soon the vibration too has stopped. I have no way of knowing if he's made it to the bottom. If he falls would I even hear him hit? The bottom is 33 floors away. More than that. There's a basement floor, maybe a few basement floors. I begin to think now, better than I have in days.

"Jo!" I yell down the shaft.

There is no answer. I yell his name again. Then I do hear something, a faint, whining cry that makes my skin tighten.

"Jo! Are you hurt? Are you ok? Jo!"

But still, there is no sound but that crying. I take it then to be Jo reaching the very end of himself, but the long shaft is twisting the sound, filling it up from behind into something else.

I spend the next hour, trying to get him to answer me. The crying has stopped, but every few minutes a piercing sound comes up from the darkness. I can't make it out as a scream or a shout or anything that humans do with their voice. By the time the sound reaches me, it is all mixed notes and echoes. But even these slow to just a few over the next hour, and then nothing at all.

I am at the end now. Jo and I are both at our ends. We've run through every option but one, and I would spend the next hours putting that one in motion.

One of the first things we'd done after being locked in was to break out a window from another conference room on the westward-facing side. It hadn't been hard. We just set the legs of the heavy table onto two roller chairs and ran the whole thing into the glass. Our purpose had been varied. We wanted to see if the outside of the building could be scaled. It couldn't. We also wanted a place to dump our trash.

I use the same method now to knock out the windows of our east-side conference room and apartment. Then I flip the table onto its side and against the open windows to make room. I carry in boxes of files, stacking them high on the north and south walls.

As I work, a part of my mind knows that I am moving to a point of action that can't be stopped or reversed. But I also know that if I slow and think at all about what I am doing, I will falter. And I had already decided as I lay with my head over the elevator shaft listening for Jo's death sounds to come up, that I must not falter here. Better to die in this attempt than to die waiting, attempting nothing.

I empty the boxes, one file at a time at first, wadding the forms and reports and documents into balls and piling them in the middle of the room. Soon I have a mound of paper that fills the space. Then I pile on the boxes themselves, the cardboard ones, partly flattened. The plastic boxes I pitch out the window. Over this I dump the remaining file boxes until the mound is chest-high, then I throw a set of wooden folding chairs on top of that.

The trick to lighting a good fire is letting it breathe. It needs air. So I prop open every door between this room and the west-side conference room. For good measure I throw the fire extinguisher through a lobby window.

I go back to our room and crouch down next to the pyre of paper and wood. In one hand I hold a can of WD-40 I'd found in the room that Jo had opened, and in the other I hold a lighter. Here is where my determination will falter and I will set these down to pick up my wire rope and my CD signal mirror while Jo dies slowly in any number of ways.

I give the lighter a flick with my thumb and hold the nozzle behind it. I think about the hour and whether this might not be the best time to start the fire. How long will it take to get a good smoke going? Will it be dusk by then? Will it still be smoking at dawn? Too much thinking. The lighter gets hot and I let go.

Then I see what my mind is doing. It's creating for itself a way out. It's trying to reason a way to be safe for a few more hours and days. I talk to myself aloud. I say that I don't know how long the fire will take to smoke or how long it will burn after or whether or not anyone in all the world will ever see it. I can't know any of that. I'm not entitled to know any of that. I do know that my friend might be dying, that we've done everything we can to survive and to escape, and that this is our last chance.

I ask God to bless me, then I flick the lighter and squeeze the can and a spout of yellow flame hits the paper. I step back and watch it. I know fire, and it doesn't take long to see that this one will take a sure hold and grow.

I go into the next room and pick up an old shoulder bag. In it are the last three bottles of Perrier, a few glow sticks, and the .38. I put my head and one arm through the strap and cinch it tight. Then I walk to the elevator shaft and sit in the opening and wait. There is no sound from below. My legs hang over the edge like I am dockside. The yardstick is still there, so I pick it up and hold it in front of me like I'm fishing. I pretend to be fishing. I can't see the space below me – it is just black – but there is a thin gleam of oil on the cable in front of me that disappears at about the level of my dangling feet. It is my line disappearing into the water. I hold the yardstick so that the gleam on the cable passes through its end. It is a convincing illusion. I am drawn into it, and I let my eyes go just out of focus.

The sound of fire reaches me now, and it is a campfire on the beach, and I am fishing from a dock. It is summer, and my family, my mom and dad and Jack and the twins, are laughing in the sun. The water below me looks cool and deep, and I stare into it for a long time, thinking that I can see things on the bottom. There's a coin. I scoot to the edge. A fifty-cent piece. Do they still make fifty-cent pieces? I could drop in quick, grab it, be out before the fish are scared away.

But there is something strange about the fire. The smell of it is different now, a chemical smell. Jack likes to put plastic cups in the flames and watch them shrivel. I do too, but I hate the smell.

A lot of plastic in the fire.

A lot of bad smell in the air.

I see myself falling into water, but it isn't water. It is a concrete shaft and Jo is at the bottom. I feel the blackness swallow me and a rush of air speed past, beating against me harder and louder like wind preceding a storm. I cough once, a hacking jolt to my chest, and my eyes start to water. Then I roll backward and away from the shaft, and the dockside illusion and the falling visions scatter in the smoke.

The sound of fire is above me now. The fire is in the ceiling, and I can feel the heat of it. I can see the ceiling tiles begin to bulge and curl. I step again to the edge, step over the steel bar holding the door open.

I am thankful that there is only blackness below me, that I can't see the bottom. Then I lean out. My hands release the edge of the open door and I hang between standing and falling.

Then I jump toward the gleaming cable.

Chapter 21

I am sliding too far, I think, sliding toward the earth's center. The darkness is utter, and my eyes can pick up no fixed reference. The only perception of descent is the paying out of the cable through the insides of my coiled legs and through my burning hands.

But when I yell out Jo's name, the echo comes right back to me. I am getting closer. I yell his name over and over, bat-like. Each time the echo comes back quicker, clearer. By the time my voice sounds again like my own, I can hear Jo sliding around in the dirt at the bottom.

I come down onto a piece of machinery. I can make nothing of it with my feet and hands except that it is steel and that the cable disappears into a big metal housing, a box-shaped cover about the size of a dog house. Another cable is attached to the far side of this. It runs up and parallel to the one I came down, but I hadn't known it was there. I know all of this by greasy, dusty touch.

"Jo?" I say quietly into the dark. I step down from the housing into an open space between it and the wall. The ground under me is steel, not concrete. And it's hollow. This isn't the bottom of the shaft at all but the top of an elevator car. I should have figured that out before. Cables wouldn't hang below an elevator. They're for lifting it.

I say into the dark, "I'm surprised you didn't figure that out earlier, smart guy." But there is still no answer.

I crawl over the top of the car, moving slowly, feeling the ground with one hand and shielding my eyes with the other. When I was little,

I walked into a broken-off tree limb in the dark and nearly lost an eye, had two surgeries to fix it. I've been shy of walking through dark places ever since.

My groping hand finds Jo's foot. The rest of him is curled up in a corner. I whisper his name and put my ear close to his face. He is breathing, but I can't tell if his eyes are open.

"Liam?" he says to me as though waking from sleep.

"I'm here. How ya doin?"

"Liam?"

"I'm here."

"Liam, this is my place then."

"What's that?"

"This is my place, where I die and dry up. It's not a bad place is it?"

"You're not dyin. Don't say that. I put out a signal that the whole city will see."

"Ain't no city."

"Sure there is. There's people out there. They're just hid away, like we are. But one of em will peek out their window and see my signal, and they'll come. You'll see."

"What signal?"

"A good one."

"What signal did you make, Liam?"

"It's a good one I said." I open my bag. "Here's some water. You've been down here a long time. You gotta be thirsty."

I pull one of the Perriers out and twist off the cap.

Jo scoots himself up, takes a big drink and sits there very still. A minute goes by and he says, "Never mind. I know what you did. I can smell it."

The air is full of dust, and it isn't until I sit next to Jo with my back against the shaft wall that I notice the wind. Air is blowing up from between the car and the wall. It's being sucked up the shaft by the fire 33 floors above us. I can taste the dust. It tastes of oil.

"How do we smell it when the fire's so far up above us?" I ask.

A moment passes. I picture him with eyes narrowed.

"There's smoke outside the building," he says. "It's getting sucked in and pulled back up to feed the fire. Like a drafting fireplace. We're in a stovepipe."

I am relieved that Jo's mind is working like it should, but still, there is a brittleness in his voice.

"No one's comin," he adds.

"Someone will come."

"Even if they do, how would we know? Why would they come here? We're in a pit."

"We'll bang on the doors till they hear us."

"With what?"

"With our fists. With this." I knock the Perrier bottle against the elevator roof.

"You shoulda brought that piece of bed frame down."

"Yeah, I shoulda. I was thinkin about other things."

For a long time after that we are silent. Once, I ask Jo if he's looked for a way into the elevator. He says he's found the way but it's bolted shut.

Then things start falling down the shaft. Not big things, or heavy things yet. I hadn't thought about fire causing things to break apart and fall. I'd only thought of everything going up.

"What's your Bible say about this?" asks Jo.

"About what?"

"About bein stuck and havin no way of getting yourself out."

"It says a lot about that."

A cloud of small pieces, like flakes of rust, rains over us.

"You could say that's what the whole Bible is about. Us getting ourselves stuck and God getting us out."

"Never heard it like that before. God getting us out. Seems like a lot of things we have to do to make right with him, but that ain't like being stuck. That's climbing up out of the pit yourself."

"That's God's law. It's what you gotta keep, but no one keeps it."

"Then why have law at all?"

The adrenalin from my long slide down is spent, and there is none left to help me think.

112

"The law shows us God, and that we can't keep it without him. But Jesus kept it. So then the thing to do…the thing to do is believe it…believe he kept it for you."

"And how do you that?"

"Well, it's like…it's like a – "

A clang of metal echoes down from far above us, and we stop to listen. It clangs again but closer.

"Cover your head!"

Something hits the steel housing with such force that my ears ring. There's a clatter at my feet, and I reach down to feel the bed frame lying over my toes.

"Got something to bang now," I say, and then I stand and whack it against the door above us until my hands tingle. More adrenalin, but with it comes a dizziness that makes me grab the wall for balance.

Another bang rings out.

"Ow!" Jo yells.

"What?!"

"Something bit me."

"Where?"

"On the leg. A rat!" Just then something bullet-like hits the elevator roof on the other side of the housing. It bounces high and comes down again between us. I hear it rolling on the steel floor. I catch it under my feet and pick it up – a marble-sized ball of metal, warm to the touch.

"What is it?" asks Jo. He is gasping between words.

"I don't know," I say.

"Oh God," says Jo.

"There's no rats. It's stuff fallin from up there."

"Oh God," he says again.

I want to tell him about Christ, but the words are thick in my mouth. "The cross," I manage to say.

"Huh?" Jo is crying now.

"Jesus gets punished on it," I say, "but it's like us. That's what I meant."

"Us?" asked Jo.

Another ball hits the roof, and the sound of it makes me flinch.

113

"Stand up. Make a smaller target."

I am willing my body to squeeze into the space under my two forearms, which cover the top of my head. I feel Jo slide up the wall and stand next to me.

"Like who?" he asks again.

"Like us. Believers."

"What if I'm not one?"

"You're one if you believe Jesus did it for you."

"That's it?"

"I think so."

"I don't get it,"

"Not sure I do either, or at least I'm not telling it right."

Another ball ricochets off the housing and hits me in the hip. The pain of it shocks the air out of me.

"It hurts, I know it." says Jo. He takes the bed frame from my hands and beats it hard against the door above us.

"I don't want to die," he says, breathless now. "Not here. Not in this place."

The pain is spinning off in waves, and when I can speak again, I say, "My dad would make us pray."

"When?"

"Whenever. times like this."

"You had times like this?"

"Not just like this. But he'd for sure make us pray if he was here now."

"All right then, you pray."

"Ok."

I don't wait or pause to bow heads or hold hands. The words just come out of me.

"Lord, we don't want to die here. Please help us, God. Amen."

"That's it?"

"Yeah. What else do I need?"

"I don't know. It just didn't seem like much."

"It's all I have."

There is the sound of metal scraping above us, then a ball hits the elevator roof.

114

"Does God ever say no when you pray?" asks Jo.

"Sure."

There is a new sound above us now.

"Liam, what's that up there?"

I don't want to look up now. That same fear of walking blind is gripping me. Things are falling. Things that hurt when they hit you. I can't look up.

"Liam, look!"

"I am!" I lie.

Jo's voice begins to break, his lungs heave like he's taking air through a pin hole.

"What is it?...Oh God!...What is it?"

I look up now and hold my hands over my eyes, shading them from whatever might fall. I can't see the top of the shaft, just a light that is shapeless, without edges, like a fog. And it is full of color, full of growing color.

"Fire," says Jo. "It's falling down. It's coming at us. We're gonna burn!"

If I hadn't been looking, I would have told Jo he was nuts, but I am looking, and the fire is falling. It billows out at us, the leading edge like a swollen balloon, continually bursting downward and being filled again from behind. It is growing bigger, like an on-coming train in free-fall.

It makes no sound, and it dazzles me. My hands slip away from the sides of my face as I watch it fall. And then the heat comes.

"People die from smoke, not fire!" shouts Jo.

"What?"

"That's what they die from in fires, smoke! Breath it in deep before the fire gets here!" He shouts the words out between big, labored breaths.

"There's no smoke," I say. I want to smell smoke, smell it in great, choking clouds, but there is only the heat.

"I'm sorry," I say.

Jo gasps, then spits out, "For what?"

"For the fire," I say. "I made it."

"I know."

115

"I'm sorry."

The fire comes closer. Like racing water filling a cavern, it curls toward us. The heat grows, and I can feel the skin on my face start to itch and then to burn, and I wonder if taking a lung full of fire will do the same to me as smoke.

Jo lets out a scream, but it is not terror. It is a plea, the very last drop squeezed out of an agonized soul. It is the word mercy. I join him and scream the word too.

The fire is on us now, the colors have all burned to white, and I am blinded by brightness.

Smoke is there, and other things – shouting, screams, voices, hands slapping and clawing.

In the white heat and smoke, hands pull at me, at my hair, my collar, my knees and feet.

I breathe in the smoke.

I bite it off and swallow it.

I am lifted up, lifted up into the brightness before all goes black. I swim in it, in the blackness. It is cool like deep lake water under a summer sky. I swim without effort, then hang there in its depths, and there is no fighting at all, not for breath, not for warmth. The smell of campfire and melting styrene is still in my nose, and it is pleasant as summer. I hear my name, and I know the voice. It says my name quietly, or maybe from a long way off, and the sound draws my body upward as on a current. I rise toward sunlight, and the blackness around me warms and gives way, and I break the surface gently.

I awake, and the space around me is hard and cold. It is concrete and wind. The black silhouette of a face hovers over mine, shouting at me, yelling my name. I cough in reply, but with the next breath of cool air I speak.

"Am I in Heaven?" I ask the face.

"No," it says. "You're in Lansing."

The brightness fades. The face rises from the depths around it into color and shadow. It is Jack. Behind him Maya is crouched down with hands on knees. Her smiling face is framed by a sky that is a washed-out gray. At the edge of my vision, on the other side of Jack, I see smoke, black and alive, climbing up and around the spire of Boji

Tower. I am lying on a sidewalk half a block east up Allegan. The skin on my face feels scalded. My lungs are full of dirt and heat.

"We saw your smoke," says Jack.

I reach up for him, grabbing at his coat collar. He winces like he thinks I am going to hit him, but when I pull him to me, he starts crying and saying over and over, "We saw your smoke." He heaves in my arms, and between us I can feel the piled weight of grief going lighter.

Part II

Time has done me a courtesy. It's parceled my memories into movable loads. What I'd once thought was a dense landscape too full of small detail to draw sense from was really a panorama of big things. The details were there, but I needed to step back to see that here were features as distinct as forests on mountainsides, as sharp as mountain peaks on horizons.

I hold the first parcel in my thoughts as being marked out by two images – the death of Josiah's father at one end and the smoking, scorched top of Boji Tower at the other. The events between are precise and hold their sequence as fixedly as fairytale. But the next, in the few years that follow, have such a plodding uniformity, have been so worked over by the recursive hand of time that they're now compressed into a few mundane sketches.

The working of the soil and the vicissitudes of four growing seasons have worn into my memory the deepest marks. There is the first year of scarcity when we'd gone at it with the clumsy, blundering care of children. Our harvest came up withered, diseased, infested, or in such over-abundance that it rotted on the vine before it could be eaten or canned.

There is the second year of complete failure, a year of vanity. We'd saved seed from that first meager garden for the next year's planting. In vain we prepared and planted and watched for months for the seedlings to break out, but they lay dead in the dirt, a thousand little miscarriages. It was Josiah who'd come across some piece of learning about how the old wise had improved things by making plants that couldn't make more plants. Those little packets of seeds from the grocery store – what a cruel trick – produced only barren children.

And then there are the first years of true farming. These stand as wide, green images in my memory. There is one where all of us – Jack, Josiah, Becka, Nate, and I – work side by side in our small, fenced-in field, work the ground with our hands until darkness sends us indoors for food and sleep. I have this entry from August of that year:

118

"Five straight days of 90+ degrees. Tomatoes splitting on the vines, cucs huge and green and too big with seeds. Chickens will eat well this month. Corn is bugged. Need to figure out what it is. Raccoons won't touch it. Melons are fat. Becka will pickle the rines this year. Calf still ailing, may have to put down soon before other one gets it. Don't know what the fever is so no meat this time. Frustrating. Knowledge once so close is buried, maybe gone for a thousand years until we have the time to figure it out..."

There is a winter memory too, a dreamy hibernation of tending the fire, mending things, reading, games, and boredom. In January of 2017, I wrote this:

"Snowed another foot last night. Took Bella to Josiah's for dinner, Becka, Nate, and twins in tow on a sled. Jack read first 2 c's of Nick Nickelby while Josiah re-caned his snow shoes with cord from three table lamps."

There is also the constant activity of hunting and scavenging which spans all the months, connects all the years. A meal-entry from February catches it well:

"Catfish for breakfast, canned tomatoes and eggs for lunch, a dinner of squirrel, apples, pine nuts for supper..."

But the next parcel in my head has an altogether different quality to it. Here there are the first hints of clarity and straight lines. Here we are just starting to see that we have it in us to make something fixed in the shifting uncertainty of life without the old wise.

Chapter 22

A late July sun shines through a dry blue sky and burns my cheeks. I am walking, in scarecrow posture, between rows of corn. The sharp top leaves trace lightly against the underside skin of my arms. To my left, toward the shade of the tree line, the rows shorten. But to my right they rise up to neck height, a full acre's swell of green.

We know it's an acre because we measured it off. The idea of merely planting the backyard would not satisfy Josiah. What kind of measure is a backyard? he would ask. What is the standard backyard unit? How are we to compare ourselves with the Spencer twins if we have to say we're farming a backyard? Turns out our backyard was about ten feet shy in length of one acre, so we pushed out the fence, cut down two pines, and reclaimed the space beneath as farmland.

We now farm an acre of corn. I'm thinking about this when I'm startled out of my thoughts by the sound of a farting horse.

"Say excuse me, Bella," says Jack. He is at the fence in the shade of the trees.

"Why do you sneak up?" I say. I sound more annoyed than I really am, but that's how we talk to each other.

"I didn't. I came by the lake at a gallop. What were you thinkin so hard about anyway?"

I smile and shake my head to say nothing and never mind. "Why a gallop? Thought you were helping Josiah do a well."

"I am. Will's cow is in a ditch. Thought you might want to help. Then I thought we'd stop by Davey Alvoord's."

"Something wrong with him?"

"The cow?"

"Cow's a she. Davey."

"There's a lot wrong with him, but no, nothing particular. We just haven't checked on him a while."

"I haven't checked on him because he doesn't want to be checked on."

"Then I guess he doesn't have a choice cause I'm doing the checking today. You're just coming along."

"He can't have a say in who he hangs out with? Even if it's nobody?"

"No he can't, not as long as he lives here in a house that we walk by every day. He lives here, so I'll knock on his door, and say hello until he tells me to stop. Besides…I got him to trade something with me."

I am ready to let the argument go – it is an old one – but at the word *trade* I give Jack a look.

"A jar of Becka's hot peppers for a stack of *Car and Driver*."

"Hmm," I say. "Since when do you – "

" – It was a trade. That's all that mattered. He's practically a member of the community now. Be runnin for mayor next."

Every once in a while we'd run into a puzzle like Davey Alvoord. At a glance, you'd say there was nothing there to promise survival of another winter. Yet every spring, there he'd be, plodding through his days, scratching out just enough from the space around us to keep some dim candle burning in his breast. He would take no help, invite no society. He tolerated Jack, who was probably his best and only friend on earth, but it amounted to a cat's tolerance.

We go first to the Wagonmakers. This is another set of twins, a boy and a girl about my age. (We never did make sense of the twin phenomena. There was a genetic favoring there, of course, but the science that might have explained it is lost to us still.) One of their milk cows is standing confounded in a drainage ditch that runs along a flat, mile-square field of grass, weed, and shrub. We stand at the lip – Jack, Josiah, William Wagonmaker, and I – and we are just as confounded.

"We could tie on to her with the horses and pull," says Jack.

"I tried that," says William. "Didn't budge her. Up to her knees in mud, and she doesn't seem to want to come anyway."

"What about leading her along the edge? We could get in there and dig a terrace, real shallow, and walk her right up. Like walking the trails up the Grand Canyon walls."

"Could do that," says Josiah. "But it'd take a whole day of digging. She'd lay down before we had it ready, and likely she'd never get up again."

121

Libby Wagonmaker is coming down the road on her bike. She stops.

"Watcha doin?" She asks. Libby is deeply freckled, wears black, thick-rimmed glasses, and her red hair is pulled up under a floppy white hat that looks to be tied too tightly under her chin. Despite such outward liability, she has an awkward grace that comes from a lack of self-consciousness. Most of the boys think she's cute.

"Tessa's in the ditch," says William.

"She hurt?"

"Just stupid."

"Hmm," is all she can add, then, "I got things to do. See ya."

"Bye, Libby," says Jack. "I like your hat."

"Thanks."

We sit at the edge of the ditch now and squint in the sun and think.

"What if we filled the ditch up with water and floated her out?" proposes Jack.

"Where'd we get the water from?" asks William. "And how would we dam it up?"

"I don't know. I'm just thinking out loud."

We turn together at the sound of footsteps, six of them. It's Libby with a calf in tow. She says nothing but walks to the edge of the ditch, takes something small from her pocket, and gives the calf a poke in the flank.

In one long exchange of bovine sounds – a cry from the calf stuck by a thumb tack, a bellow from the protective mother – Tessa the milk cow climbs the ditch wall like a trail horse, scatters the four of us, and before we can figure out what's just happened, is walking the road back to the farm with her calf and Libby.

"Hmm," says William from the bottom of the ditch.

"She pulled instead of pushed," says Josiah.

"We'd a thought of that eventually," says Jack.

We say nothing more and let Jack's pronouncement stand as final word. At the house, Josiah wastes no time in resuming the work of affixing a homemade hand pump to the Wagonmaker's old electric well. I don't know the intricacies of the system except that it requires a lot of pvc pipe, pistons, valves, and levers. I say something to that effect, and as Josiah works, he teaches me – again – the rudiments.

"Two foot valves, one at the bottom below the water line and one at the top just under the spout. The pump pulls up a few feet of water at each draw, the bottom valve locks it there. Pump away and up and up it climbs. When it hits the top and you pump down, the water above the higher valve can't go nowhere except out. It's like suckin on a long straw, you pinch it to keep it from falling back then suck again. Get it?"

I say I do, just like I said it after the last time he explained it. He gives me a grin and shakes his head.

I had failed to understand Jack's meaning that we would stop at Davey Alvoord's after he finished the well, so I'm left standing idly to watch Josiah and Jack at their work.

"Goin to the meeting tonight?" asks William, who is standing with me, also ready to lend a hand or suggestion.

"Yeah," I say. "We won't get much done, but I think it's needed. If nothing else we can at least say we met." Then I forget who I'm talking to and add, "And the music will be worth the trip."

"The trip and two jars of peppers," says William with a punch to my soldier.

"Right."

Before the dying came, Libby was something of a prodigy on piano. Folks still talk about it now in hushed tones and shaking heads. She would have gone to the best schools, had it paid for even. She would have been famous. She would have been the best in the world. Such assumptions left uncorrected take on a stony quality in the heads of children, so we believed all of that about Libby Wagonmaker. She is a fine piano player, but whether she'd have found a way into Carnegie Hall, who knows.

To his credit, William worked hard to keep a fan to the flame. He made her practice daily, kept her challenged with new pieces, even learned how to keep the piano tuned. William was good at preserving things. He was a good farmer, and maintained his parents' home well. Libby's talent was just one more thing within his purview that could be nurtured and improved until it moved under its own power.

Making a business of it happened as a matter of course.

In year two, we made a survey – it was Jack's idea – of the 30 square miles or so south of us. (I-96 just a quarter mile north acted as border just as convincingly as a wide river might have.) We then invited the fourteen households we'd found to meet at the township hall on Holt Road. There was a piano there, horribly out of tune. But under Libby's hands it brought a living sound to the room. She played for an hour or so while we waited for all to arrive. The meeting was short – introductions and an agreement to meet again in a month. Then Libby entertained us for another hour, asking the keys on the old piano to do things they had no business doing. We didn't know what we were hearing, but we knew it wasn't a common thing.

The next month's meeting went likewise, except that a few of the more thoughtful brought little gifts for the piano player – a jar of honey, a loaf of bread, butter. This opened William's eyes. He would let her play a few songs before the meetings, but those wishing to stay for the concert after had to barter for the privilege. It was the first of our many forays into commerce, and it emerged from the simplest iteration of supply and demand: she could play, and we wanted to hear it.

I can recall no indignation at the Wagonmakers' plan to profit from her ability. We all understand by now the value of time, can see that much effort and practice comprised the talent in those slender, girl's hands. Those hands should be practicing, and we are only too happy to give them more time to do it, just as the Wagonmakers are happy to pay Josiah a half bushel of dried beef and a smoked ham for the well.

He too has spent hours building talent into his hands. By the end of that second winter, he could read anything in the English language. The more he read, the more ideas he would have for improving the world around us. All of those ideas of course required more reading, so it was a list of improvements that grew faster than it could be whittled down. Getting water from the old wells just proved to be in highest demand.

I watch a shady spot beneath the Wagonmakers' back deck – a cat is there torturing a bird – when the sound of water hitting the ground pulls my eyes away. Josiah is pumping a handle, the kind you'd see on a railroad hand car, except that it's one sided and made of wood. From the other side of the pipe that sticks up from the ground a few feet, a jet of water falls in long lengths against the dirt and gravel.

"Need a tub to catch it," says William.

I turn to Jack.

"That mean you're done?" I ask.

"I want us all to go to the meeting tonight," says Jack to the four of us, ignoring my question.

Libby brings two five-gallon buckets and sets them next to the well.

"Why?" asks Josiah, still pumping but slower so that the water falls at an angle the buckets can catch.

"Cuz I got something I want to propose," says Jack.

"To the whole town?"

"Thought we were calling it a county," says Libby.

"Town, county, whatever," says Jack. "But I want as many there as we can get."

"Why?" asks Josiah again.

"Cuz it's important. Don't ask any more questions. I'm not telling you what I want to say till I say it. And yes we're done. Right, Josiah?"

"Right."

Chapter 23

Davey Alvoord lives on a stretch of country road that isn't quite country. A dozen houses bunched together on both sides of Willoughby create a neighborhood island in a sea of fallow fields. But it's a sinking island. The once manicured lawns are fields themselves, growing whatever grass or weed the wind brings. Bushes and trees have grown up and out, and moss has taken deep root on the shaded roofs, so that even the tallest houses sit nestled down in green.

125

Davey's house is the worst of the twelve. His dad had been a master gardener and tended the space around the big ranch-style with care and an inclination for fruit trees. When the dying came, nature on the Alvoord place simply took advantage of a long head start. That seemed to suit Davey just fine. He'd always looked as though he might welcome the idea of being subsumed by the colors around him.

Jack's horse knows the way, and mine follows it up the short drive. The growth on both sides is heavy and leans toward the center, forcing us into single-file. The house has the same un-lived-in look of most every other house in the world except that two small, broken windows are boarded over from the inside, the broken shards still hanging in their casements.

The drive wraps around to the back of the house. There the grass and weeds are worn down in patterns. A path from the back deck to the pole barn, one to the detached garage, another to a greenhouse and meager vegetable garden seem to mark out all the wanderings of Davey Alvoord. And yet the picture is a false one, for Davey's fame as a wide-ranging scavenger is considerable.

Jack knocks hard.

"He's probably in Detroit," he says, "looking for phone books."

We stand on his porch. Windows on either side of the door are shaded, but I can see cardboard boxes stacked beyond window height. The door has its own window, and by the light that comes from the front of the house, I can see a narrow passage between high stacks of boxes and storage crates.

"Wonder what all he's got in there…" says Jack. He knocks again and yells Davey's name.

"Don't see his bike," I say.

"Maybe we should go in," says Jack.

"You can't just walk in."

"Why not?"

I give Jack a what-are-you-stupid look.

"Maybe he's hurt in there."

"And maybe he's on his bike like he is every single other day."

"Daveyyyyy!"

"He's not here."

"Look at that!" Jack reaches down to a potted plant next to one of the porch steps.

"Look at what?"

"That! Those tomatoes. They're all rotten and black."

"So what?"

"So he hasn't been out here in a while. He wouldn't let food rot, he's too careful. I'm tellin you Liam we need to go in."

He cranes his head to look into a high kitchen window.

"What if he's dead?"

I just sigh and let the question go, and then Jack turns back to the door and gives the knob a hard turn. The door opens.

"Maybe I'll just see – "

"Maybe you'll see what?" At the sound of the voice behind us, I yell out, and Jack pulls the door shut. Davey Alvoord is standing on the bottom step with a kitten in one hand and a cider-press flywheel in the other. He is staring at our knees.

"Doesn't like what?" he says again as he brushes past me up the steps.

"Tomatoes," says Jack.

"I don't like tomatoes."

"So why…?"

Davey stops and sets the fly-wheel down, then looks at Jack's hand still on the doorknob, then at the tomato plant.

"Mom plants them every year in that pot. Not in no other pot."

Jack nods in understanding, pulls his hand quickly from the door and takes a step back.

"We thought maybe you were…you know…"

Davey doesn't know and just holds Jack in a blank stare – now at his chest – until the kitten squirms. He sets it down too. Davey is as thin as a straw. His short, black, serrated hair is self-cut. A red hooded sweatshirt and jeans hang on him like drapes on a rod.

"What do you want, Jack?" he asks.

His hands, empty now, have grasped his own elbows and seem to steady him.

127

"Just seeing how you're doing, Davey." Jack turns and smiles at me. "I really liked the *Car and Drivers*. I was hoping we might trade a little, help each other out. What do you say?"

"I don't need nothin else."

"Everyone needs something."

"I don't need nothing."

"You needed pickled hot peppers. You didn't think you did, but when it came right down to it you needed em more than you needed those magazines. Ain't that right?"

Davey purses his lips like he wants to spit, but Jack is rolling.

"Yeah, that's right, and I bet there's something you need now if you just think it over. I got more of those peppers – "

Davey shakes his head hard.

"No, no don't need no peppers. Don't need nothin, like I just said. And neither do you."

"What do you mean? You don't know what I need."

"I know you don't care about cars and…and you don't like them and you just traded to trade."

"You don't know what I like, and besides, you didn't just give them away. You got something too."

He shakes his head again. "Didn't want em."

"Didn't want the peppers?"

"I traded with you so you'd go away. I didn't want em. Didn't need em. Just like I don't need nothin right now."

As Davey is saying this last bit, he is also sliding between Jack and me, into the house. He takes a breath as if he has something more to say, then lowers his head and shuts the door. The sliding metallic sounds of a thorough locking follow.

"Why do you have to do that?" I ask.

"Do what?"

I am stuck for the right word – the notion I'm thinking of is many-sided. I find an approximation.

"Intrude."

"For his own good. And it's not intruding. It's…I'm…taking care of him. Taking care of my neighbor."

"Seems to me he doesn't want to be taken care of. Or needs to be. Will you stop buggin him now?"

"He didn't tell me to stop. Did you notice?"

"He didn't use those words, but that's what I heard."

Jack walks off the porch with his teeth dug into his bottom lip. I follow him to the horses. He takes hold of the horn and turns to me.

"You think he didn't want the peppers?"

"That's what he said."

"I know, but…"

"So what? So what if he didn't want them and just wanted you to go?"

"That woulda been fine if I'd figured it out right then, but I really thought he'd traded with me. For real, I mean, and that would have been something."

Jack swings up into the saddle, and his eyes are fixed on some distant point. He wants to keep talking, so I climb onto Bella and point her the same way. We leave Davey's place in single-file.

"We used to be friends, you know?"

Jack is in front of me, down the road now, and has to yell this.

"A long time ago when I went to school my second-grade year. He was only in the class for part of the day, and Mrs. Bernstein would put him next to me. She said I knew how to talk to him."

"I didn't know that."

"I've tried since then to get him to come out of his shell a little, but he's pretty stuck. But he's never told me to go away. Not exactly. So I haven't gone away, not yet."

As we turn onto Willoughby, Jack's horse keeps the lead, and so for the two-mile ride I have the back of my brother to consider. I am struck now – as I have been many times – by our differences. I try to imagine myself going out of my way to trade in junk with a recluse. I try to reproduce the feeling that would compel me there, but I can't.

As I watch him ride, I think that this is a good part of him, that it is better than any corresponding part in me, and yet there's something doubtful at the edge of it. I wonder about the meeting tonight and what Jack might propose, and though I try to fight them off, my last thoughts as we come down the trail between Dobie Lake and Mr. Mench's grave are dark ones.

Chapter 24

The Alaiedon Township Hall sits among farm fields in one of the flattest parts of the county. You can see it a long way off. As Jack, Josiah, and I turn onto Holt Highway, we can see from there that some have arrived already. There are the Wagonmakers' two ponies hitched to the flagpole. A hay wagon with a tent pitched on it sits horseless in the east parking lot. The two horses, which I can see now are mules, have been let loose to graze in the softball field. Luke McHugh and Isaac Quinn have walked over from their house on Okemos and are playing catch in the road.

"We're always early," says Josiah.

"Mom would be amazed," says Jack. My mom was never early, and it always seemed that she had passed the trait on to her kids. But Josiah was right, we were always early. Most everyone was.

As we approach the hall, I can make out the word *NEW* painted in bright white letters on the big sign by the road. We had talked it over briefly at the tail end of a meeting several months prior that we should change the name of this place. It seemed fitting to Josiah who'd proposed it. He then left it for me to convince the others, which was not hard. I'd forgotten about painting in the word – it was Luke's assignment – and at the sight of it now, I am surprised at a flush of pride that rises in me. It seems a silly reaction, and I say nothing more than, "Look. We're in New Alaiedon."

Jack says, "Cool."

I look over at Josiah, but he only nods.

The hall is split into two parts: offices and a big, high-ceilinged meeting room. There are only a dozen of us, and the meeting room is more than we need, but it's on the west side and the windows let in the late-day sun. On the wall opposite the windows is a chalkboard on which three items are written: *fences, growing corn, Grand Ledge.*

Josiah and I are at the board, listening to Libby play something by Mozart on the old upright piano when Jack steps up and writes the word *Jack.*

"We're gonna discuss *you*?" asks Josiah.

"Not exactly, but it's too hard to put into one word."

Josiah gives me a look that says he's curious. We both are, but we know that Jack won't give up a clue if he knows we're hooked.

Libby stops playing and that's the signal that the meeting is about to start. We sit down at tables arranged in a big square and wait for William to begin things. He is the tallest and tells Libby when to stop playing, so from the first he's always been the one to lead meetings. He's natural at it, and no one else begrudges him the job.

"The Baldwin house isn't here yet, but I talked to Aidan a few days ago, and he said they're coming."

He looks around the room and consults a legal pad in his hand.

"Anyone seen Emilio, Nick Williams, or Brandie? No? Ok. So I think we can start talking about some of the other things, then if there's a vote on anything we'll wait for the Baldwins. We can vote at the end of the meeting on stuff, right? So who wrote *fences*? It looks like Luke's writing."

"Yep," says Luke.

"Go ahead."

Luke is slight and bookish. He uncrosses his legs and pulls himself with his elbows closer to the table.

"I know this isn't the first time we've talked about this, but I think we need to figure out how to deal with it. Last week — and some of you know this because you've seen it too — last week I was bringing a load of pipe from Mason and I saw that Chandler Cunningham had made his fence go all the way around his neighbor's place, the house on his east. I've been in that house. It's clean and the guy there had a woodshop in his basement. I've taken hand tools from there more than once, but I can't now. Or at least I have to ask Chandler if I can go in now because there's no opening in the fence except on his property, and that's got a locked gate. He locks it. We've always treated houses as open property that anyone could use. I think we need to talk about the rules or write something down. I've got some ideas, but I wanted to let everyone else have a chance to talk it over. I think we need some rules about fences and houses. That's what I wanted to talk about."

"Did you tell Chandler you'd be talking about this tonight?" asks William.

"I did, and he just spit and said 'whatever.'"

"I can totally see him doing that," says Libby to several yes's, laughter, and nodding heads. The next discussion proceeds with all the order of a henhouse at breakfast.

"What did they do in the old time?"

"They didn't have places that no one owned, did they? I mean everything was owned. Either people owned it or the gov – "

"What about before that?"

"What do you mean before that? Before what?"

"Before government…"

"You mean like Indian times?"

"Yeah, before everything was owned. What did people do? Did they share it? Or just grab up whatever – "

"They put flags on it."

"Like we did on the moon."

"Like at the North Pole."

"You mean the South Pole."

"Both, I'm pretty sure."

"No land at the North – "

" – But that was governments doing it."

"I don't know what time we're talking about when there was no governments. What time is that?"

"William's right. Even in Indian times there was government. Someone would make a claim on – "

" – Native Americ – "

" – Someone would make a claim on land and tell the government back in Washington or wherever what the land was, and someone would write it all down in an office."

132

"When Christopher Columbus came over he was doing it for a government. Italy, I think it was."

"No, it was Spain. He was Spanish."

"Not Spanish. Portugan."

"Portuguese."

"Yeah, that."

"It doesn't matter what Columbus was," says Luke impatiently, "or whether or not there was government then. We don't have government now, but we need to figure this fence thing out."

"Maybe we should be talking about government then."

"Aren't we the government now? Isn't what we're doing now government?"

Silence.

"Ok. How do we talk about that?"

"What do you mean? Like, having a president or mayor or what?"

"Something like that."

"I thought we were talking about fences."

"I think we need a new item on the talk board."

Josiah has been silent until now.

"We don't need any more government than what we've got. We're each making decisions for ourselves. Why do we need someone else making them for us?"

"What if something happens?"

"Like what?"

"A war."

"A war with who?"

"Whom – "

"With anybody. Who knows? We don't know who's out there who might want to just come in and take us over, take our stuff. But what if it happened? We don't have a plan or an army or anything."

"What kind?"

"What kind of plan?"

"What kind of...leader?"

"A president!"

"A king."

"What's the difference?"

"A president has a job kind of like a king but he's only supposed to do what the constitution says. A king can do whatever he wants."

"Our president could do whatever he wanted."

"Not always. Those were executive orders – "

" – my dad would say the President has executive odor!"

" – and they could be thrown out by the next president. A King could say no more elections and just be king."

"We don't want a king then."

"We need to start with the laws. That's what our foundling fathers did. The laws that we want will decide what gov – ."

" – Foundling?"

"Whatever."

"So what kind of laws do we want?"

"We need a law about fences," says Luke.

"Ok, let's start with that."

"But who says you get to decide what laws we talk about?"

"I . . . I guess I … I don't know. We've just always done it like this."

"Let's vote on what laws we talk about today."

"Who says you get to say 'let's vote'?"

"Can't anyone say that?"

Josiah pushes back from the table and stands. His chair makes a nails-on-slate squeak that stops the talk. He walks to the talking board and stares it at long enough to establish the silence.

"Can I suggest something?" He points to the board. "Let's talk about *these* things." He points to each item and says it out loud. *Fences, growing corn, Grand Ledge, Jack.* "Let's *think* about governments and wars and Christopher Columbus for the next month and then we can talk about them at the next meeting. How does that sound? Do we need to vote on that?"

"Let's vote."

"I second that."

"All in favor say yes."

"Yes."

"All opposed."

Jack's lone *no* sounds in the room like a struck bell, and all eyes turn to him. The silence that follows is an invitation from the group to explain himself.

"My name is on the board because it's government that I want to talk about. So I had to vote no to the proposal as you worded it. I've already thought long and hard about it and I want to talk about it today. We need to talk about it today."

Luke McHugh coughs, then says, "But that's after we talk about fences, right?"

Chapter 25

Our discussion of fences goes quickly. We determine a fence can be put up wherever we like as long as its adjacent to our own property and doesn't enclose anything of public use, including, but not necessarily limited to, unoccupied houses or businesses, a body of water, or a woodlot. In effect we limit the law of first find to things that can be carried or dragged away by a horse. Anything bigger and we vote on it. We'll let Chandler Cunningham's fence stay up provided that he reads the proposed rule (Luke McHugh will deliver it), agrees to leave the gate unlocked, and attends next month's meeting where, after everyone's had time to think about it, we'll vote to make the measure a law, albeit a highly local one.

Isaac Quinn proposes to grow another's corn crop next year, if the other party agrees to take on his 5 acres of hay. It's an intriguing idea to everyone. And as it doesn't involve any but the two parties, no motion is made for any action at all, and we move on.

The Grand Ledge discussion, as it turns out, is really about mail. Jodi Conklin has two cousins alive in Grand Ledge. She won't move there and they don't want to come here, but they visit each other about monthly. She runs letters for Nick Stilwell to a friend of his whom the Conklin cousins know in Grand Ledge. She has on three separate occasions carried traded goods between them, the last being five gallons of yeast water for one month's use of a Jackson fork. The fork was heavy, so Nick's friend paid a fare of eight twelve-gauge shells in #6 field shot. Nick will pay the return post of eight shells in 00 buck. She's decided to start charging for all services and wants to know if anyone has friends or relatives in Holt, Dewitt, Bath, or Haslett.

"What about Williamston?"

"That's kind of out of the way," says Jodi. She has a round, friendly face framed in brown hair pulled back and tied at her neck. She's as tall as any boy in the room and big boned. "I know two people in Dewitt, and doesn't Dougie go out there anyway to work on horses?"

"Not every month," says Dougie. "Few times a year, I'd say. Twice in the summer."

"I'd think about it if there was enough people who'd have regular deliveries. Let's wait on Williamston. "

"I can walk to Holt."

"Not if you live on Meridian and want to send something all the way to Waverly. And she goes right through it to get to Grand Ledge anyway."

"Just seems like it's next door."

"Canada's right next door too, but you wouldn't want to walk there."

"Would you deliver them to every house? Like the mail?"

"Well, that's the thing. For Grand Ledge I just take them to Josh and Jake's and they deliver them. The other towns, I don't know, I guess I'd have to figure out where people live at first."

"What if you found one person in each town who would help you? Maybe take part of your fare."

"Or just be a place where people could pick up their stuff."

"Like Nelsons' Mercantile."

"Like what?"

"Nelson's Mercantile in Little House. Everyone went there to pick up their mail. It didn't get delivered right to their house."

"It was a post office."

"That's not right."

"Yeah it is, a post office where you had your own box inside."

"No, I mean the mail didn't go to the Nelsons' store. It went to the post office. Walnut Grove had its own post office. And it wasn't called Nelson's store. It was Olsons.'"

"Oh…yeah."

"The post office was called Olsons?"

"No!"

In the end, Jodi decides to make the full round trip next week, talk to the people she knows, and get a feel for how much demand there might be for a once-a-month mail/delivery circuit. On objection that she shouldn't go alone, Jodi agrees to ask one of her cousins to make the trip with her.

"Next item is Jack…" says William, who looks at him with raised brows.

The next minutes are burnished in my memory, for I've gone over them time enough that they shine. His forearms rest on the table. Jack is looking at the space between his hands, his body still. Then, with the deliberateness of a stage entrance, he stands and sends his chair skidding back. It doesn't squeak like Josiah's did, but he seems surprised still by his own gesture, and smiles nervously at all the raised brows.

"I…I want to see…I have an idea. Yes – I have an idea, and I want to see if it's a real idea, or if it's just been in my head so long that it seems real to me. Do you know what I mean? Does that happen to anyone else?"

"Let's hear the idea," says Josiah.

"Right. That makes most sense. I didn't mean to – "

Jack now begins to walk behind the chairs. His body visibly relaxes as he finds a slow rhythm of step, step, hand on a chair, step, step…It occurs to me that I am watching someone I don't really know, and a discordant knowledge that it's my brother comes over me and I'm suddenly tired. As he takes his hand from my chair, there is a flashing, familiar image of him moving away from me, into uncertainty. My stomach clutches as I remember it. I cough hard to dispel the confusion, and then he begins to talk to the room.

"When I was little, my dad built us a fort under the basement stairs. He put a little light in it, and a book shelf, put a little door on it with a real door knob. It was a great fort."

Jack stops behind Libby Wagonmaker's chair and pauses for a moment to look out a window. He starts walking again.

"But I never used it. I mean – I did. When we had to do quiet time, I'd do it there sometimes, but I never went there on my own. I was never drawn to it the way Liam was."

I knew this to be true, but had never put words to it. To hear him now point out this small and passing distinction between us only pushes him further from me. I cough again, but the sensation is fixed.

"Then he built us a tree house. I liked the tree house, but not for the reason he meant it. It was like the fort. It was a place to go and hide and be by yourself, but I never went into it thinking about that. I liked the tree house because you could see for a long way, and you could climb from the roof up higher into the tree and see fishing boats on Dobie Lake and send flashlight messages to the Spedoske boys. When you climbed the tree there was so much more of the world happening right then. It was happening always, of course, when I was on the ground and not seeing it, but not really. I let myself think that the boats appeared only after I got to the highest branches. The boats needed me to climb up and see them, or they wouldn't be…there."

He is still pacing around the tables, but he's moved out in his orbit, no longer touching the chair backs. His voice has lost its hesitance, and he is speaking as though alone. There is a faint tension of embarrassment over the room.

"I feel like I'm on the ground now, like I've been there for a long time, and I want so much to climb some huge tree, a bean stalk if I could, and see what's happening in the world. I want to make boats appear on oceans. I've wanted to do that for a long time, but I couldn't. There was always the next day to get through, and that's always how it was, getting through days, pieces of days little bits at a time. But then we started thinking in weeks and getting through them one at a time, and we did, and we learned and got better and then it was months and we did that too, learned how to plan and work and get through a whole month like we knew what we were doing. But all

138

the time I've wanted to get off the ground and see farther. And now, now that we've got a whole growing season planned and now that it's working and the corn's up and there's wells in our yards and we're teaching the young ones to read, I feel – don't you all feel? – like we're doing it. We're not waking up every night screaming about the Fear, but we're alive and thinking about how to keep living and we're starting to know that we can…can live, I mean."

Jack stops again. He is at the south window of the big room. I have a sense that had the wall not been there, he would be speaking from somewhere in the softball field.

"I said I wanted to talk about government, and I am getting to that, but I feel like you needed to know why I'm proposing what I'm about to. We're already making decisions and voting and stuff like that, so we have a kind of government. But really, how can you govern something if you don't know what it is, or how big it is." He points to a map on the wall. "We've got our little township marked out and counted, and we know of some people in the places around Lansing. I'm sure Jodi will learn a lot more taking the mail around. But what about the other cities?"

Jack goes to the piano and takes something from the top of it. It is a map, and he unfolds it as he walks to the bulletin board. He tacks it next to the township map. It is our state of Michigan.

He points and talks to the map. "What about Jackson or Grand Rapids or Flint or Ann Arbor? Who lives there? Does anyone? Some of us have made trips looking for family or friends, but really we don't know. What about Detroit or even Chicago? They're not that far. And maybe" – Jack pauses, seems to weigh words as he turns around – "maybe they're not dead like Lansing is…maybe we find city people. Or maybe we find – because it's still possible, just because we haven't seen anything here – maybe we find a grown up."

This glances off me. I don't really hear it. I have buried the hope of rescue so deep that it can give no answering note to the word. I suspect the others are like me in this, for there is no noise, no gasps or sighs, not even a shifting of limbs.

"We can't talk about government until we know who we are. I want to find out. I want to go and find out, that's all."

"We know who we are."

It's Josiah, and he speaks as one dropping a pronouncement. There is no attempt at persuasion, just the quiet plunk of fact.

"We know who we are," he says again.

"Ok. Then there might be others like us. Wouldn't it be better to know?"

"How better?"

Jack looks us over slowly. He is drawing from his memory, priming it with our faces, drawing up recollections as though from deep waters.

"We've learned a lot in the last four years," he says slowly. "We've learned things we shouldn't have been able to learn. Who would have thought that Josiah, who couldn't read when the dying came, would figure out how to give us water? Would any of you have ever thought four years ago that we'd be building farms or making medicines or teaching classes...or doing the million other things we've learned to do to stay alive? And we're not just staying alive now, we're living lives. We're actually living. Sort of. Aren't we? Well, there must be others out there doing things like we are, figuring out the world and how to use it. But not the exact same things. New things. Different things."

"What do we need from anyone?" asks Josiah. "We have food, water, good shelter. We're warm all winter. We have horses and – "

"And maybe someone else needs what we have. Not every little tribe is going to figure out how to get water from old wells. We could help them with that. Why do you – "

" – they might not want help, Jack. Have you thought of that?"

"I'm not thinking of any of that. I mean, I'm only thinking of it now because you're bringing it up. I'm just trying to give you good reasons to see who else is out there, but I only want to go to...to..."

" – to take care of them," I say.

This stops Jack, and he goes quickly from Josiah's eyes to mine. And though I feel foolish for having said it, I hold his stare, unwilling to back away from it or from the words.

He holds mine too and says, "Not to help or take care of anyone. Just to know. I want to know what's out there. Who's out there."

A long silence falls on us. The susurration of moving clothes, blood in the ears, and wind through open windows fills it until I cough it away.

"Why bring it up then?" I say. "There's nothing stopping you from just going."

His stare, still on me, turns from impatience to astonishment to something else, but before I can fix the look, he smiles.

"I guess I was thinking there might be something to stop me. But I guess you're right. I can just go…can't I?"

The changing moods in the room have piled up like charges in a cloud and seem to release at these words and at Jack's falling into his chair again. Suddenly everyone has an errand to do, a whispering neighbor, a coughing fit. Libby passes around a basket of cherry tomatoes, while William begins the end-of-meeting language that so much suggests a falling off of action.

"Well…I guess if there are no more items to talk about, then I guess this meeting is adjourned and we'll see everyone back on Monday the – "

"Hang on," says Josiah, shaking his head. "I don't think Jack is done."

Jack does not object to this. Again his eyes go from Josiah to me, and there is a hardness in his stare now.

"What is it you were wanting from us?" asks Josiah. "You didn't just bring this up to inform us. You didn't need to put it on the board for that."

Jack is silent.

"Did you want advice?" asks Josiah.

But Jack is sullen, his arms crossed. His eyes are still on me. I can feel them there.

"No?" says Josiah, "Then what? Did you want company? I could understand that, but none of us would be able to leave now. Too much work to do. You would have figured that. Oh wait." He glances at the talking board. "I think I know."

The charge is building again. The basket of tomatoes has stopped its circuit, and even the chewing has paused.

"I know what you want from us. You don't just want to go. You want permission. More than that, maybe. You want to be sent. Is that why you wanted to tell us this way?"

At the word sent, Jack's eyes meet Josiah's, but only for a moment. He turns to William and says, "I said I wanted to talk about government, and now's as good a time as any."

Chapter 26

I'm spraying my acre of corn with a dish soap-and-hot-pepper mixture in hopes of stopping an invasion of chinch bugs when I see Jack standing at the fence, watching me. It is his sending-off day. Josiah, William, and I are to help him load up.

I had tried to talk him out of it – not to the extent that Josiah had tried, but I knew well Jack's bending points and sensed right away a firmness that surprised me. I knew I couldn't prevail, and in a way I didn't want to. I found myself rehearsing survival stories I knew – Shackelton, that soccer team from Argentina – stories in which they'd put all hopes in a few intrepid souls willing to leave the security of the shelter and risk all for rescue. It was always very romantic, those stories, very harrowing, and I would scold myself out of the daydream saying, "this is not the same thing."

And it isn't. We are in no danger of starvation. This is no all-or-nothing push to fend off our sure demise. It is an adventure born of boredom. And yet, it is the parallel that keeps drawing me into these old stories. I do want to make contact with a world apart, to see our little shelter connected somehow to the others adrift as we are. Jack is the one setting out on the long-shot push. He is the one being sent by this community. We've agreed to take up his labor, to supply him for the journey. He is the Lewis to our Jefferson, and I am envious.

I am also annoyed with him. So today I exact a final punishment by making him wait. I apply the spray to two more rows than I'd planned. He is patient, and this only irritates me more.

"You gotta see this thing William put together for me," he says when I'm finished. He is wearing a new hat, a beaten-up brimmed leather thing out of Indiana Jones. I wonder if he is trying to rub this in, but just as quickly excuse him. Such a thing would be my style, not his.

"Your Mayflower?"

"You could say that."

In the drive sits a horse-drawn conveyance without category, so I'll attempt to build it one. It begins as a harness-racing sulky with a lawn chair attached for better view frontward. Under the chair is an open space for stowage, behind that is hitched an aluminum and nylon two-wheeled cart, the kind you used to see behind bikes, for gear or toddlers. The whole impression is one of spareness.

"I was expecting something bigger."

"It's perfect. It's light. Look at these wheels. They're one piece but made of some fancy composite stuff. William's a genius."

"What if you pick up a hitch-hiker?"

"Bella's got a saddle."

Working cars are rare now. There are simply too many hurdles to getting and keeping one running – stale gas, failing batteries, gummed up generators. It is getting easier to do things with horse and mule. They don't usually quit. Grass is abundant along every road. Besides, for any speed beyond horse and rider, the roads themselves are a hazard. Four years of neglect show in debris, abandoned cars, broken-up pavement, all hidden in grass and weeds. Even trees are now sprouting up from the seams.

"I'm still not sure why you're doing this."

"I told you. I just want to see what's out – "

" – don't say it."

The thought of walking away and making that my farewell tempts me, but I will my feet to stay planted.

"You see something I don't see, and I want to know what it is, and it's more than who's out there or what's happening in other towns or anything like that. You don't walk away from life and from your family just to see things."

143

Jack is working at the tack, giving his hands something to do. He pulls hard at a girth cinch, and Bella throws her head at him.

"Sorry," he says, and he resets it.

He takes two big steps backward and lets his arms drop, and he looks at me.

"You know how Josiah can always see what needs to be fixed and how to do it?"

"Sure," I say through set teeth. "I guess."

His eyes go to the nearest horizon, which requires him to turn full around until he faces west down Stillman Road. Then he says, "It's kind of like that. I think I see something broken, but I can't really see it. I can feel it, sense it somehow. A brokenness everywhere, and I can hardly hold myself back anymore from trying to see what it is and fixing it." He looks at me and says, "That didn't come out good, I know, but it's the best I can do, Liam. I don't talk like you."

He steps to Bella again and lays a hand against her flank.

"I can't stay here any longer. I'll come back, but I can't say how long I'll be gone."

In exasperation I shake my head and say, "I don't get you."

"But you believe me?"

"I believe you think you have to go, but I don't understand."

I am angry with Jack, though I try to disguise it. I want there to be a heaviness to my words, so I measure them to land hard, but I don't want them to be taken as anger. It's a mistake. He had a claim on me that I should not have denied him. He was my brother. Since then I catch myself thinking that I helped somehow to push him to his fate. I am usually able to talk myself out of that delusion, but sometimes it sticks close to me for days.

William and Josiah arrive to say good-bye, and for the next hour the three of us help Jack gather up provision. The night prior, Josiah, Jack, William, Libby, and I had sat around the Wagonmakers' kitchen table finalizing a list. We decide to pack him with the long view in mind: food, shelter, clothing to keep him alive, the rest to be got at creatively. He has a few days' food, but enough .22, .30-.30, and 12-guage ammunition for a year of hunting. He carries only one extra set of clothes, but a sewing kit for repairs or tailoring up clothes from

144

whatever closets he finds along the way. The rest of his gear looks like a shopping list from Tractor Supply: two bit axes and a hatchet, tool box, 100 feet of hemp in both ½ and ¼ inch, 100 feet of 18-gauge wire, a bolt of linen, a tarp, fishing gear, two roles of duct tape, three knives and sharpening stone, matches, lighter, flint steel and magnesium, a small gas stove and a gallon of denatured alcohol, sleeping bag, one frying pan, salt, pepper, 20 lbs. of lard, a .357 snub-nosed revolver and ammo, first-aid kit, camp saw, bike repair kit, tire pump. I am sure that I've since forgotten as much as I've listed here.

Most of it fits inside two sealable 5-gallon buckets which ride side by side in the rear-most bike trailer. The rest fits under the driver's seat and in a wire-basket arrangement that hangs beneath the sulky's frame. It is a dense conveyance, but somehow elegant, and William is visibly proud as he works his way around sulky, trailer, and horse, double-checking the many cinches, ropes, and bungee tie-downs. When he seems satisfied, he looks up at Jack.

"Sure you don't want to wait till morning and get a full day's ride before you camp?"

"No, I've still got six hours of travel time. That's a good stretch to get used to it, for me and for Bella."

Josiah has a gift for him. He hands him a two-foot piece of pvc. "It's a bailer bucket," he says. "There's 200 feet of line inside. Just drop it valve-down into any well head and you got water."

"Thanks, man."

"Should probably still boil it."

"Right."

"And Libby sent this." William hands Jack a jar of pickled eggs and a paper bag full of jerky.

"That was nice of her," says Jack. "Tell her thanks."

I bike with him as far as Okemos Road. Our good-bye is simple, a handshake. I say something about being home in time for spring plowing, he laughs and is gone. My last sight of him is unremarkable. He is hunched down on the make-shift chair, pulling at a piece of jerky, headed dead south.

Chapter 27

Davey Alvoord is not one to seek the company of others, but on this morning something upsets his sense of order to the degree that he stops at our mailbox and waits there on his bike, standing, straddling it. I am in darkness at the back of the garage building tomato cages from wire fence. I hear Becka yelling to him from her upstairs bedroom window.

"What are you doin there, Davey Alvoord?"

Davey shifts on his feet, looks at them like he's muddied a carpet, looks up the road east and west, then shrugs his shoulders.

"You want something to drink? Just made cider last week. Oh wait! You knew that already cuz we used your press. Anyway, you can have some if you're thirsty. Or just water."

He shakes his head and looks north this time, but there is only the Davis house and a tall tree line behind it. His left hand goes up as though he's going to point, but it drops just as quickly and goes into his pocket.

I step out of the garage and begin walking down the drive.

Becka is persistent.

"Something to eat? There's bread from breakfast. It's just the butt ends, but there's plenty of butter, and I bet there's a fried egg."

He is getting agitated. I can see that his right hand is opening and clenching. Davey doesn't like to talk, but he's not usually this shut up. I wave my arms.

"Hi, Davey! Hey! Is there something wrong?"

I am near the bottom of the drive when he looks at me, and I stop. I've never made eye contact with him before, never seen him look anyone except Jack in the eye. It's only for a moment, and then he looks north again.

"There's fires."

"Fire?"

"Fires. Lots of em north of here. You can't see them from here, but they're there. I saw them this morning."

"Where are the fires, Davey?"

146

"Bath. Dewitt, maybe. I was riding up Marsh, to I-69, past Haslett, and saw the smoke. I counted 5, but there might have been more. Some were so close together."

"Could you see what was burning?"

"I couldn't see. Just the smoke."

"A forest fire maybe?"

"I told you, I couldn't see what was burning, just smoke rising up in the sky. But no, now that I think about it, I don't think it could have been a forest fire. The smoke was coming from points on the ground, little points. Houses more likely. Yes. Houses."

"Davey, do you think you could ride to the Wagonmakers and tell them the same thing?"

"But I was going..." he twists around to look west up Stillman, "...going to my house."

"You can get to your house from Every Road. The Wagonmakers are just a ways past Every."

"I've always gone...this way. Stillman, Dobie, Willoughby, home...I don't ever...but Every is a good road though."

"It's a very good road."

Davey grips the handlebars tightly and dips his head into the space of the V, holding it there. He is breathing deep, and I sense a struggle. He lifts his head and puts one foot on a pedal. "I'll tell the Wagonmakers, then go up Every. It's a good road."

"It's a very good road."

"Yes."

"And Davey?"

"Yes?"

"I need you to tell them something else."

He breathes deep again but keeps his head up. His thin forearms are knotted and clenched.

"Tell them what?"

"Tell William to meet me here. I'm going to find the others and come back here, but it may take an hour or two. I have to go all the way to Hagadorn and then – never mind. Just tell William to come back here."

He nods.

"Tell them about the fires. Tell them to come back here."

He nods again, but before he rides, he says, "Liam?"

"Yes, Davey?"

"You heard from him yet? You heard from Jack?"

"No, Davey, not yet. But there's no mail beyond Grand Ledge. He'd have to send a letter with a traveler. I'm sure he's fine. But I promise if we hear from Jack, I'll let you know."

Davey lifts himself and pushes a skinny leg down on the pedal, and he repeats his orders.

"Tell them about the fires. Tell them to come back to Liam's. Every is a good road."

"You got it."

Everyone heats with fire now, cooks with fire, clears fields with fire. Fire at night has taken the place of TV as our end-of-day amusement. So smoke on the horizon, rising up over a burning house or barn is not an uncommon sight. But many homes burning at once has a malice behind it. It may be an undirected kind – the fever of destroying taking hold of a few bored souls for a night. Or it may be more purposeful than that.

This is the thought that compels me to pull together as many friends as I can, so I spend the next two hours riding the horse trails between the houses of Alaiedon Township. By noon I return with Luke McHugh and Josiah on horseback, Chandler Cunningham and Mio Garcia on bikes. We find William, also a biker, waiting.

We eat the lunch that Becka and Nate have prepared. Then the horses ride north, through the grove of dead ash trees, across I-96 to the northern stretch of Dobie Road. The bikers will take the paved roads to the overpass and meet us at the roundabout on Hamilton.

As we move into the miles-long stretch of neighborhoods, I think of Ricky and his band of lost boys and wonder if any have remained. The Westgates had long ago failed in their own clumsy attempt at community. According to Maya, they never learned how to live beyond scavenging because they'd never learned how to work. When the first winter hit, the littlest ones would go off, compelled into the cold by hunger, and not be seen again until their bodies poked through the melting snow.

148

By the time the second spring came, there was no one younger than eight or nine. The fact went unacknowledged but put a cloud over the house, and things began to fall apart. One day Ricky took the last of the canned meat and a few of his favorite guns, climbed onto a quad and just left. Without their leader, the sheep scattered or starved.

Our rescue from Boji Tower had been the last we'd seen of Maya for some years. Then one day Davey Alvoord told Jack that he'd seen her and a little boy in Okemos tending a garden in one of the houses along the Red Cedar. Another year passed before Jack and I, on a scavenging errand to the library, decided to check on her.

We too found her in the garden. The wild boy was clothed now and clean. He kept himself at Maya's hip like a wary dog. She told us then about Ricky and the kids who'd called themselves the Westgates. Jack tried to talk her into the idea of community, into taking one of the houses near us, but she wouldn't give it a thought. She was proud of her hermit life. She grew flowers in boxes and huge pots on her back patio, something we had not seen in the new age.

I think of her now, as Josiah and I are crossing the bridge over the Red Cedar. I think of telling her about the fires but decide not to. There is no alarm yet, and knowing what I do about Maya, I don't imagine she would change a step in her day for the news.

The bikers have beat us to the roundabout by an hour and are taking up the slack in time by napping in the high grass of the circular median. The old and new rub together at places – bike and horse are one of these.

"We should have just met you there," says Mio.

"We don't know where there is yet," says Josiah, but he knows his real complaint. "We might need the horses – if we have to leave the road, or carry something back, or – whatever."

"And they're carrying the food, remember," says William.

But Mio is not up for arguing and silently mounts his bike. He is not a contentious type, and I suspect he has a fear of horses or animals in general.

An hour later we are at the intersection of Marsh and Saginaw, about where Davey said he could see the columns of smoke. But the view to the north is blocked by a tree-lined hill. As we follow Saginaw up toward the 1-69 ramps, the hills descend to road level, and the road rises into an overpass. Even before we reach the top of the east-bound exit ramp, our view is clear to the north and northwest, and we can see that the five smoke columns of Davey's memory have grown to seven. They appear to be in a line of maybe a mile, and we are some miles off the eastern extreme. We continue toward the ramp but stop ourselves just as it begins to descend.

"Is there a road that runs north up there?" Mio is pointing west, up the expressway. This is farther than anyone of us has ever gone since the dying.

"There's got to be an exit up there, right?" asks Luke.

"We don't want to go too far up it," says Josiah. "Not sure even a horse could get up those ditches, and I think they're fenced."

On Dobie Lake is a high willow tree. When I was a child I would watch the older boys jump from it. I made the climb once with the intention of jumping. In the abstract it was just a step from limb to water with a long interval between. But when I stood perched on that high notch, I could think of nothing but that the space below me was hostile. Now, the long ramp at our feet and the stretch of highway at the end of it has the same quality to it. We would be moving exposed – a condition we avoid naturally now – with no exit, maybe for miles, into a country where houses are burned in ranks. I take a deep breath and start my horse down the ramp that will take us onto the expressway. I turn to the others.

"Let's see what we see."

Minutes later, as we round a big bend in the road, what we see is a sign that tells us US 127 is a mile and a half farther. The long turn onto it puts us south of the first smoke column. Another two miles and we put the horses to a gallop along the soft, green shoulder, then up the embankment onto Howe Road. Here, the horses sense our relief and break into a trot. We head east again and soon are at the intersection of a long, straight country road. On the corner is what remains of a house – a pile of glowing embers and two chimneys sticking up ghost-like through the heat and smoke. The horses want to continue past it, but we muscle them into a stand of trees opposite the house and hitch them there. From here we can see a body on the lawn, so we pull the 12 gauge and the .243 out of their scabbards. The bikers all carry pistols.

It's a boy. He lies at the bottom of the steps of a stone porch. The heat is too great to get close to him, but we can see that the front part of his head from the eyes upward is gone. We find another body on the other side of the gravel drive, also a boy. He is sitting on the ground with his elbows on his knees, his head hanging down like he's tired. There is a small hole in his back and a pool of black blood beneath him. At a nudge, he tips over woodenly, as if the lower parts of him are rooted in the ground.

"Let's walk around the house," says Josiah, "make sure there's not someone hiding in the weeds."

We find no one else and head up the road a few hundred yards to the next house. This one too has burned nearly to ground level. A high stone arch in the front stands alone and gives it a grinning appearance. We search the property carefully but find nothing, no one. Then we head west again, down to the next smoke column, a mile away this time. Here, the fire seems to have quit before the whole structure was consumed, as one low wing of the house stands defiant against a dense field of smoking timbers and a single, scorched chimney. Again, we find nothing.

"These were lived-in houses," says Luke. Both houses have large kitchen gardens, and this one looks like its lawns have been mown with sheep.

"There's tack in the barn," says Chandler, "and fresh hay in four of the stalls, but no horses."

"A raid?"

"Likely," says Josiah, "but who? And where from?"

Over the next mile, two more houses are settling down into their basements, the smoke over them thinning to ribbons. A barn and a detached garage are burning too. Then, at the last house, which is set well off the road at the edge of a wooded hillside, we find sign of a battle. Scattered around the house, from all angles are spent shells of half a dozen different loads. Two of the attackers, skinny boys with tattooed cheeks, lie face down behind a retaining wall, both head shot.

151

Even the burnt hulk of the house has a bunker heft to it, as though the timbers above have come to rest over thick walls. It appears a house that has yielded itself grudgingly.

After some minutes wandering the area, we slowly gather together again as if by gravity. We are at the low wall where the two raiders lie. The gray sheen of death is over them now. Flies make familiar use of the bodies' holes, and the blood is congealed and black. Oddly, this is an unfamiliar scene to us. We've watched many die, but not out of a quick violence. Our dead were wrung out from the inside, and then buried quickly or shut up in rooms for months or years. This is new, and the old fascination has taken hold of us again.

"Look here," says Chandler. He points to an area around one of the boys. It is an arc, one arm's length from the boy's shoulder, scraped in the dirt and weeds. Clumps of purselane and creeping charlie are pulled from the ground by the roots and lie piled within the crescent. The hand is pulled in close now but still holds a fist of green leaves.

"Took a while to die," says Luke. The thought of living for even a minute after a bullet through the head silences us. For a few minutes we watch the horizons, kick at the shells, and listen to sounds of the house settling. Mio breaks the quiet.

"How do you think...?"

He looks back down the long line of thin gray ribbons, then says to no one, "I mean...what happened?"

"Here's what I think," says Luke. He points down the road. "The first house was surprised. That's why they were caught in the open like that. Nobody killed at the others until here."

"The others heard the shots," I add.

"Right, and came this way."

"Instead of fighting?" asks Chandler.

Luke looks eastward again. He is working through the mechanisms of people in panic. "Maybe they knew there was no point. The fighting might've been over in two shots. Or maybe they had a plan all along. They went west, warning the other houses along the way and holed up in this one."

Just as we'd been drawn to the death scene by its novelty, we are now repelled from it as though we'd taken it in too long. We separate and then gather again on the level surface of the drive.

"But how do we know there wasn't just one or two in there?" Asks Chandler, picking up the conversation.

"A lot of shots fired to dig out just one or two," I say, "and there's more than that living in the other houses, judging by their gardens."

Mio turns again to the house and says, "So I wonder how many are…"

We all stare toward the smoking wreck of wood and brick. We are tired – out of words, weary of circumspection – and I realize that Josiah has not helped with these speculations, that he's not doing his job. Then I realize he's not with us.

"Anybody seen Josiah?"

"He went around back right when we got here," says Mio. "I guess I ain't seen him since."

At the back of the house is a clipped yard sloping up steeply toward a narrow skirt of field along the wood line. A notch in the grass suggests a broken trail and we all converge on it. Luke points out a wide spatter of blood, then another just inside the trees.

"He probably followed it in," he says. "Blood's a few hours old."

At the edge of the wood, we stand as in the mouth of a cave, a threshold between light and gloom. The forest is older pine, planted in long, close rows. We shade our eyes and blink away the sun as we peer into it, but the darkness is deep.

"Why would he have gone in there?" asks Mio, more in rebuke than question.

I yell Josiah's name, but the softness of white-pine needles wicks the sound right from my lips. It is as though I've yelled into a sock drawer.

"Let's just go," says Luke, and he heads into the murky wood.

"Watch out for dead limbs," I say. "They grow at eye level."

We don't follow Luke but move off into parallel rows. It puts into mind driving deer with my dad and uncles up in Gaylord. We are a few hundred feet into it when I hear a low sob from a different row. I cross two, and up ahead of me I see Josiah squatting next to a body on the ground. When he hears my footfalls, he swings the .38 on me.

"It's me! It's Liam!"

On the ground is a girl around twelve or thirteen. Becka's age. Her eyes are open, but they look past us to something that causes her face to contort between what looks like terror and grief. I call the others over.

"She's got a fever," says Josiah.

"There's a lot of blood where we came in," says Chandler.

"Grazed on the back of the head," says Josiah.

I realize now that Josiah is shirtless under his jacket, that his sweater is wadded up under her head.

"But it's stopped...I think."

Josiah turns to us, is about to speak, then he stands and whispers, "She thought I was gonna kill her. Like she really thought she was gonna die right there. You shoulda seen her... I've never seen anyone scared like that before. It made me...feel bad. Not bad like sick, but bad like I was bad."

We all consider her, and just as I am thinking these words, Josiah says them.

"I wonder what she saw."

He kneels again, then lifts her head gently and inspects the sweater. "It's clotted shut."

"Head bleeds a lot," says Luke. "Always worse than it looks. I got hit on the forehead with a metal lampshade once and thought I was gonna die. Blood eeeeverywhere."

A whispering conversation ensues among us about bleeding heads, stitches, and shocking wounds in general.

"What do you want to do, Josiah?" I ask. The whispering stops now. Even here the law of first-find establishes an order of things. Josiah will decide what to do with the girl. He will probably consult us, though we are already disposed to agree with him.

But he doesn't consult. He stands, glances quickly round the dense wood, and says, "We take her to New Alaiedon."

Chapter 28

Her name is Molly. She saw much that day. Over the following week or so, as Libby Wagonmaker helps her to heal in body and soul, Molly shares it with her. Libby shares it with us.

The attack had not been a complete surprise. Some weeks earlier a raid on a settlement in St. Johns had left three dead and three homes burned to their footings. The raiders had struck fast and with a purpose, less intent on killing than on stealing what food and livestock could be carted off.

But in Laingsburg they showed a change in tactics. Luke had been partly right in working out the events. They had caught the first house by surprise. At dawn, they'd killed the boy by the driveway when he'd come out to quiet their barking dog. The other had stepped out onto the porch at the sound of the shot, then called to the boy who was sitting with his elbows on his knees, looking at something on the ground beneath him. Checking on his friend, the other one was a few steps down the walk when the shooter in the trees across the road took him down. We know this now because Molly watched from behind lace curtains in an upstairs room. The boys were her twin brother and one of their cousins from Owosso.

When the attackers – Molly described them as filthy and face-painted – gathered at the front of the house to set it on fire, she slipped out a basement window and sprinted to the field that stretched a mile or so to an empty house. From there she watched the last of her neighbors reach the safe house at the road's end. She watched the raiders move there too, a few of them peeling off to set fire to the houses along the way.

She moved the last quarter half mile slowly, stooped to stay hidden behind a low ridge, crawling when the land flattened. Crouched in the weeds, she watched as the murderers huddled up behind landscape boulders and two fat pines. Her friends were now firing from behind curtains and rooftop chimney stacks.

She saw two of the invaders shot behind the same little wall. The boy she had liked in 3rd grade had climbed the wide stone chimney in the house's middle to get the angle. Two quick shots before a third

155

knocked him from the roof and crumpled him on the front lawn, and bullets from many guns went into him. She had turned, first in horror at the sight, then in disbelief at the sound of a truck coming up the drive, when a thump on the back of her head knocked her flat.

She woke later to the sound of voices only. The guns had quit firing. She doesn't know how long she'd been out, but when she pushed herself up in the grass she could see that a surrender had taken place. Her people sat on the floor of the long covered porch, their backs against the house. The house was above her, so she could see only their faces. A boy with a shotgun at one end of the porch stood guard over them.

A knot of boys was in the yard talking, laughing, looking back at the prisoners. They were deliberating on some point of action. After a few minutes of this, a consensus seems to have been reached. Two boys broke from the group and ambled up the yard to the house. They didn't take the steps onto the porch but went right to the balusters, one boy at each end. Some words were said to those lined up – Molly couldn't hear them – then each boy took out a pistol. Molly felt her head begin to swell and her vision go watery, as though she would faint, but she didn't. She watched as each shooter, with a plodding deliberateness, moved toward the other, firing between the balusters. One or two shots, then a step toward the center, another shot, another step. When the screaming stopped, and the two boys were shoulder to shoulder, they simply fired at whatever movements drew their aim.

An older boy flew from the porch, bleeding from the mouth and chest, sobbing in animal terror. He leaped down the steps, fell hard, and scrabbled frantically on hands and knees along the side of the house. He was heading for the trees. The two turned and watched as the boy with the shotgun walked easily down the steps, turned when he hit the walk, and took careful aim. The boy was at the corner, a step from cover and a sprint to the dark woods when the shotgun barked. He folded up like the one on the lawn. One of his legs went up like it was kicking at something in the air. The shotgun boy walked to him, pushed the leg down with his own. He put the gun barrel somewhere close to him – Molly was too low in the grass to see – and fired once.

156

She spent the next hours crawling a wide, slow arc around the house through the high grass. She was aiming at the same dark woods the boy from the porch had hoped for. At one point, seeing that they were all gathered near the truck, intent upon their burning work, she cut the corner across the lawn and plunged into the waiting trees. There she would let death come for her. She didn't know yet that such visions as she had seen do not kill the seer, not directly anyway. It made perfect sense that she thought Josiah her killer, there for the reckoning.

Her coming to Alaiedon was as the peel of a bell, a struck note that hung in the air so long we never marked its passing out of hearing. The note was the knowledge of war, and we would add it to our long list of deaths to be wary of. Starvation was an old pest. We could usually see it coming. If we got too close to it one winter, we'd double efforts in the spring. But hostility could strike wildly, in pre-dawn darkness or deep in a long season of peace. It was the unrelenting threat of it that made us weary.

Josiah and I sit on the front porch of the Quinn house, me in an old camp chair, and Josiah on the bench swing. It's a cool dusk, a luxury, as this fall day has been warm and humid. Gray clouds to our north are lit from under by a setting sun. For the next minutes they are all colors but gray, with gold and crimson predominant.

The house sits almost on a line between mine and Josiah's trailer. It is the highest land in the area and gives us the most comprehensive view of what's around us. Far down the sloping field I can see Becka and the twins weeding the box gardens in our backyard.

"This is a good place," says Josiah, emphasizing the pronoun. He has a pellet gun – break-barrel with a red-dot scope – that he found in the Quinn's pole barn. He has his feet on the railing to steady the swing while he shoots at a lamppost by the drive.

"You still thinking about the move then? I thought you'd decided."

"I have decided. I just said it's a good place."

"You sound like you're still discussing it with yourself."

"No. I'm not. This is a good place. I'll start moving things over tomorrow."

"I'll help you."

He cocks the gun again but doesn't put it to his shoulder right away. He is thinking. When he moves on in his thoughts, he shoulders it and pulls the trigger, but there is no plink of metal on metal, just the release of the spring.

"Forgot to load."

"You can still see the lake, you know."

Josiah looks at me and nods.

"Yeah, I know."

He takes his time loading the gun and shoots again. The pellet ricochets straight up and after a few seconds we hear it fall onto the porch roof over our heads.

"And the twins won't have near as far to walk. I worry about them going all the way to the trailer by themselves. Saw a couple dogs around last week. At least I think they were dogs. Mighta been coyotes, wolves even. But now they can just run through the back yard and there's Uncle Josiah."

"The twins," says Josiah, grinning. "Wolves. Right."

"It's a long walk to the lake is all."

"Yep."

Years ago, Josiah had suggested moving the trailer to my backyard. It's the closest he's ever gotten to leaving the lake. That was the day we lost Jack to Ricky's bunch and then spent the next few weeks trapped in a high rise in Lansing. We all stayed for a month at the house on Walline, but when we came back to the Stillman Road house, Josiah took up again in the trailer and has been there ever since.

But the raid on Molly's settlement has struck us all deeply. He brought up the move himself, which surprised and relieved me. I was afraid of what sort of persuasion it might take to pry him out.

"It'll always be there too," I say, still trying to plug any gaps in his commitment to this.

"I said I'll do it."

"Ok."

Josiah takes aim again when a bird, a yellow finch, alights on the top of the post. He lifts his head and considers it, then puts his eye back to the scope.

"Should I shoot it?"

"You gonna eat it?"

"Heck no."

I wait for the sound of the spring and a puff of yellow feathers, but he takes too long. The bird disappears. He shoots the shade of the lamp instead.

"You didn't want to shoot it?"

"No, I did want to."

"So why didn't you?"

"Because I didn't want to at the same time."

"Hmm."

"Yeah."

We sit for a while and are entertained by small movements in the distance. One of the twins, the boy, has a stick in his hands and pounds at something moving on the ground. Becka, squatted among the leafy stalks of brussel sprouts, waves away bugs with her hand. Closer to us, a red squirrel hangs between limbs of two white pines before swinging to lower branches. We're both content with the sights, and the weight that once came with a long silence is gone now. It is no longer a fearful thing, so it is many minutes before Josiah speaks.

"How are we different from them?"

"From the twins?"

"No, from *them.*"

He flings an arm northward, toward Laingsburg.

"They were kids once, just like us, right?"

The other twin is with her brother now, intent upon a rescue. The stick, apparently, is the key to the argument. Yes, I think to myself, they were kids once.

"How do people get to be…that bad?"

"I'm pretty sure they don't go to bed good and wake up bad."

"So they get bad slowly? Like a piece of fruit?"

"Maybe," I say, but I don't try to hide my uncertainty.

159

He puts the gun in his lap, and his eyes narrow as though he's stepped into sunlight.

"So they start by doing a little something bad. They even feel bad about it for a while. Then it gets to be easy and so the next little bad something comes along and it's worse than the first..."

I realize now he's already spent some time working out this puzzle – I recognize a practiced cadence in his thinking – but for how long I can't tell.

"...But just a little worse, and it doesn't seem that way to them. It seems a lot like the time before. It's just the next step."

Josiah pushes against the rail with his feet and plants them on the deck. He holds himself there in a state of potential energy, nearly standing in the swing.

"And that next thing gets easy too, and something worse comes along, and so it goes. Until one day you're stealing horses from your neighbors, and then you're killing them if they try to stop you. Then you're killing them just to kill."

He turns now and looks at me with tilted head. "So really, maybe, we're not much different than them."

He leans back against the bench, lifts his feet and swings forward. He is energy kinetic now.

"Yes we are," I say. "I don't see us murdering the nearest settlement."

"No, but what's stopping us?"

"It's wrong is what's stopping us."

"Wrong. Ok. But where are your lines for wrong, Liam? And how do you know to put them there? You're not perfect and neither am I, and we've both done that next little something bad."

"I know it's wrong, that's all. Our parents taught us that."

"So have you gone against what your parents taught you in the last five years?"

I have no good answer to that, and decide that it's an unfair question. These are unusual times. But then I think I have him when I say, "You didn't shoot that bird. You wanted to but you knew it was wrong so you didn't."

"Yeah? Well, I shot a groundhog last week for no reason at all. I was just bored. Didn't even wait until it got away from its hole so I could at least eat it. Just shot it and down it went to its den where it's still rotting. This time I just wasn't in a killing mood so I didn't shoot."

"What's the point? So there are good guys and bad guys, and we're the good guys."

"The point *is* the bad guys. We've only been in this for five years but something happened to those normal boys that made them killers. I don't know what to be more afraid of – whatever the something was or the fact that they were normal."

His talk is threatening my good mood, so I stand to go.

"There's an oak tree behind the trailer," he says, ignoring my attempt at adjournment, "It's u-shaped and gnarled. It's an ugly tree and all the more so because it's in a big stand of old straight ones. Dad says it was damaged as a sapling but kept on growing." He turns his gaze from the far-off sky to me and says. "We're saplings. That's the point. And you of all people should be thinking about that."

"Why me?"

"You were always the one who knew we needed to think beyond the next day or the next week to survive. That's all I'm doing. Those kids probably woke up every day thinking they were doing just fine, surviving. They can't see what they are now, and we won't be able to see what we'll become."

"Saplings?" I want him to smile at that and de-escalate. I want to keep his genius trained on crops and wells and nearby things, but he won't come down yet. He doesn't hear my tone, just the word.

"The whole world's a sapling right now. Can't you see that? Every little thing we do goes out into time, and it…it – "

" – but it's always been like that. Time hasn't changed."

"Time hasn't changed, but it was different then. What you and I did in the time before didn't matter. It got swallowed up in the real things. Adult things. That's what mattered. But even our moms and dads never sat where we are now. The things we do now are like…like…I don't know. I can't think of what they're like because it's never happened to anyone I know. It's something new, and it has been for these five years, but I'm just now seeing it. If our decisions now are bad I'm afraid we'll end up – our whole world will end up all gnarled and bent and ugly."

"Noah."

"What?"

"It's like Noah. You know, Noah and the ark. They get off the ark and the world is new but there they are. Noah, his sons, their wives, a little settlement on Mount … something."

"Ararat."

"Right."

"And what did they do?"

"I don't know. They started a city, I suppose." But then I do remember what they did at the very first, and it wasn't building a city. Their first thing had always been the whole point of the story.

"They built an altar," I say. "They sacrificed on it and gave thanks."

"Then the rainbow."

"Right. Then the rainbow."

Josiah stands and faces me. He is taller than me now, and I am just realizing it for the first time. I wonder if he's noticed it yet. He hands me the gun and steps off the porch.

"I'll start moving my things tomorrow," he says over his shoulder.

"I'll bring Ann," I say. Ann is our mule, Antigone. "We can go get William too."

"Ain't got that much stuff," he says. But he is around the corner of the house and gone before I know if he means Ann or William.

He is right about my not thinking far enough ahead. Where I worry over what crops to plant next year or how to teach the younger ones to read – good things to be sure – Josiah sees a civilization growing. He sees that it either thrives and blesses itself and others with it or it turns against its own like the Midianites under Gideon's torches and trumpets. Like the face-painted kids in Laingsburg.

And yet he's strangely provincial in his convictions, subduing only that earth closest to him. He had argued against Jack's wandering mission, not with my reasons against it, and not at all by my motives. He simply believed that the greatest need for Jack's efforts were here in New Alaiedon. But it was too simple an argument, and Josiah was

162

not persuasive. I suspect now that he was arguing from half-formed notions.

I have no doubts that they are much more formed now, and if I mark a place when Josiah moves beyond me as leader, it is this evening on Quinn's front porch as I realize that his vision has outstripped mine.

That night Josiah's words work down into me like a poultice, and the next morning I record this in my journal:

"I had a dream last night, dreamt of a tree. I knew it was an oak but there was nothing oak about it. As I stood at the foot of it and watched it grow I would swat at anything that threatened it. Bugs chewed at it birds pecked at it larger animals like beaver and horses nipped at it and pulled the bark away in strips. But I was faster and could stay ahead of the attackers and the tree kept growing. But it grew so fast that soon I couldn't see its top, only a little way into the limbs that sprouted above my head. I couldn't tell how it was growing. I could only protect the few feet of trunk I could reach and hope that the top still grew straight."

I don't think it is a portentous dream. I'm no prophet and I've never been one to look for signs. Rather, I see it as a re-casting of ideas to myself, a rehearsing of words that did not settle in my understanding as Josiah spoke them. The dream stays with me for days. If Josiah were walking with me morning to night whispering visions of deformed saplings, the truth could not have come home clearer: We stand at a frontier, and heaven and hell are both on the horizon, but no trails are yet broken for us. Like Noah, the flood is over, and here we are.

Chapter 29

We've gotten good at taming the world around us. We farm. We conjure water from great depths. We are masters over flocks and herds. But it took Davey Alvoord to subdue the calendar.

At first, when the old paper calendars failed us and we couldn't be sure of a date to within a week's error, we resorted to the moon. We liked the phrasing more than we did its efficacy. Meeting for harvest at the first quarter, or driving deer at the new moon had more romance to it than did ennumerated months and days. But the truth is we were no good at it. We didn't know waxing from waning then, and then Davey made it so we needn't bother.

In May of the year, he began observations of the sun's rising. Every day, he'd peek through a welder's hood and a tiny eye hook screwed into one of his back porch posts. The dark glass would reduce the sun to a bright point down in the trees. On the day that it quit its march north, the day it stopped and began its swing back the other way, Davey cut down the very tree the sun had climbed. The effect was a notch on the eastern horizon. He called that day June 21, walked off 364 more, and we had ourselves a year.

We don't know of his astronomical work until the October meeting when, for the first time in New Alaiedon's history, Davey Alvoord writes a word on the talking board. The word is *year*, and when Luke calls us to order and turns the floor over to Davey, he says nothing. Instead, he pushes his Solstice calendar to the center of the table, points to the ceiling, puts his fingers on his mouth as though struck by conflicting thoughts, and walks out.

A month later, the word *Year* is on the board still, and it triggers a series of thoughts that turn out to be prophetic. Josiah is with me on this day, and so is Nate, the boy we stole from Ricky's camp six years earlier. They are out back affixing a hand pump to the old well head. I am at the conference table reading something from Judges when my eyes wander to the talking board and the word *Year* in Davey's precise hand. I think of seeing Davey, that I don't check on Davey enough. There is a lingering memory of a promise made, that the promise will require me to go see Davey. Then I remember Jack. If I hear from

Jack, so I promised, I would let Davey know. The thoughts come in that order, but are compressed into a moment.

They are prophetic in that as I am thinking of Jack's letter that will require me to go see Davey, I hear horse sounds. It is Jodi Conklin bringing her big chestnut filly up the drive. I meet her as she hitches up to the softball backstop. She sees me coming and waves.

"Good timing. Got something for ya."

She reaches into a saddle bag and pulls out an envelope, which she hands to me. She punches my shoulder with her other hand and laughs. Jodi is big natured, one of my favorite people.

There are only two words on the outside of the envelope, and while the writing is blocky, like Jack's hand, Alaiedon is spelled right. Jack never bothered with getting the vowels straight. He would just use an all-purpose a and write it Aladan. The other word is my name.

"Who...?" I start to wonder out loud.

"Not from Jack?"

Jodi is surprised, snatches the envelope back and looks at it.

"Meghan Parmeter in Leslie had two cousins from Jackson move in with her last week. One of em had this. Don't know how long it sat in Jackson, though. Maybe whoever wrote it dated it?"

"Maybe. Thanks."

I take it into the hall and sit at the table again. It's a fat envelope, the manila kind. I try to think of who I might know in Jackson, but the state of Michigan south of us has always been a vast blank. There is simply nothing between Lansing and Holcomb, Missouri where I have cousins.

Inside I find a letter that's been taped over a bundle of others bound up in rubber bands. I don't recognize the hand on the wrapper, so instead of beginning there, I tear into the bundle. I am relieved at seeing the angular scratches I've known since our homeschool days and begin with the topmost letter. Here is what I read, and it's word for word Jack, poor grammar and all...

"Hey as it turns out Paul doesn't care much about baseball so the team idea is out the window I guess. Im a little disappointed cause Max and Dom are getting

good at ground balls. Max can even catch a short hop without thinking hard about it. But if your not playing real games, it doesn't mean much. But that's fine. It's not like we won't get something really cool done instead. Did I tell you he was an engineer once? Not like on a train, but he could build things and weld and stuff. He worked on gas wells all around Michigan. His wife and kids went with him which I think would be cool because youd get to do school right in a hotel or car or something. He did other things too but that was how he knew about the lights. They're still on even though I said they wouldn't be. There. Im admitting for the first time ever I was wrong about something."

I put the letter down and lift my head to the sounds of Nate laughing and the blubbery snort of the horse. I've read something wrong and have to back up. I do this all the time with books and have to read the same paragraph 3 or 4 times. It usually means I'm tired. But I'm not tired now; in fact, my heart is beating like I've just climbed a hill.

I pick it up again and start over, and as I'm reading I find myself slowing down, stepping carefully onto each word. When I come to these, I say them aloud: *"He worked on gas wells all around Michigan. His wife and kids went with him…that was how he knew about the lights. They're still on …"* I stop reading there. Something has seized me. Something from deep in, like a hypnotist's spell buried until it's called up by a signal.

I force myself to pick up all the letters and separate them, laying them out on the table before me. There are nine. No, he hasn't even tried to date them, so I quickly read through beginnings and endings, trying to sequence the parts by their transitions, but there are no transitions. He is a horrible writer. No organization at all, just a stream-of-consciousness spewing between "hey" and "see ya soon." My eyes fly over the words searching out anything to mark time.

Here is a sentence with "the last of Libby's pickled eggs." I put it to my left, above the others. It's letter one.

He writes of sleeping in various places between Spring Arbor and Jonesville, then of staying a week in Quincy where he camped at the edge of Marble Lake with six kids, brothers and sisters all from the same family. "They're all left-handed," he writes. "Ever seen anything like that?" I haven't, and I keep sorting.

166

In another letter he writes this: "…had supper with Max and his friends. There good hunters but there the dirtiest kids I ever saw and still live on river water." Still no mention of a leader in this one, so I put it to the right of the others.

Another letter mentions fishing from a bridge and meeting a boy who floats by in a canoe with a dead swan in its bottom. The boy's name is Max, and Jack is somewhere between Quincy and Three Rivers. And so it goes. I piece the word puzzle together like any other, looking for shapes to fit against other shapes.

The last letter I put into place is in the middle of the line, number five.

He writes, *"Hey again, Your not going to believe this and I wish I could stand right there in front of you and everyone and see your faces when I say it but I guess this letter will have to do. Maybe I can read this to you out loud some day when Im back in NA. Anyway, here it is. I found one. A man, I mean, a grown-up. You heard me right. And not an older who just turned 20, but a real grown up with gray hair who had a job and a house and a family before the dying. And I tell you what if there was one man to live through it and be left behind here to help us its Mr. Smith. But he lets us call him Paul, which is cool. I told you about Jack and the canoe and how we came to Three Rivers…"*

I find the part about Three Rivers in letter two, the one I'd started earlier. I'll include the original letter here:

"Hey, spent the last two nights under a covered bridge over the St. Joe river. It was nice to be able to garage Bella and the sulky and pitch the tent and still feel like I was outside. Quiet few days, and haven't seen a soul for almost two weeks, but yesterday I ran into a kid named Max while I was fishing for breakfast. He stopped and pulled out his own tackle and so we fished an hour or so. He knows the river well, especially the spots along this bridge likely to hold fish. When I asked him about where he lived, he pointed east and said, "Ten miles that way." He makes this same trip downriver every seven days. Just like us, they don't have a calendar they can trust, so Max's been counting off seven days since the very first trip in Spring. He floats the river and hunts for whatever he runs into — duck, wood duck mostly, but he'll surprise mallards and pintails on some of the wider inlets, and an occasional goose. He doesn't use a shotgun or even a .22 but a pellet gun the kind where you have to cock the barrel. And no scope! Just iron sites and he pops them right in the head. This time, he's got a huge swan that takes up a

whole section of the boat. He trails a fishing line too for trout and even salmon in the late fall. Anyway, he does this every seven days, and the end of trip is just a mile down from this very bridge that I set up camp on. A friend lives there who takes one of every three in trade for a wagon ride back to Max's house which is about five miles by road. So after we fished I met Max a mile downstream at his friend's place and thought I'd just ride Bella along with them since I had nowhere to be except with people, except his friend wasn't there. The place was locked up and there were notes on the door to different people and one to Max that said "meet me at the Assembly of God in Three Rivers. I'm living there for a while." I asked if that was on his way back home and he said sort of, that he'd just float another mile or two to the cemetery by the river, and since I hadn't seen Three Rivers yet, and didn't even know there was a Three Rivers in Michigan I agreed to meet him there. So I did. When we got here, we found Max's friend Henry, who actually doesn't live in the church but in a tent across the street which is kind of weird. And when he hitched his wagon up to Bella (his horse was gone, but he didn't say where it had gone) and pulled the canoe up near the high school, one of the kids in charge took the dozen or so ducks, the swan, and the three trout and said there was some new kids there who were really hungry. And so of course no one stopped him, and Max and Henry were ok with it. I decided to stop the night here. There's room in Max's tent, so I won't need to pitch mine. I'll pick up again later in the week if anything interesting happens. See ya!"

And here's the rest of the first letter I'd picked up, the one about finding a grown up:

"...Not a very exciting name I know but he lets us call him Paul instead of Mr. Smith, which is cool. The kids gathered in the church after dinner and then he came out. I pushed my way down to the front to see if it was true, and it was. He's old, with gray hair and a beard, and taller than just about anyone I know, except maybe Gabe Vanderwey. And he spoke. I don't even remember much of what he said. It wasn't a speech or sermon or anything, just talking to the kids like it was a family meeting. Things that needed to be done, a rule changed or added. He talked about their progress on projects with names I didn't get. What I do remember was how the kids acted when he spoke. Their eyes were all big and wide, and they were leaned forward where before he came out, they were lying around every which way like kids do then they all went straight up as soon as he coughed into the microphone. I didn't mention that, did I? You can plug things in here if you

have them, and if you sign up for a time to use the electricity. I guess there's not a lot or it's not strong enough. I don't really get how it works. Max has a Nintendo he's going to play tonight at like one o'clock in the morning. He has a half hour of plug time. I'd like to watch him. I was telling you about Paul. I'm planning on talking to him tomorrow. I want to explain what I'm doing out on my own. Maybe he can help me or point me in a good direction. Anyway, its been a long day and a lot has happened. Im goin to bed now. See ya soon!"

The next letter seems to have been written a week or two later. He's excited and the words have a frenetic energy on the paper. Less like he is hurried, more like he is carving with the pencil lead.

"Hey! It's been a few days. I've been so busy I haven't had time to write. Here's the thing. Paul's sending me to a place called Catastropolis. Isn't that a crazy name? It's actually Cassopolis, but the kids there changed the big sign to read Catastropolis. From what Paul says they're a rebelious bunch. He wants to bring them "into the fold" as he says. He's hoping I can go and make some straight paths for him. Those were his words too. So I was right Liam. He knew exactly what I wanted to do like he'd been thinking it himself. I've never felt like this before, like I'm part of something bigger than me. Wish me luck in Catastropolis. What a name!"

He goes on to introduce me to his friends. Most are attached somehow to Max, and I sense that there are tribes within the tribe.

He ends with this: *"No chance I'm home before Spring. If there's a long thaw and pasture enough for Bella to make the trip, maybe, but don't count on me."*

"Whatcha got?"

Jo is at the door. I jump back and look over the spread of letters. The surprise makes me feel like I've been caught at something. I wave my hand over them.

"From Jack."

Jo nods as though I've told him the hens have laid and walks back out. I don't get Jo's problem with Jack and right now I don't care. The mental work of ordering my brother's nonsense has me tired. When I finally have what I think is the right sequence, I begin to pack them up to read again later. I reach for the wrapper they came in and remember that it too is a letter.

169

It reads, "You dont know me but I know your brother. He spent a few days here in Decatur. I took him all around and meet the people here. There are about 20 I know but not that many close to town. He left these in my house. He didnt come back. I waited a couple weeks but he didnt come back. He was going to Benton Harbor and then Holind and then going to Muskegin I think. I will give these to Jake Menzel. He has a neighbor moving to Jackson. Thats a little closer. He was nice and I hope you get these. Bye."

I stand there for a long moment and let the hope of seeing Jack before Christmas shrink down and die. By the time I walk out of the hall, hope has been replaced by a bitter little knot of anger.

Chapter 30

The next day, I remember my promise to Davey, that I would let him know when I hear from Jack. I ride to his house and knock on the back porch door. When he doesn't answer, I yell his name through the kitchen window, which is ajar an inch or two. As I do, a sense of familiarity comes over me. It is one that formed over opening a thousand such windows, breaking into a thousand houses once occupied by the living. And though I'm about to take those actions again, it is the smell that brings it.

I don't climb through the window yet, but walk to the garage where my fears find confirmation. Davey's bike with the empty wagon attached is there. I am angry with myself now for not inviting Josiah or picking up William on the way, and I consider going back to correct the error. But I don't. There is no surprise left in a corpse, I tell myself. There is no more spook in a dead body than there is in a fallen tree. This is the last thought I have as I climb through the kitchen window.

Inside, I don't need to search far. As my feet hit the floor, I can see that the once high and straight stacks of crates and boxes in the dining room have lost their flushness and right angles. They are piled. I walk through the kitchen where the collection of things is abbreviated some. On one of the counters a space big enough to eat a meal at has been kept clear. A bar stool sits under it.

As I step into the dining room, I understand what has happened. A wall of stacks, several rows thick has fallen outward and collapsed against a china cabinet. The rows of the boxes have buckled in such a way that the very bottom under which Davey's body is pressed is the point of a V. So it is a concentrated weight of junk over his slight spine. At the thought that something else may have died in the house, his cat maybe, I kneel down to check his pulse but see right away that there is no need. The room is dim for the high stacks of crates and boxes in the living room to which it is adjacent, but I can see the recession of flesh from the mouth and eye sockets. The contrast in shade increases with decay.

When I leave through the back door, I see the tomato plant. It is dead too. I think of his mother now, and what must have been an attachment beyond my knowing. Then I think of Jack's schemes to get Davey pulled into the life of the community, of the calendar and the meeting where we heard him speak. I think of the day he stopped at my mailbox and told us of the fires, and I realize that he was every bit a part of New Alaiedon, that Jack may have accomplished at least that much.

I sit down on the steps and cry hard. At the time it feels like a satisfying cry, like when I'm in the grip of hard laughter, but when I'm done I feel heavier, like I've been stained by it. Davey is part of the sadness but not its object. It is a sadness that casts a gray light over anything I turn my thoughts to. It is cold and vague, and for days after it keeps me at the edge of another sobbing fit.

That afternoon I find Josiah at work in the woods near Dobie Lake. He has been building a house of fieldstone at the top of a knoll just north of his trailer. At least I assume it's a house. He has the footings dug and the dimensions are house-like, but when I ask him what he's planning, he won't elaborate beyond a shrug and a "not sure yet."

When I tell him about Davey, he stops in his work and sits down on the slip forms. I take a seat next to him. In the silence I consider the spot we're on. It sits above the trail that runs between the houses and Josiah's trailer, just west of us. I'd never noticed that there was high ground here. From the trail that I've walked since I was a little kid, the woods are simply two walls of trees filling my peripheral vision to the left and right. I hadn't noticed the landscape beneath the trees.

"Nice spot," I say.

"Yeah."

"Lot of work though. Why not just take a new house? You got a million to choose from."

"Maybe it's not a house I'm building."

"What is it then?"

He shrugs, then adds, "I said maybe."

"Nice spot anyway."

He looks around and nods.

"I've always liked it here. I'd sit up there with my dad in October."

He points to the back of the clearing where a side-by-side tree blind still hangs from high up in a beech tree.

"You can see the lake from there and your house. You wouldn't know the woods around the lake had such a high place as this."

I tell him I was just thinking that.

"We never shot a deer here, though. It's too high above the trails they like. My dad knew it but he put it up there anyway. I think he just liked this spot too."

We talk about deer, the rut, what rubs we've come across. Josiah has been watching several on the east side of the lake and a big one in the swamp between the Minnaars and I-96. He'd found the shed antlers of a 14-point there over the summer.

"You know," he says – his tone tells me he has changed subjects – "Davey was one of the few things Jack and I agreed on. We both thought he needed to be brought in."

I don't respond to this. I want him to think I am just being a polite listener, but I am simply conscious of what my position on the matter had been.

172

"Though our motives were different," he says.

"Different how?"

"Davey was just on Jack's frontier, the next thing to pull within his influence. But he was always pushing that line farther and farther out."

I am not following, so I just turn and look at him.

"That's what he's doing now, pushing his frontier out to include all that he can. He's admitted as much himself."

Josiah reads my perplexity.

"I don't mean he's an egomaniac or anything. He's just . . . progressive. He sees organization as a savior, and the bigger the better. There will be a lot of guys like Jack in the years to come. They'll want to count and build systems and govern. Right now he's just recording, getting the lay of the land, but soon enough he'll want to make things formal, give it all structure. And from there…"

"What are you talking about?"

My head is thick, and I have to keep reminding myself that we're talking about my little brother.

"He's a kid exploring a big backyard. He's just out having himself an adventure."

"Maybe that's all it is. Yeah, I think you're probably right, but still, that's saying a lot. I mean, why do we explore, really? There's a way of thinking in people that – I don't know – it always tends to…I just think if we've got this chance at doing things different we might do whatever we can to avoid it."

"I still don't – "

"We need very few things is all. Our family and a few others around us, people who we can look after and they can look after us. That's all we really ever need. But as soon we get ourselves into groups bigger than that it's like we forget how to just live and be decent to each other. And there's a thinking in some people that works against that ideal. It's just a spark in Jack, but I've seen it as fever in others. It's a hunger to take care of and take responsibility for others, but that's not what it really is. That's just a cover."

"Where have you seen this in people?"

"In history. In the Bible. In us."

"In us?"

173

"Did you forget about Nate?"

"Forget what?"

"That we stole him."

"We had to take him."

"We used our own reasons to do it, and we'll always be able to find our own reasons for doing whatever we want, but in that case we were man-stealers."

I feel myself on the defensive and am indignant at being maneuvered there.

"We probably saved his life taking him with us."

"See? There's always a handy reason. It's taken me a long time to see that about Nate. I only bring it up so you can start to think about these things too. As far as I can make out, there's only two things driving people – mastering others and not being mastered. And I keep thinking there's got to be something else because I don't feel like that. But when I read the Bible I realize I lie to myself like nothin. I'm no different. I want those things too."

"But you are different."

"Only in the specifics of who and whom."

"What does that mean?"

"The Lord is over me, and I am over only what he gives me."

"What does he give you?"

"So far, my body and mind, the ground here. Not Nate. I never had that. That Nate chose to stay with us has nothing to do with it, and maybe God will discipline me yet for that sin."

He comes down off the slip form and goes to the stone pile. Two by two, he begins walking them to the forms and dropping them down between the boards. I am relieved. These strange ideas have stacked up in my head, and I feel it may take days to find places for them all. I join him.

"Those are too small," he says to me. "Six or eight inches are good, ten at the most. Any bigger won't fit between. But those are small."

He has driven rebar stakes into the ground. Between these are ten-foot-long planks with a gap between. Cement and stones go into the gap, and when the section is cured, another set of planks is stacked on top. The building rises in twelve-inch spurts.

"You don't have enough planks to go very high."

"Four feet. I'll do the rest with a trowel, one stone at a time."

We work silently for a while, laying down a row of stones along the 30-foot section of forms that will make up the east wall. Josiah is careful to turn each stone so that the right surface is exposed when the forms are removed. The work has about it both the brute and refined.

As he begins troweling cement in over this stretch, he says, "In Samuel – the first one, I think – the people all want a king, but God tells Samuel to warn them about what they'll get if they insist on a king, that they'll be taxed heavily and their children will be taken and land taken. They'll be mastered by someone other than God. So Samuel tells the people that, and do you know what their response was?"

I know it, but I want to hear the answer from Josiah's mouth, so I just wait.

"They say fine! Great! We'll take it, just give us our king. We want to be like the nations around us. And that's what they get, and it's exactly as God said it would be. For the rest of their history, they're slaves to whatever king sits on the throne."

"What alternative did they have?"

Josiah gives me a look that makes me feel foolish.

"Plenty," he says patiently. "They could have asked for a king who loved God's word. That's what they were really rejecting. They were living a good alternative," he says patiently. "The judges were ruling them. No kings, no palaces or armies, just a judge with God's law open on his lap settling disputes. It was very simple, and He promised them it would be enough if they would keep up their end of the covenant."

As Josiah speaks, I am pushed gently off-balance by his words, and it is not unlike my catching up to the fact of his height. At some point in the past he has lost the blunt phrasing formed in those first years of illiteracy. He's found an eloquence. I don't know at the time if it is this or the force of his arguments that has me unsettled.

"What's this got to do with Jack again?"

"Maybe nothing. I'm not saying that Jack wants to be a king or anything like that. Or even that he would want a king or leader like it.

175

It's just that I can see in him a seed of that thinking. You get enough kids like him together who think they can create some new society, bring up a…a *phoenix* from the ashes, then it just takes a clever word from someone with that ambition and we'll have our king. We'll be standing in line to become slaves. I see that seed in him as plain as anything."

I don't mention Paul Smith yet, or his blessings over Jack's plan to map out the state. I want to withhold that, look at it myself before I expose it to the heat of Josiah's zeal. I tell myself that I am protecting Jack from him, but the stronger sense is that I'm protecting myself.

"You've got your eyes wandering everywhere, Jo," I say. I am flustered and want to diffuse the aim of his thoughts. "You see yourself in those marauders from the north and you expect the worse from it. You see Jack as some…I don't know, some well-meaning fascist and – "

" – can't help what I see, but I never said Jack was – "

" – and now you're looking into the future and saying we need to watch out for people who haven't even come along yet."

He drops the trowel and turns his eyes on me. He doesn't yell, but his voice holds down something that wants to fly.

"Where else are we to look but the future? I'm not reading the stars here, Liam. I'm just seeing what should be plain to anyone who looks. People are screwed up. Broken. And it's got nothing at all to do with the dying. It's always been there."

He picks the trowel up, and resumes the work, but his movements are quicker now, more angular.

"When we were talking on the Quinn's porch, I wasn't letting my eyes wander. I was thinking of me more than anyone else, but I'm not now. I'm thinking of every single one of us, and not just us in New Alaiedon, but us a generation from now. Ten generations from now."

The step from us to our generations catches me. It's not the conclusion I thought he was aiming at, and it throws questions over all of his words. And mine. I have to walk backward now along my own thinking, look for logic that may have taken a bad step. I can't think, though. My head is cloudy. I want to hear Josiah say more. His words next to mine are as sharp and clear as broken glass. I try to think of a

176

question to keep the momentum of the subject moving, but even in that I am dull. I decide to set loose the one sentence I had planned to hold back.

"Jack found an adult."

Josiah stops in the act of lifting a trowel of mortar. He holds it suspended for a moment and then turns it over slowly, lets the gray mud slop into the burrow in one, long, plopping stream. He wipes the trowel clean, first against the edge of the burrow, then on his pants.

"How old?" he asks.

"Gray hair. He had a wife and kids."

"A man. Just one?" he asks.

"Yeah."

"Where?"

"In Three Rivers."

"Never heard of it."

"Southeast, toward the border."

He glances in that direction. He always has the compass points at hand.

"Three Rivers."

He puts the trowel down and sits again on the forms. He is bent forward, hands on knees like he's catching breath.

"That's a lot for one day," he says. "Not sure where to point myself."

I've forgotten that I just told him about Davey too.

"What should we do?" he asks me.

The same question is forming in my mouth as he says this. He will not be the clarifying voice I am hoping for.

"Do we need to do anything?" I reply.

"I don't know. I used to wonder about this. What I would do if I found a grown up. But now – " he shakes his head " – it just seems too late for any good. We're grown-ups ourselves. What could he do for us?"

"Jack says he knows a lot. He was an engineer or something. Figured out how to turn the lights on in a church."

"Lights..."

"If he can figure out a church maybe he can get electricity to a whole city."

Josiah shakes his head.

"It'd take too many people to get a whole grid up, even a small part of one."

Jo takes up the subject as if relieved to be thinking of something else.

"If we want electricity that bad we'll have to make it ourselves, at least for now, every house making its own. I've read up on it. Thought it'd make a good business model. You know, clean up the generators, figure out how to get batteries charged again. But it's too much work right now."

His arms relax, and between us a stillness is achieved for a few long seconds. Then he says, "Maybe I'll let my sons take up that work."

I chuckle at this, but he doesn't hear me, and I can see that these last words were spoken from some future time where he can see such things with clarity. I feel self-conscious, like I'm in the presence of someone praying silently.

I leave Josiah to his work and walk back to the house. The trail descends from the knoll and opens into a field that once grew corn and soybean in alternating years. Now it is meadow and shrub. The air is cool where it passes over the sweat on my face and neck. The ground receives my footfall with a gentle push. I am loose-legged, and my stride is long and fast. I feel I can walk forever. As I settle into the rhythm of the familiar quarter-mile, an impression of well-being rises up alongside the sadness. I am surprised by it, and for a time I can't place its source. Then I realize that an anxiety has been remitted.

Over the past months, and probably longer, a space has opened between Josiah and me. I had feared it as a loss of affection, that we were each moving from the other by virtue of growth, like trees of different species seeking their own heights.

But it is not that. The difference is simply a matter of perspective and acuity of vision. I have only ever seen society as concentric circles moving out from me in degrees. There is the immediacy of Jack and Josiah, of Becka, Nate, and the twins. There is New Alaiedon, and the pale of our wanderings since the Dying, encompassing a few

178

townships around Lansing. And then there is all the voided continent beyond that I don't suspect I will ever see.

But for Josiah, society is not cut up into such orbits, but by levels moving down through time. It is located in stonier, deeper-rooted things, in a place of generations and centuries. This is a perspective I have never considered, but standing at the edge of it, I feel myself drawn there. Having been deprived the mysteries of growing up into an adult world, I feel this to be like one of those, and I want the clear, sharp words – or maybe the confidence behind them – to be my own. I want to set aside my flimsy things and work in mortar and stone, as Josiah does.

Chapter 31

In the first week of November, a light snow falls, and we will not see the ground again until Spring. The snow lends urgency to the last of our autumn chores. We finish wood in snow, harvest corn in snow, gather windfall apples and press cider in snow. On this day, one of November's last, the work of butchering is made lighter as the skies are clear and blue.

Nate and I have our hog Buster up on an engine hoist. He's been bled, scalded, and scraped. We have just taken off the head and are about to open the belly when Josiah comes in from shingling the roof of his stone hermitage. He is breathless.

"Smoke north again. Can't tell what though. One big one, or maybe more than one."

We are working behind the garage, blind to everything in that direction. The three of us climb to the rooftop of the house, where we can better gauge distance and direction.

"Closer this time. Okemos, I'd say. Here." As Josiah hands me the binoculars, I see that his hand is shaking. I remark it to myself only.

There is a breeze today, just enough to wipe out distinction in the rising smoke. We see it only as a dense gray cloud on the horizon, stretching up and westward.

"Josiah, you wanna take Bella to the Wagonmakers? I can go to the hall and fire the gun."

179

"Have them come armed," says Josiah. "Heavily. That smoke wasn't there this morning."

"Can I go?" asks Nate.

"Sorry. Someone needs to stay here and get Buster split and packed in snow. Can you handle that?"

I see shades of disappointment and pride both wash over his face, and then the settled look of compromise as he says ok.

We move quickly, Josiah on Jade, the new mare, I on Bella. At the hall I fire the gun 3 times as quickly as I can load it. It is a small hobby cannon about two feet long, a bronze replica of something from Civil War days. We found it in the front window of a gun shop in Mason. And though it can fire a one-inch ball to a prodigious distance, we use it only as a signal. Three shots means come quick.

It is a half hour later, when I am still alone behind the town hall's garage that I remember Isaac West is raising a barn on Harper, five miles south. Most of the township is gathered there. I curse myself for not remembering, and when I meet with Josiah again at the house, he too is alone.

"Will went scrounging for a wood stove for his barn," says Josiah.

"What do you want to do?" I ask.

Memories of the last expedition north rise up of their own buoyancy and argue against our going alone.

"Maya lives that way," says Josiah as he begins to climb down from the roof.

Two hours later we have the horses hitched in a neighborhood in Okemos. A block or two away, we are deep under an old, sprawling evergreen shrub at the edge of a golf course on the south side of the Red Cedar. Across the water, Maya's home is untouched, but smoke darkens the sky behind it. Josiah has the binoculars and narrates what he sees.

"Sliding door is open a little, but I don't see anyone. Something's on the floor, a chair back maybe. There's heat from the stove, but no smoke. Hasn't been fed in a while."

"It's gotta be cold in there," I say.

It's cold where we are, our bellies against the dirt.

"She's not there. Can't be."

180

I think of finding Davey in his dining room, but don't share the thought.

"Check the other houses."

In a forest, a log on the ground can have a look to it that suggests rot. The look is not in the wood itself, but in the settled incorporation of it into the soil. If you could crop out the surroundings, the log would appear as solid as standing wood, but push your foot against it and it collapses into compost. The houses around Maya's — a brick cottage to the east and a cedar craftsman to the west — have that look, the hollowed quality of long abandonment. All houses now seem as logs on the forest floor.

For a minute, Josiah glasses both but sees nothing unusual. The snow around them is unbroken. We walk east another block to a bridge that crosses the river, then come back down Maya's street, moving as though we were stalking game — quietly, watchfully, masking our silhouettes against the hard shapes of tree and house. We see that the tracks of a lone horse cut between two houses on the opposite side, go up the center of the street, and stop at Maya's. There the horse had been hitched to a lamp-post long enough to melt the snow and stamp the high grass flat. A set of boot tracks leads to a door in the garage, out the front door, and back to the horse.

"He left and cut through there," says Josiah.

He points across the street where the tracks disappear behind a little cape cod and then looks closely at the tracks coming out the front door.

"What do you see?" I ask.

"Something's wrong," he says. He takes two big steps to the first set and follows them to the garage, walking deliberately. He goes to the front door then takes the same stilted steps back to the lamppost.

"Steps are shorter comin out."

"Walking slower?"

"Yeah."

"Why?"

Josiah drops on his hands and knees to look at the boot print, then crawls to the first track, craning his head to catch light from different angles.

"'Cause he was carrying something heavy."

Josiah runs to the front door, hitting it hard with his shoulder. It's open, and he is yelling Maya's name through the house. In the kitchen, where the sliding door is open a foot, we find not a chair back on the floor but a shelf torn from a wall. Across the kitchen is scattered a mix of dried beans and peppers, little figurines of animals in clothes, angels, dominoes, and buttons. Two chairs are overturned and the table is shoved into a corner. We run up to the second floor and look into each dark room, but the house is empty.

Josiah's voice is measured, held back as though to make himself heard clearly.

"Get the horses."

We are in agreement without saying anything. We'll follow the tracks until we find Maya.

It is the beginning of a remarkable memory. He pursues the raiders along their tracks with the fixedness of a hound, as if he were simply incapable of lesser action. I am reminded of his decision to take Molly back to New Alaiedon – the same unchallengeable resolve is here.

We are on the track of a meandering retreat, eight horses strong. There is nothing studied or deliberate in their movements, just a curious poking about in the neighborhoods of eastern Okemos, Haslett, and further east toward Williamston.

At one point, the group has stopped at a greenhouse and nursery along Haslett Road. Inside one of the long glass buildings, they've built a fire and cooked the back straps of a yearling whitetail. The coals under the ash are still hot and the carcass fresh when we find it.

"They left the inside loins," says Josiah as he pulls out his knife. "Idiots."

"They're not more than a couple hours ahead of us now," I say. My tone suggests we should keep moving.

"They'll stop somewhere soon. One of these houses on Haslett probably. There's moon enough to track by. Besides, I want to find them in the dark."

The full meaning of this will not be clear to me that night.

We cook the venison over the old coals and eat it unseasoned, with some cheese, and dried apples we'd brought along. Then we move slowly on their tracks. At dusk we stable the horses at an old dairy farm and finish the hunt on foot.

From Haslet Road, a couple of miles farther, the group moves off to cross a broad field. Here the narrow file spreads into a wide rank, crossing the field shoulder to shoulder. In the twilight we can see that the tracks angle to the southeast corner of the field, making a triangle with the road and the tree line to the east. To avoid the open space we continue on the road then cut south through the trees. At the corner, a wide and well-worn trail cuts diagonally from the field into another open space, a quarter-mile square of rolling hills. In the center of it stands an enormous brick house in the Tudor style. Smoke rises from chimneys at both ends.

We move in the trees, along one side of the square until we are directly west of the house. From here there is but one second-floor window over the garage that might have watching eyes. Second floors are generally shut up now, especially in bigger homes, but with such a large group inside, there's no telling. Either way, it is our best angle for coming at them across the snowy, moonlit field.

"We'll wait a few hours," says Josiah.

He looks at the moon, then scans the horizon for a sign of cloud cover, but it is clear and starry. We take shelter from the breeze behind the root ball of a wind-toppled willow.

"Liam," says Josiah. "I should tell you something before we go in there."

His tone, though whispered, is both confessional and direct, like he's pushing through with a gathered courage.

"I've seen Maya. A few times, actually."

I wait for more.

"Lately, I mean."

"Ok."

"I've kept it from you . . .but I'm not sure why. Well, I'm not sure why I didn't tell you the very first time. When I didn't tell you, I turned it into a secret, and then it was easy not to tell you after that. I'm sorry. It seemed like a private thing, I guess."

183

"You don't have to be sorry. You didn't do anything wrong."

I shift myself down into the hollowed-out earth so that I am looking upwards. Josiah is already reclined.

"Did you?" I add. "Do anything wrong?"

"No."

Within the span of a single breath, two shooting stars scribe parallel lines across the sky, but neither of us remarks on it.

"I stopped there the first time going to Home Depot for pex pipe. Remember? I asked if you wanted to go, but you were doing something – '

"Burying chicken wire around the lettuce.."

"Right. I wasn't planning on even stopping there. It just came to me. She needed help fixing a gutter but she wouldn't ask for it. But after that time I found myself just wanting to see her."

Another meteor draws a long, slow line across the black.

"And all the time too. Like I could hardly do anything but think of reasons to go into town."

We wait for more atmospherics. Every few minutes is punctuated by a streak or two, all on a south-to-north bearing. Josiah is thinking about his last comment, or at least he is chasing after the thoughts that follow it. I know this by his next words.

"We haven't talked yet about what to do when…it – you know – when that happens."

"That?"

"Yeah. Women. Marriage. That."

"No, we haven't. You thought about it?"

"Oh yeah. A lot lately. It's the next thing, you know. Families. We need to start families."

"But we're only kids still."

"Really? You think that?"

I don't think it, but the conventions of age are still strong with me. You don't marry at 17. You do that in your twenties. At least I think you still do – no one's gotten married yet in the new age. No one that we know of. It is another mystery we find ourselves at the edge of.

To see movement in the woods when I hunt, I let my eyes go just out of focus and bring in the periphery. I do this now to catch

184

movement of the shooting stars through the tree branches. It works, but it's not a star I catch. It's the blinking eyes of a boy in a tree. A boy watching us.

"Josiah?" I whisper.

"Yeah?"

"Someone's up there."

"Huh?"

"Up in the tree above us. Behind you, where my feet are pointing now."

"Something you mean. A possum probably."

"No. Not a possum. A someone."

Josiah turns to look and shoulders the shotgun in the same movement. He relaxes his aim, then lets the gun drop. He steps from our hole to the base of the tree that holds the eyes.

"Marcellus?" He whispers. "It's me. It's Josiah. You come down here."

As Josiah whispers, the boy's eyes are on me. I can see the whites blinking in the low moon light. Josiah sees this too.

"He's ok. He's a friend. He's here to help Maya. Come down now and we'll tell you what we're doing."

The boy lowers himself from the limbs to the long trunk, then slides down it pole-like. At the bottom, he springs lightly behind the tree.

"Ok, then," says Josiah. "Liam, this here is Marcellus. You remember him? Last time you saw those eyes they were starin out of a pile of stuffed animals in a bunk bed."

It is indeed the same boy – an older, cleaner version, but the animal stare is the same.

We sit for another hour, and the boy takes much of it to crawl to us and take up a spot down in the dirt and roots. Josiah has a twig and leaf fire going at the bottom of the divot. It is just big enough to warm our fingers, but the idea of it – a fire under the nose of our enemies – warms me deeper.

"They think they're safe," says Josiah. "They take what they want, and no one's challenged them yet. They don't even put a guard outside or on the roof. We should be able to get inside without a problem, walk around like we were one of them. We'll find Maya, try not to scare her, and if she's not tied down, we walk her right out. They'll see how safe they are. Sound good?"

"Umm…"

"Ok. Which part?"

"The part about going inside."

"How else are we gonna do this?"

"How 'bout the way that doesn't get us killed. We peek in, we find Maya and tell her to sneak out."

"You think she'll be next to a window and we can just talk to her?"

"I was just never planning on sneaking in is all."

"Then I'll do it. If I'm caught, you can go back to New Alaiedon and get our friends."

I am in that hateful position between desires. I want both to match Josiah's courage and to save my skin. I envy him that clear sense of action. But then, I didn't think of Maya the way he did.

"Never mind," I say.

Josiah gives Marcellus the job of keeping the fire going. He convinces him that Maya will want the fire when we bring her back. Then we cross the field at a sprint and sit for a minute breathing heavily under a shuttered garage window. On hands and knees, we creep the perimeter of the entire house, peeking up at each ground floor window, moving quickly past the basement wells. We are near to the end of the circuit when we find a basement walkout and an unlocked door. We step inside and shut the door gently behind us.

Chapter 32

It is deepest night, mid-way between dusk and dawn, and the house is quiet above us. A cough sounds from a great distance, behind many walls. It is a big house.

Josiah grips my wrist.

"Stay here. I'll look for Maya. If I'm caught, I'll make noise. You take Marcellus back to New Alaiedon. Ride up the creeks in case they follow. They won't catch me, though. Hold these."

He shoves hat and gloves into pockets, takes his coat off, and gives it to me.

"I need to look like them if they see me walking around."

He takes his boots off too.

I feel like I've abandoned him. I want to make myself a part of this if only by helping him think it through.

"What's your plan?"

"I'll tip toe around the house like I'm looking for something and like I belong there. If anyone says anything to me, I'll shush them quiet and keep moving. I'm counting on them wanting to sleep more than caring about what one them is doing walking around."

From the bottom of the basement steps, I watch him go up. The moon light is low now, coming in from windows on the ground floor, so he moves from the darkness of the basement to light. He takes the last step at the top, turns and is gone.

Beneath the basement stairs is a closet. I spend the next few minutes exploring it carefully with my hands. It will be my fallback if something keeps me from getting out the door.

In the stillness I can hear nothing but the movement of the house. Even the gentle breeze of the night works against the high, flat surfaces and brings out creaks and groans. But for what feels like an hour there is no other sound. No footsteps, no voices, no opening or shutting of doors. I begin to lose sense of passing time. It has pooled around me in darkness and noises that don't change. So I set a metronome going in my head, something to knock the time around me back into the linear. I recite memorized things. There is Psalm 16 and 23 and 100. There is the Frost poem of the diverging roads. There is the Gettysburg address that I recited in a homeschool co-op, and there's the Lord's Prayer.

Above me is a crash, then voices. Feet move quickly down the steps, then stop at the bottom. Out of the sudden silence, I hear Josiah whisper my name. I reach out from the closet and pull him in. Now there is laughter above us.

"What happened?"

"Two of em woke up at the same time."

"What was that noise?"

"I tripped on a bench. They both think the other one did it."

We wait in the quiet for a few minutes until our tired legs give way to gravity and we sit.

"I should have thought of that," says Josiah.

"Thought of what?"

"Second sleep."

"What sleep?"

"Second sleep. It used to be a normal thing for people who lived by the sun. They'd wake up in the middle of the night for an hour or two then go back for second sleep. Sometimes neighbors would meet up under the moon, talk, play cards, pray, whatever. You haven't noticed? We're starting to do it again."

He's right. At least I've noticed it with me. I wake up most nights and lie there. Sometimes I read. I didn't know it had a name.

"We'll give them an hour and a half."

"You got a watch?"

Josiah chuckles and says, "Can't you just tell?"

"No," I say, "My brain goes funny."

"I found Maya."

"Is she ok?"

"Yeah. For now. She's chained to a bed and I can't lift it alone. I came down here to get you. The two of us could lift the bed, slip the chain off."

Josiah sounds off the time as he sees it passing. He whispers *an hour more*, then *half hour to go*, then he says, "You ready?"

I am not ready, but I stand up and I carry the fear that has leached up into me like cold.

"Take your boots off."

My jacket is already off and piled with Josiah's things next to me. I put my boots there too.

"We'll either have plenty of time to get dressed again, or we'll be running for the horses in our bare feet. No in-betweens. If they decide to chase, they'll have to saddle their horses."

"Right."

I'm hearing him with only part of my attention.

"Two of us together might look weird," says Josiah at the bottom of the steps. "At the top of these, you'll see the kitchen. Walk through it. Take a right when you can see the big open room on the left. Stairs are in the foyer to the right. It'll be darker there. Follow the wall along your left till you hit the banister. Take a right at the top of the stairs. She's in the last room on your left, end of the hall. Got all that?"

"Got it."

"Say it back to me."

I close my eyes and repeat the directions.

"Good. Give me five minutes. If I make a lot of noise, get out of here, yell for Marcellus and head for the horses."

"He might not come."

"I know. Don't wait for him. Tell him to get up a tree and sneak home when he can."

"Five minutes."

"Five minutes."

Again, the silence of the house twirls time into circles, and when I start up the stairs I don't know if it's been two minutes or ten. I don't have Josiah's internal clock. The moon is low and throws a horizontal light into the great room and kitchen. It casts my shadow onto the white cupboards like it's been cut from black paper.

I step over a bench that is still on its side. I see why Josiah tripped over it. It sticks out between two islands and cuts the aisle where there should be no bench. At the intersection where kitchen, great room and foyer meet, I look to my left and see covered lumps on couches, loveseats, one in a recliner. Even in the racing of my heart, I wonder at the idea that these killers need to sleep together in the same room. None of the lumps move, and I turn toward the foyer. But I let my

189

body turn before my eyes do, and as I step I kick a spoon that tinkles like a bell as it skips across the tile. The noise is incredible and even echoes in the big, still silence of the house. I freeze.

The lump on the couch lifts itself and says, "Where was it?"

I don't move. The head is covered, and I can't see which way he's looking, or if he's looking at all. He lays down, and I wait again for more waking sounds, but there are none.

I can hear my heart beating in my ears and am afraid it will wake the room. When it slows to where I can only feel it, I finish my steps into the foyer, leading with my eyes this time. The moon light doesn't reach here, and the darkness is absolute. But the banister is there, and I follow its curve up the steps. At the top I turn right. I walk with feeling toes. My fingertips guide me along the left wall.

I find that the last door is ajar. I listen for voices or movement, but hear nothing. I push it open and wait in the doorway. There is a clicking sound, and then again, and then a lighter flame shows me Maya's face on the bed.

"Come here," says Josiah. "What took so long? I thought maybe you got spooked."

I start to explain, but he says never mind.

The bed is an old-fashioned one with four tall posts at the corners. It is oak and heavy as a car. The two of us are just able to get the one leg off the floor enough that Maya can slip the loop of chain from under it. She puts a pair of tennis shoes on and we repeat the method going down – one at a time, every five minutes. I go first, then Maya, then Josiah.

The trip in reverse is less eventful. I make no missteps. And before I have my jacket on, I am met by Maya. She carries her chain wadded in a ball and pulled taught against her ankle so that it doesn't clink.

"The boy is with us," I say.

"Jo told me."

In the quiet, as we listen for Josiah, I feel myself reaching for things to say. I say this: "You should stay with us now."

Maya's response is close at hand. She says, "I know."

Feet step lightly down the stairs, and the three of us finish dressing without a word spoken. We slip out the door and move across the field at the speed of Maya's hobbled gait. At the tree we find Marcellus and the fire waiting faithfully.

"Take them back to the horses," says Josiah to me. "I'm going back in."

Maya comprehends his words quicker than I do.

"What are you talking about? What are you doing?"

There is panic in her words.

My brain catches up, and I say, "Wait...Josiah? What –"

"We're not done yet...Maya?" –Josiah takes Maya's jacket in his fist, not in a threatening way, but as a way to speak through her fear – "Where does he sleep?"

"I won't," says Maya, shaking her head. "You can't. Let's just go."

"Which room is his?" Josiah's voice is harder. His whisper is a croak. "Tell me where he sleeps, or I'll have to check every room, look into every face."

"Who are you talking about?" I ask.

Josiah lets go of Maya's coat and stands. He takes his jacket off and puts it around Marcellus's shoulder. Then he begins to walk back out of the wood line, into the field toward the house.

Maya says Josiah's name in a tone that stops him, and he turns around to listen.

"He has the big bedroom," she says, "right below mine."

As Josiah begins to walk again, I start to follow him, to bring him back, but Maya grabs a hold of me.

"He won't listen," she says. I pull away and catch Josiah in the field.

"What are you doing?"

"Take them back to New Alaiedon. The boy's freezing. He's gonna die if you don't get him warm. Leave Jade for me. I'll be right behind you."

"So I'll help you. We'll do it together. Whatever you're doin–"

" – this might take a while, and Marcellus can't wait. You can help by taking them back."

Josiah turns and breaks into a sprint to the house, and again I am between my wants. But this time a bigger one comes along, and I curse Josiah under my breath.

He is right about Marcellus. He is showing signs of hypothermia. By the time we are back at the barn where the horses are hitched, he is shivering uncontrollably. I put Maya in the stirrups and Marcellus in front of her. I slip his legs through the sleeves of my jacket, and then lead Bella home to New Alaiedon. It is a long, long trip, and I walk for some miles in my sleep. At one point, when I stop to rub the boy's feet, I ask Maya who Josiah is after, but when I look up I see that she is sleeping too.

It is two hours after sun up when we arrive home. Becka and Nate set up a bed in the living room of Josiah's house. There they bury Maya and Marcellus in quilts warmed on racks by the wood stove. For the next hour I wander between them and the front porch where I watch for a silhouette on Stillman Road to the east. I must just miss him on one of these checks, because when I do see Josiah leading Bella, he is already crossing the hay field to the east of my corn. I meet him in the open space between my house and his. There is a body in the saddle, slumped forward, wrists tied around Bella's neck.

"Who?" I ask.

Josiah hands the lead to me, and pulls the head up by the hair, showing me a dark-complected, but unconscious face.

"Should I know him?" I ask.

"Maybe. Look here." Josiah points to his mouth. "Blue?"

"Ricky?"

Chapter 33

"He'd always wanted her."

"But I thought he was – "

" – her brother? Yeah. Step brother. That didn't stop him."

We are unsaddling Bella in my garage. Josiah has begun to rub her down.

"He even got into some trouble for doing...whatever, something gross. They had to move him out of his house, have him live with his

192

aunt in Lansing. He came back. Everyone thought he'd gotten himself straightened out, but Maya knew him better. So when he came back, she left, and found her own trouble. When the dying came, Ricky went after her for good, made her his very own."

"Nate said he tried to kill her."

"Maybe he did. Maybe Nate was just seeing something he didn't understand. Anyway, Maya did manage to get away from him – finally. That's about when we met up with her. Remember the tattoo?"

"The westgates."

"Those boys at Molly's place, the two dead ones, they had something similar on their faces."

I hadn't noticed the similarity until now. The tattoos on the two boys were more sophisticated, but that would make sense. The design would get tweaked over time.

"So that first winter, when Ricky couldn't feed everyone – maybe he didn't even try – he takes off, goes to Mt. Pleasant where he has a cousin and a few friends, and he starts over."

"So what are we doing with him?"

"He's a rapist and a murderer. What do you think we should do with him?"

"I don't know. That's why I'm asking you."

"I know what we need to do. The hard part will be talking everyone into it. I could use your help there, but then I may have to talk you into it first."

"Into what?"

"And there's kidnapping too."

"You're gonna talk me into kidnapping?"

"No. I was just thinking he's a kidnapper. Another crime that forfeits your life. That's what I'm talking you into."

"You think we should kill him?"

"I know we should kill him."

"But we didn't kill people for rape or kidnapping before the Dying."

"We did a lot of things wrong before the Dying. I don't find anything in the Bible about prisons as punishment."

193

"Joseph and Daniel." I was surprised at how quickly the examples came to me. "Both prison stories."

"Joseph was in Egypt, Daniel was in Babylonia. God never prescribed prisons. Sure makes it simple, doesn't it?"

"But is it right?"

"What's right? I mean ultimately. For most people right is whatever feels best."

"It should feel good, being right I mean."

"People can feel anything they want if they want it bad enough. Our hearts lie to us. Something outside of us has to say what's right and wrong. Could be a code of some kind. A feeling that everyone shares. But it's always something. Everyone uses something."

"Then how does everyone know that murder is wrong? We all feel it's wrong, so it's wrong."

"We all feel it because we're made in God's image. Deep down we know right and wrong. We just go our own way. 'For what can be known about God is plain to them, because God has shown it to them. For his invisible attributes, namely, his eternal power and divine nature, have been clearly perceived, ever since the creation of the world...' We're without excuse."

That's twice now he's quoted scripture to me, and it feels like I'm being jabbed with a stick. I taught him to read after all.

"Then why don't we have this death penalty law written there too?"

"We do. If someone does something bad enough, even the most soft-hearted will say 'kill him! He doesn't deserve to live!' So it's there, it's just perverted."

"By what?"

"By our own inventions – false mercy, revenge, blood lust. Anything but the sense that God's holiness has been offended."

He is walking in circles around the garage. He's forgotten what he was looking for, so I hand him the pitchfork.

"Thanks."

Once he's moved two loads to the stall, he says, "If we deviate from how God tells us to live, there will be consequences. Every single time. That's why I went back for Ricky. When we talked back in the fall – You remember? My front porch? – I said we were at a point where we could go one way and be a blessing or go another and follow the same road as the kids who butchered Molly's friends."

I take the fork from him before he can stab another load. He doesn't notice and keeps talking.

"And that's still the choice. We can bless God and obey him, or make this little choice to set him aside. I think the way we choose now will set us on one road or the other."

It's hardly fair to credit Josiah with changing my mind since I was halfway there to begin with. Where I will credit Josiah is in getting the entirety of New Alaiedon to go along with him.

Ricky is chained to a heavy ring bolt in the corner of Josiah's stone house, and as I look at him a part of me wonders if the structure was not made just for that purpose. He is much bigger than I remember him, and I think I remember him as a brute. Now he has the look of a caged bear. When Josiah takes a stool to the limit of the chain and sits down on it, I am struck by the difference in their sizes. Josiah is tall and lean. But Ricky is tall and thick, twice Jo's size, maybe more.

Earlier that day, after I'd helped get Ricky down off Jade and chained here in our jail, Josiah had recounted, without embellishment, the events of the previous night.

He'd found Ricky where Maya had said, in the large master bedroom. He slipped a belt around his neck while he slept and simply cinched it tight. Ricky awoke and tossed Josiah up and down on the bed for a minute before passing out. Josiah then rolled him out the window – I have trouble imagining that, but then Josiah has always been good at applying leverage to things – and dragged him to our willow tree where he hog-tied and gagged him until he could get Jade. Ricky saddled up just fine with the encouragement of the .38 at his neck. But when he tried to bolt with Jade under him – Jade would have none of it – Josiah was obliged to brain him with a piece of 2x4 pulled from a dilapidated vegetable stand.

The effects of his rough night are showing. Ricky's eyes are bloodshot, and he holds his head motionless as if he were guarding it against unforeseen shock.

"You need anything?" asks Josiah. "We got aspirin, Rolaids… What else we got, Liam? That pink stuff. Tea? You want some tea? We're outa coffee, but Becka makes a sort of counterfeit from…something. I don't recommend it, but we have it if you want."

The words go right past him. He holds Josiah in a stare of simple hatred.

"Ok then. You should probably know what we plan to do here. It'd be cruel to draw it out any, and we're not here – that is, you're not here – for cruelty's sake. You need to know that."

"Our plan, Ricky, is to see that justice is done. You'll get a trial where we'll present the facts of the case. You'll get a chance to see your accusers and question them. You'll get a chance to defend yourself. But my goal here is to see that justice gets done. And that means I'll be arguing for your quick execution. Hanging, I think, will be the way of it."

When Ricky doesn't blink at the words execution and hanging, Josiah feels he needs to repeat himself.

"It's your execution I'll be arguing for, Ricky. Do you understand that? We're going to kill you, and I say going to because I have no doubt that I can prove your guilt in this."

Ricky doesn't answer but launches a ball of phlegm that hits Josiah on the neck.

"Ok then," says Josiah. "As long as we're clear."

Chapter 34

Our knowledge of law and courts is skimpy and drawn entirely from the TV shows and movies of our childhoods. Josiah takes the opportunity our ignorance provides and in his opening remarks teaches us from scripture the necessary elements of investigation and verdict.

196

When a crime is committed against a community member, two witnesses are required to bring a charge against the accused. Maya, of course, will be the first. The second will be the boy Marcellus. He can't – or won't – talk, but Josiah does not seem concerned by it. These two will claim they saw Ricky rape and kidnap Maya. As to the killings at Molly's homestead earlier that fall, Molly can not only place Ricky there but can testify that he was one of the two shooters firing through the balusters at the front porch. But she is alone in this, so Ricky is safe from a charge of murder.

The witnesses understand, explains Josiah, that an intentional falsehood here will return the intended punishment back on their own heads. If they are lying, then they've put their own lives at stake for it. He reads a passage from Deuteronomy 19 to establish this, and leaves the crowd in a stir for some minutes after.

We are in the township hall. It is the largest group we've ever assembled, the entire population of New Alaiedon. William Wagonmaker, Luke McHugh, and Isaac Quinn sit as judges. Josiah will prosecute, and Ricky is allowed to defend himself with questions for the accusers and clarifications as to points of law. Because I came with Josiah and Ricky, I am made bailiff and must stand for the duration. I am also given the only gun – my own .38 that Josiah has brought.

The space is set up in typical courtroom fashion – the principal players at the edges, with an open area in the center for the drama to play out. At the south end of the room is a long conference table. Behind it sit the three judges. To the judges' right is an empty stool, the witness stand. To their left sits Ricky in an office chair. He is chained by his right ankle to the piano. The north half of the room is taken up with spectators in folding chairs. They are not in rows, but spread out in clumps of two's and three's. We have added the job of county clerk for the occasion: Libby Wagonmaker will take notes on the proceedings. She sits at her own table along the east wall, opposite the door. As I tell her that I've counted twenty-two people present, William raps the table with a heavy mug and says, "Let's get started. Josiah, you can" – he has to retrieve the right phrasing – "*call* your first witness."

197

He calls Maya, who tells her story without passion, in the voice of one seeing it from a distance. She adds nothing to compel us to pity for her or to contempt for Ricky. The details of the crime in their barest prose are enough.

William asks Ricky to respond to his accuser, gives him time to formulate a question, a rebuttal, a refutation of her testimony, but he is sullen and silent.

Josiah calls Marcellus next. He still can't speak, and what might have proven the technicality that sets Ricky free, becomes a testimony of exquisite clarity. The terror in the eyes, the agitation in the body that racks him in the witness chair shout out Ricky's guilt.

And when the accused is given another chance to defend himself, when he rises to speak, Marcellus is unstrung, leaps from the chair, and runs to Maya who holds him tightly. All the while he is facing Ricky, keeping himself between him and Maya, as if in her defense. It is an unfeigned performance, more damning by far than speech.

One of the judges, Isaac Quinn, has a keen sense of the judicial, and questions the court as to the validity of such an implicit account. He gets an answer in an unforeseen way. Nate volunteers himself as a third witness and offers his own version of Ricky's attempt to kill Maya years earlier. As the details emerge, it becomes clear to us all that his recollection of attempted murder is, in fact, the memory of a rape captured by young and naïve eyes. Isaac concedes the testimony as that of a second witness, and the prosecution resumes.

But here Ricky finds his voice and objects.

"You said community!"

It's unclear to us all what he means.

"Who did?" asks William.

"He did." Ricky points to Josiah. "He said the community. Maya's not part of this community, never was. Neither am I, so how is it you think you can judge me?"

"So is that an objection?" asks William.

"Yeah it is." Ricky stomps his chained foot. "I object."

From the time Josiah returned with Ricky strapped like a prize buck to his horse, I've not seen him waver in this. But now there is uncertainty in his narrowed eyes. I can see him wondering if he's left an opening for Ricky to slip through.

Almost before I can think about what to say, I hear myself speaking.

"She's a part of us. She has been since the first months of the dying."

"You'll need to be called up as a witness," says William.

"All right then, call me."

I pick up in my story after Isaac swears me in.

"That first spring after the dying was over, Maya helped us find Jack. She didn't have to do it, but she did. And she wasn't part of Ricky's group by this time. She'd already left. She lived in her own place. Heck, you can almost see the deer blind from our house. It's closer to our house than a lot of you in this room."

You can see the expressway from our roof, and the blind isn't a mile from there. I am being accurate in a broad sense. I finish with iron-clad logic: "If that's not community, then I don't know what is."

After a consultation with Isaac and Luke, William says, "Objection is overruled. Maya is a part of this community."

Josiah is relieved. It's a rare thing for me to be even a short step ahead of Josiah, so it's not without some pride that I resume my spot next to Libby.

The closing arguments are simple and concise. Josiah makes a quick tour of the evidence against Ricky and the requirements for witnesses and testimony. Ricky offers nothing but a snide, "I ain't done nothin to hang for."

As the evidence against Ricky has been mounting, so has a sense of collective shame. We have seen much since the Dying, but for most of us, the shock has been a natural aversion to death and decay. Here it is a moral affront, and we want it far from us. We want the thing removed.

When the judges return with a verdict of guilty, the air in the room seems to clear and the desire for justice in its many iterations – punishment, recompense, reconciliation, cleansing – fills the void. It is an easy transaction and has the simple force of a clear guilt behind it. Josiah senses the momentum. He moves across the court in full vision of us all and puts his head outside to check for...for what? Clouds? Rain? Then he turns and fills the door. The sun is descending, and he is a dark silhouette in the frame as he begins to speak the words that most of New Alaiedon will remember him by.

"Doesn't it seem like every day we wake up with a new job to do?" he asks.

He is not hurried. He knows he speaks to a room full of friends.

"We're still just kids, in a way, aren't we? But we've had to become a lot more than that."

He takes a step inside the room, and I can see his eyes sweep the audience.

"We're farmers now, and doctors, and businessmen. We're parents, a lot of us, to our siblings, to orphans too little to make it on their own. We'll be real parents someday, God willing. And here, today, we woke up and we're– " He gestures to those occupying these new roles, " –judge and prosecutor ...clerk and bailiff...and..." He looks at Ricky then back at his audience and says, "We'll need to be more yet before this is done."

Josiah doesn't step into the open space in front of the table and the judges. Instead, he takes slow steps along the wall toward the back of the room. He will encircle us in a net of words.

"We'll have to be something new today, I think. New because it won't be just one job that one person can sign up for."

He stoops to pick up something. It is a child's shoe. He works out a knot in the laces as he speaks.

"New because it will be something that only a whole community can do. No one else should do it. Only – all – of us. New Alaiedon, every one of us here together, will have a new responsibility today. We've done things together before, but never anything quite like this. Never anything with this much... weight to it. But before we go there, I need to say a little about what we'll not be doing as a community."

He is at the back of the room now, and most are craned around in their chairs to follow him with their eyes. He's done with the shoe and tosses it to Alex Pratt, who hands it to his blushing little sister.

200

"We're not going to pass this on to someone else, not to another town, and not to some authority higher up the line. Because there is no one else up the line."

He stops and faces the room with his hands in his pockets. The next words come slowly, each phrase pitched for its own sake. It has the effect of whispered words, and our focus on each builds a tension over our heads like collected lightning.

"We're it. But we all know that by now, don't we? We know it in our bones. Every night when we go to bed tired and sore after every day of fighting the ground for our bread, we know it. We're it. There's no one else. We know it when we're made to watch someone we love go sick, when there's no one to call but our own as the end is coming, when we have to put them in the ground with our own shovels. We know beyond a doubt at times like those that we're all there is. But it's not all bad, is it? that knowing?"

Here, Josiah begins to move again, and the breath in us is released. But that charge is still in the air.

"At harvest time this year, did anyone else feel like God was pouring strength into them? Like you had energy enough for a hundred harvests? I sure felt it, and I know those who worked at my side felt it too. It was hard. We've never worked harder, but it was a…a joyful hard. We knew it then too, that we were it, the end of the line. So there can be no passing on of this…this terrible…responsibility. No. It is our own to put away."

Though the talking board is cleared of all business, Josiah studies it, the empty space, for a full minute. He is letting us, the stragglers and the slow among us, catch up for the next push. And we all know that he'll argue now for killing. We knew it before we walked in, but we're at the business of it now, and he's helping us toward it.

Josiah turns around and says, "I don't know about you, but this whole business scares me."

He takes a deep breath and lets it out with raised brows. It is a friendly gesture. Then he says, "So another thing we're not going to do is we're not going to leave this decision up to us."

Now he gives us a look like he's waiting for us to catch the pun, the private joke.

201

"I'm not being contrary. We will see to it that this responsibility is done. But if it's gonna be done right, we'll need wisdom beyond ourselves. Beyond me at least. I can hardly put two good decisions together in a day. Seems like I'm saying or doing or thinking the wrong thing before I'm out of bed. I don't know about you, but I seem to make a lot of choices based on...on my stomach...on the condition of my crops...how much meat I have salted for the winter, too much rain, too little rain, too much heat, too much cold. Toothaches! I make more decisions by mood than just about anything else that comes into my head. But friends, what we're doing today cannot be informed by things like mood. Because even on my best days, when I'm feeling full of wisdom and my thinking is sharp, even then I screw it up!"

His voice is rising in gentle swells, like music composed to build up.

"I don't know about the rest of you, but I don't trust myself. I'm fallible."

He is now in front of the judges, back to the space from which he's argued Ricky's guilt.

"And we cannot be fallible when it comes to what we're doing here today. We have to be right. We *have* to be right. Isaiah says the Lord is a God of justice, that it's a part of him. David tells us the Lord loves righteousness and justice. He *loves* it! We have to love it too, and so we cannot look to ourselves to find what is and what is not just. We can't do that because we don't know ourselves. Only the one who made us knows us. Only our maker can tell us what is right and what is wrong. And not only can he tell us, but he does tell us. He gives us his law and in that law he tells us that we can't trust our own hearts, and he tells us exactly what to do with the law breaker!"

Josiah is pointing now at Ricky, but I cannot mark the place in his speech where he's raised his arm. It is as if he'd been raising it slowly from his first words when he stepped out of the sunlit door frame. He holds it there now, and as the next words come, the hubris in Ricky goes flat, and he seems to shrink before us.

"Who here can say that he knows right and wrong? And if you say you know it, tell me this: what are you pointing to and calling law? Is it

202

us? Are we the law? Are we calling such fallibility as our collection of senses the law? Surely we can do better than that."

Josiah turns to us now. He lets his arm fall, lets his eyes soften, but there is still an awful note in his words. This is not the boy I knocked off the log or heard whimpering in the elevator shaft, and it's there in the township hall that I first think of the word that will go with him in my thinking from this time on – preacher.

Josiah Mench is a preacher.

"It is God's law or it is man's law. And you've seen what man will do when left to himself. This is the decision we make today. Not whether or not to execute a rapist. We can arrive at yes's and no's by all manner of reasoning. People have always been too blood-thirsty, and people have always been too lenient with evil. Those are easy. If we're following moods, just catch us in the right one and we'll choose anything. What we're deciding today is what we'll point to as law!"

At the word *law* he raises a finger, and several in the crowd flinch as if he's poked them with it.

"Yes. This should scare the deepest parts of you. It scares me. God scares me."

He shifts his gaze around the room, but holds his finger out, like he's sighting down a gun barrel.

"If we let a man live whom God has appointed to die, are we not guilty? Does God not then have a law to hold over *our* heads? And make no mistake in this – God will bring about what he's appointed. Ricky will die, and God will find us faithful. Or Ricky will die, and God will find us rebels. We can try to hide from this, New Alaiedon, but we cannot hide from God."

Now Josiah swings his arm to Ricky again, and says to the roomful of friends, "I know you want this evil removed from you. So remove it."

But he is not done. The middle chair of the front row is empty, but on it sits a book. From his first words, Josiah has been moving toward it, like a satellite in decomposing orbit. The book is a Bible. It is the fiery surface of the sun.

He picks it up. From where I stand I can see that he has several passages marked for reading. Slips of paper hold the places. The last words of the prosecution to argue for a penalty of death will not rise up new out of Josiah's eloquence or persuasion. They will be ancient words working in their own power. He opens at the first spot and without exposition or commentary begins to read the familiar words of Genesis 1.

From nothing, God creates the universe, earth, all that is in them, and man. He stops at these words: "*So God created man in his own image, in the image of God he created him; male and female he created them.*"

From there, Josiah moves forward in themes. He shows the inseparability of creation and law, that spoken words of God are both creative and legislative. God speaks the seas and land and in the speaking sets their boundaries. He speaks life forms into existence and sets their natures "each according to its kind." And God sees his good creation, affirming it as such. God's spoken things are expressions of himself. God's law is an expression of himself, and we are made in his image.

And yet Josiah is not preaching now, he is only reading. I know the words well. I've heard them from childhood. But it is as if they had always, until now, been unstrung, scattered like beads, and here in the courtroom, Josiah is carefully stringing them again.

I stand against the east wall with Libby on my right and the profiles of the three judges in front of me. When I think that it is only I who hear Josiah fashioning something new for us out of God's word, I look to them and see that each is rapt with the same astonishment.

He is deep in the book now. I don't know which scriptures, but they have the sound of the prophets, an Old Testament heaviness. He reads of a restoration of Israel, of all nations looking to Jerusalem. He reads of new hearts, new covenants, of swords beaten into plowshares. He reads this: "I will put my Spirit within you, and cause you to walk in my statutes and be careful to obey my rules."

He finishes with a cautionary tale. It is the story of King Ahab's mercy to Ben-hadad. It is an unlawful mercy, like Pilate's to Barabbas. Behind a disguise of bloody bandages, God's prophet gets Ahab to condemn himself. And the prophet replies, "Thus says the LORD, 'Because you have let go out of your hand the man whom I had devoted to destruction, therefore your life shall be for his life, and your people for his people.'"

If he has added effect to the words, it is no more than a slow and deliberate enunciation. His inflection is wooden but clear as light. He closes the Bible and puts it under the chair. He offers a simple closing remark.

"God, who created everything, reveals his character in his law, and he writes that law on our hearts. New Alaiedon, God deserves our obedience in this."

He is done, but his sitting down and the silence that follows have come just a measure too quickly, and the air in the room, heavy as a rain cloud, is still full — the holy words, their terrible glory — and before the judges return with the sentence, we know it already, for we've heard God speak it. Ricky must die. But even this pronouncement, as heavy as it is, stands attendant to something greater: New Alaiedon has chosen the authority that it will follow.

Chapter 35

"We should stone him," says Chandler. He is a fire-eater and needs tempering even in mundane things like putting up fences.

"That's asking too much," says Josiah.

"Too much of who?"

"Everyone."

"So where do we draw the line?" asks Luke. "I mean there's a lot of law in the Bible. Are we gonna only plant our gardens with one kind of seed? Or make our clothes out of one kind of cloth? You say we've already asked a lot of our people, but it looks like we haven't even started."

"There's a lot to straighten out, and I'm just now starting to see that we can draw lines. I feel like we're at the edge of something good though. And learning it will be good."

Josiah looks around the room, catching our eyes. He is inviting us into this, appealing for allies, co-workers.

"So we hang him?" asks Chandler.

Josiah nods. "Together. As a...as a *covenant* community."

"Why together? And what's a covenant?"

"That's how God deals with us – together. Covenant is like a promise. When two are bound together, like in marriage, they're in covenant."

"I thought he saved sinners, one at a time. What about all that stuff about a personal relationship with Jesus?"

"He saves us and puts us in covenant with others. He saves us to his body. For his body. Sometimes the covenant community is the means he uses."

"Whatever." Chandler has reached his limit for the abstract. "So how do we all hang someone?"

Josiah looks at me and nods, as if to say, "You tell 'em."

So I do. I tell them a story my dad read to us about a Confederate spy who gets hung from a railroad bridge. He stands on the edge of a long board that just sticks out over the river. At the other end, the safe end, it doesn't take much for someone to keep the board from flipping up because it's so long.

"The fulcrum," says Josiah.

"Right. The condemned stands near the fulcrum." We could do the same thing, I explain, but on the roof at the front of the building. It's not too steep. There's a long shelf in the garage. It's one board. We put a little of it – enough for Ricky to stand on – over the edge and a bag of sand at the other end with a rope tied to it. We screw a heavy ring bolt into the ridge beam for the noose.

"Then we all tug," says William.

"Together," says Josiah.

There is no other response to this, and we sit in the quiet for a few minutes. The sun has long been down, and only a camp stove gives us light. The quiet is slowly filled with a sense of unreality, and I begin to walk back the events that have brought us here. Suddenly I feel a resentment for Ricky and want the deed done quickly. So when Josiah

206

suggests I go talk to him, to hold out God's grace to him, I am struck stupid.

"Do what?"

"Talk to him. Tell him the gospel. I don't think he'd listen to me."

Chandler is astonished. "You think God will have mercy on...*him*?" he asks.

"Why not?"

"He's a rapist. And a murderer."

"That's no answer."

"You're nuts."

"No, but apart from Christ I'm just like Ricky. The same sin."

"Ricky had a rotten life," says William. "People are saying his dad abused him pretty bad."

Josiah looks at William for a moment then holds up the pencil that's in his hand. "If you treated this pencil real bad – and I mean really bad – you think it'd poke you?"

All Josiah gets back is a suspicious look. Is it a trick question? it asks.

"Why not?" asks Josiah.

"That's stupid. It's – "

" – Why not?"

"Because it can't."

"Because it's not in its nature?"

"Sure, you could say that."

"You couldn't make it do anything that's not there already. Right? You can't make it fly or sing or tie itself into a knot."

"I haven't murdered anyone."

"Not yet," says Josiah. "But that doesn't mean anything."

"I'm not like Ricky."

Josiah is done talking. He hands the Bible to me.

"I'm goin to bed."

But instead of sleep Josiah takes up the task of preacher and spends the dark hours exhorting Ricky to a repentance. I am amazed at this. Not that Josiah would choose to do it – not at all at that – but that Ricky would choose him. I'd tried it earlier, as Jo had suggested. I sat down on an unsplit round of firewood, opened the Bible and gave him a little of God's holiness and our sin and Jesus' redemption. It was a poor attempt, resting solely on logic. In answer, Ricky only glared at me, then asked for the tall guy with the words. He wanted preaching, so Josiah gave it to him.

The next morning we are gathered again at the hall, and again I count 24. There is little ceremony, and we have no liturgy to lean on for such occasion, so a quickness in the matter has risen out of an implicit consent. No one wants to draw this out, except for the condemned.

Four of us have him hemmed in at the foot of the ladder that he'll mount to the roof of the hall, but as he is taking a step to the first rung, he twists violently, breaks free of the circle and runs head-long toward the road. His hands are bound at this back, and in his momentum, his legs can't quite catch his body, and he pitches forward into the gravel.

When we've pulled him to his feet and presented him again to the scaffold, it is a bloody, tear-stained boy who faces death. He is pitiful, and it is Josiah who shows him pity. He takes him aside, and the image of Josiah, his hand on Ricky's shoulder, his lips whispering urgently at Ricky's ear lays hold of our imaginations and quiets us all. For several minutes, the county of New Alaiedon, scattered in its clumps and pairs, is as still as a portrait. The only movements in the scene are Josiah's lips and Ricky's big frame drawing breath like a bull in the ring. I can't help but wonder if Josiah's preaching has only served to harden Ricky's heart rather that break it.

Into this stillness, the distant sound of knocking penetrates and turns every head except those grappling with eternal matters. We look west, far up Holt Road, where two riders are approaching on horseback. No one speaks. We only watch, and by the time I think to warn Josiah that someone's coming, I'm able to say to him, "Jack is here and he's not alone. He brought his adult with him."

Chapter 36

Jack swings from his horse, a gray, spotted Walker. Bella is hitched behind, loaded down with gear. In saddle next to him is a tall, thin man of gray hair and a neat, white beard. He wears a straw hat for the sun and Carhart bibs over a flannel shirt. He is lanky, and when he swings out of the saddle, he lands on the drive with a youthful bounce. He turns and whips off the hat in greeting, sweeping long gray hair back with his free hand.

"Liam, Jo, guys, I want you to meet Governor Smith. Governor, this is my brother Liam, and that's Josiah Mench. That's William and Luke, Isaac and Chandler…and I guess…the whole town. Hey guys."

Jack looks at Ricky, questioningly at first, then he recognizes him, then he sees that he's not standing politely with hands behind him, but that he's bound that way.

"What's happening here, boys?" says Smith.

William and I have a simultaneous thought and move ourselves to either side of Ricky.

"County business," says Josiah. "And pardon my bad manners, but I don't remember voting for a governor."

"A little young to vote, aren't you?"

"I'm 18. And what is it you govern? Sir?"

Smith laughs. It's been years since we've heard a full-throated, adult laugh. It is an attempt to be cordial, but there is a contrived familiarity behind it, the kind that authority presumes in the presence of its lessers.

"Well . . . Jo, was it?"

"Josiah."

"Well, Josiah. That's a good question and the right place to start. In fact, that was a question Jack and I had. Jack was quite fervent in his desire to… survey our boundaries, so to speak. So that's what we've been at for these last months, and it seems safe to say that I am the only adult—"

"Just said I was 18."

Smith gives a conceding nod.

"—That at the time of the pandemic's conclusion, I was the only adult, and as such was, at that time, by default in the succession of the governing chain of authority, the governor of the state of Michigan and quite possibly the President of the United States." More laughter. "But we're not making plans for that office just yet."

Smith hands the reins of his horse to Jack and takes a step toward Josiah. His interest has shifted to Ricky. "Your hands are tied, son."

Ricky's eyes flit between Josiah and the adult. I have a hold on his right arm and feel it clench. His feet have shifted and his legs bent. He is a spring winding slowly.

Josiah steps between them.

"You've interrupted us, Mr. Smith. I suggest you leave or you step back with the rest of the folks of New Alaiedon and let us finish our business. It's government business."

"In that case I think I need to know what business you're into, Josiah, before I do anything."

Josiah's eyes narrow. I know the look. He is weighing knowns against unknowns, seeing the machinery at work behind the keyholes. But when he looks at me now, his expression is unique. It is settled and right, but it is profoundly sad.

"This man," says Josiah, "has been found guilty of kidnapping and rape. He has confessed his crimes, confessed his sins before God, and will be executed this morning."

"Executed."

"By hanging."

"Well, now, Mr. Mench, I'm afraid – " He laughs and takes in the whole crowd with a quick turn of his head. "I think you're kidding, right? You're kidding."

Josiah returns a cold look as answer.

"Hanging? As in by the neck until dead? I do hope you're kidding." But Josiah's look convinces him. "This is the 21ˢᵗ century, kids. No, I'm afraid that I can't let you do that. You see, Josiah, there's a thing called due process. Maybe you haven't heard—"

"—I know what due process is, and he got it."

"Says you?"

"Says this community…in which you are a guest."

Smith takes a big step backward and turns to those gathered behind him now in a wide crescent. He has set aside the laugh and puts on a scolding face.

"Kids!" he shouts. "Hear me! This is serious business."

"They know that," says Josiah.

"More serious than you know. You're all very close to getting into more trouble than you've ever imagined. Killing a man without the state, apart from the state, is murder itself. Now go on home! Take your horses and go home! And I'll forget all about this!"

There is a stir like a breeze has come through and made everyone to brace against it. A few of the faces seek each other out in nervous looks.

"Don't listen to him, Friends! The state is us!"

"*I* am the state!"

"There is no state where there is no law and he brings no law! Think! God's law is eternal and perfect, and it must be so here in New Alaiedon."

Smith turns again, and this time he pauses and takes in Josiah with untempered wonder.

"God's law?"

Josiah meets his gaze.

"God's law?" Smith laughs again, but it is not cordial. "You were gonna hang a kid because the Bible said to do it?"

Ricky tenses up in my grip, and just as I'm sure he's going to break free, Josiah pulls the .38 from under his jacket and puts it to Ricky's head.

"He's no kid, and yes, because the Bible says to do it."

Smith steps forward, and in the same movement extends his arm. He holds a small semi-auto to the side of Josiah's head.

"Put the gun down," he says.

"I can't."

"Why not?"

"This life's forfeited."

"What's that supposed to mean?"

"This evil must be removed."

Smith moves around Josiah so that the gun barrel is at his forehead now. He takes Ricky by the right elbow, but I still have him by the arm higher up.

"Let me take him," says Smith.

"It has to be removed."

"Let me take him."

"Not if you won't kill him."

"Has he murdered?"

"Probably. But he's raped and kidnapped. We told you that."

"If he's murdered, then I can kill him."

"You would kill a murderer?"

"I would have to if I found him guilty."

"Would you think me a murderer if I shot him now?"

"I would."

"And you'd have to shoot me?"

"I'm prepared to."

"Then we're both prepared. Liam..."

He motions with his head for me to step back and in a flash of comprehension, I see behind Josiah's earlier look. He has seen ahead to what must happen if he pushes through in this obedience.

"Put your gun down," says Smith.

"Can't...can't do that."

"You're leaving me no choice."

Josiah's jaws clench. He swallows.

"I suppose not."

The four of us, attached by hands and gun barrels, are a knot of drama, a tableau of small movements. I see the long tendons in Josiah's gun hand go taut, feel Ricky pull against my grip. At the edge of my vision Smith shifts his weight forward like he's bracing against something formidable. The still spaces around us where our neighbors hold breath have gone thin and stretch away from me like a shadowed audience before a bright stage. The only thing happening is us. In all the world there is only silence and these tensions of threatened action.

And then there is more, and things happen at once. I see the flesh of Smith's finger press into the trigger. I yell No and pull down hard on Ricky's arm. Both guns fire, but there is distinction in the sounds –

a boom, a crack, the workings of the semi-auto's slide. The sounds explode over me as I fall with Ricky. My ears ring. The tang of gunpowder is already in my nose, on my tongue. And something else – the sharp smell of burning hair.

Ricky kicks against me, springs up and away, and I see Josiah take a slow step backward. He catches himself as he settles onto his butt an arm's length from me and sits in the snow. His face is stunned and pale, his eyes perplexed. As I move to help him, he reaches for me but at the same time lays back like he wants to gaze at the clouds. There is a hole just above his left eyebrow, and now it begins to run. It runs out in two distinct streams, one right and one left. The snow under his head is reddening. The bullet has passed through.

As quickly as the shooting noises have cleared, shouts begin rising up out of the crowd, wailing cries from boys and girls. Smith is taken by surprise at this and moves defensively back toward his horse. Ricky, not sure of his status now, is there already, holding his scorched scalp.

Smith begins shouting. His deeper voice rises up just above the sounds of grief.

"This is...this didn't have to happen. None of this had to happen!"

He turns to the right and left, but no one listens.

"You see what a waste this is? You see this foolishness now?"

I have lifted Josiah's head out of the snow and cradle it in my lap. Blood and other matter falls from the hole at the back of his head. I press the end of my finger into it. It is an instinct. I am holding the life in. I look up and see my friends moving to me, and for a moment I think they will close in on Smith and have their vengeance, but they pass around him like he's a ghost. He turns and turns and looks for understanding, but he is a ghost, and New Alaiedon does not see him.

Part III

Chapter 37

I keep the next year in my warmest affections. It is a kind of matriculation into full life. Most of us see it that way.

We hold our first election. William Wagonmaker is unanimously voted in as sheriff. It is an unpaid office, and he has no opponent. It is a peaceful affair. We cast our votes with raised hands, and there is apple pie on little plates in our laps.

We have our first birth: Maya's girl on the fifth of July. I know the date because it is my birthday too. She names her Zora and tells us it means new beginning, but in what language, she can't say.

Our first weddings happen that summer too. Haddy and Isaac are married on one of the two rainy days that August. The next month, Mio and Jodi are wed. There will be two more weddings by Christmas: Libby and I are married in the township hall on a clear day in October. Oddly enough, I have no journal entry for it, but I can see a bouquet of fall colors at the edge of the fields as plain as if I were there now.

And on Christmas Eve, we gather in Josiah's stone chapel where he and Maya are joined in the first of many ceremonies there. It is less than a year since the shooting. Josiah is in his wheelchair, and his *I do* comes through his bride interpreter. He whispers to her a brief set of vows which she repeats to us falteringly.

Next to her stands Libby who holds Maya's daughter. She is 5 months old now, but as big as a yearling, dark-haired and happy. Marcellus stands between Libby and me. Maya has civilized him well, but he is still as live as a set trap, and I wonder if he'll make it through the ceremony or spring out the window we've left open to cool the room. As I pray a blessing and benediction both, I keep one hand on Marcellus's shoulder. At amen, I release him and out the door he goes. Before the bride and groom are done kissing, Luke has pulled the plugs on two big carboys of the season's hard cider. I see Josiah whisper something to Maya, and she stands.

"Drunkenness is a sin, Luke McHugh!" She yells with the inflection we have all come to know as Josiah's. Then in her own, she adds, "And so is spillin on these floors. Take your drinkin to the porch." At this the room erupts in laughter, and Josiah breaks out in a big, lopsided grin.

Though much has happened over the preceding 13 months, it is this happy day in winter that forever succeeds the memory of Josiah's head in my lap. It seems fitting. He was as good as dead. Blood and brains in my hands proved it. And now he lives. What other pieces to the story need there be?

Of course, it was not simple like that, and I would be a poor scribe if I conveyed that sense. There were dark days between. On the day of the shooting Josiah would drop into a coma. It was a mercy, as it relieved his agony, and we marked it as the start of the end.

More than once Maya or Libby or I would have to call on another to confirm that there was no breath, no pulse. And then just as we'd reach consensus and go to pull the blankets over his head, he'd cough or gasp or his heart would race and send a wave of blood through his veins. We quit giving up on him at some point and just assumed he'd come out of it for good. And he did.

Out of a sense of that due process that Smith had invoked, William, Jack, and I paid a visit to him and his followers in Lansing. He had taken up lodgings in the most fitting of places – the capitol building. He fancied himself the governor after all. To his credit, he does give us a polite few minutes in a stately, polished, high-windowed room. We ask about Ricky, but he eludes the questions, feigning to have forgotten the incident, or at least to have misplaced it in his vast and ancient memory.

Smith changes the subject by a degree when he brings up Josiah. He is fully aware of his survival. I assume that Jack has kept him informed of events in New Alaiedon. I've long ago stopped inquiring into his days' long trips east.

"I hear he's done some teaching even," says Smith. "That's quite a recovery. I'm glad of it. Very glad."

"What teaching do you mean?" I ask. I know that Josiah has been sought out by some. The story of the shooting has gone far and wide, and words like miracle and prophet have been heard on strangers' lips.

"Maybe consulting is a better word. I've been made aware that there's at least one other community who's taken on some of the same...*odd* beliefs that your Josiah espouses."

I know the community he speaks of. It is a group from Dansville. They'd sought out Josiah for advice on setting up court to try a thief, one of their own. They're smaller in number than us but further along in some of the structures of society: They have a restaurant. It serves one meal, supper, on Friday and Saturday nights, and we're told every soul in the town turns out for both.

"*Odd* beliefs?" asks William.

"Don't jump to the defensive so quick. You know what I mean. Josiah's ideas about the Bible being a source for law. For law today, in the 21ˢᵗ century. It's ridiculous. You have a sensational story, a miraculous survival, and rumors start flying, and suddenly everyone's flocking in to see the guru. First Alaiedon's got a court, now Charlotte. This spreading message of his just undermines real authority, the state's authority."

Josiah's teachings have gone farther than I think. Charlotte is twice the distance that Dansville is. I am proud at the thought.

"You keep saying state," says William. "Mr. Smith, you're one man. One unelected man."

He seems amused at this, leans back in his chair. He twirls a hand in a circle around his head, indicating the space.

"Look at this...We all know what a dead building looks like, don't we? Hollowed out, dry as an old husk, the outside flaking away. What did you see when you came in here today, boys? Another dead building? No, you didn't. This one is alive. There are people in these offices, people like your brother Jack. Jack has his own office here, did you know that?"

"I didn't know it," I answer, "but what's a building got to do with government?"

He raises his brows and smiles like he's conjuring up a forced patience with me.

"Why...everything. It's got everything to do with it. It's a solid thing that can be seen and touched. It's real. No one living in Lansing doubts that I'm the governor of this state, and it's largely because this building lives now. A government needs a home like a family does, like a soul needs a body."

"Like a cast-out demon," says William under his breath.

"What's that?"

William speaks louder.

"What do you plan to do with your government?"

"We have lots of plans. Be more specific."

"New Alaiedon has a government, Mr. Smith. We have agreements with other communities around us for mutual defense and assistance. And we will— "

" —assistance in what?"

"In protection."

"Protection of what, Mr. Wagonmaker?"

"Our bodies and our property. What else is there?"

He shrugs with his eyebrows.

"Go on."

"And we will continue in our...*odd* beliefs. So I'd like to know if your state government plans to interfere with our lives. Can we live next to each other and keep out of each other's affairs, Governor? Or will there be other incidents like last year?"

"Last year's incident was unfortunate, tragic really, but I don't apologize for it. I had to stop that, that...lynching. Sometimes authority requires the force of law."

"But you had no law to enforce!"

"Of course I did. The same law that said your daddy couldn't shoot you no matter how much he wanted to."

"My dad consented to laws like that, and it was right for him to. But that was then, and that time's gone. We haven't consented to any authority, not yours at least. We have a government. And that wasn't a lynching. It was an execution that came after a trial. We looked at the evidence, heard witnesses, found him guilty. We have a government where there wasn't one before. Now, maybe someday all the communities and counties and villages in our part of the world will decide that we need something more, but till then, we don't recognize any state, and we don't recognize you as legitimate authority."

Smith's eyes move between William and me. He holds each of us in a stare and then smiles.

"You'd make a good leader, William."

"He's our sheriff," I reply.

"Of what again?"

"New Alaiedon."

"Right. Two dozen, Jack? Was that number right, or were you being facetious?"

Jack, who has been silent, lifts his head and says, "Twenty six. We had a birth this year, Hailey and Nik McManus moved up from Jackson, and Jess Gibbs died of tetanus. So twenty-six now."

"Oh, well, twenty-six. Have you ever wondered, Mr. Sheriff, if your gifts are being used to their potential?" He shifts his gaze to me. "You too, Liam. We need sharp guys just like you to help lead a whole state out of this nightmare, maybe the whole country. Still have a few empty...Come in!"

The door opens, and a girl about ten or twelve brings a tray with vegetables, pickled eggs, a kind of wet cheese, and sliced bread.

"Dig in, fellas," says Smith. "Thank you, Alice."

"I didn't see any gardens in your front lawn," says William. "Who grows the food?"

"We have a whole group of youngsters growing everything we need. Have you been to Frances Park, on the river?"

"I used to play flag football there," I answer.

"It's a farm now. We grow all kinds of stuff – corn, potatoes, barley, wheat, raise pigs, chickens. Float it right down river. It's quite a system."

"That's a long walk from here," says William. "How do you tend it?"

Smith laughs big.

"No, I don't tend it. No one here has to. We've got...folks suited to that work, taking care of the farm. No, the ones working here, doing the work of getting this world organized again don't need to spend time on...farm chores, I'm afraid."

"What do the youngsters get in exchange for working your farm?"

220

"They get what all the kids seem to want. Same thing you want. Protection."

"Protection from what?"

"From everything they're afraid of. From hunger, from homelessness, from predators. But more than any of that from being alone. They like to know that they're part of something, part of something bigger than them. They're making a way for us to rise up. All of us, of course. I assure you, William, they're not only safe, they're proud of the part they play, and I'm proud of them too."

"Mr. Smith," I ask, "do you know where Ricky is or not?"

"Why do you want to know that?"

"Because we have our own to protect."

I am dogged now by thoughts of Ricky. He lives because of me. Josiah has not held my actions from that day last winter against me; in fact he's been the one to remind me that God's sovereignty ruled there too. Still, I want the process that we'd begun to be finished. My hopes today – though they were slim – were that Smith had done that.

He now sets aside any pretense of ignorance and leans forward onto his elbows.

"He's safe gentlemen. And I can assure you, your people are safe from him."

I can hear in the sharpened tones that we will get nothing more about Ricky.

"You make a lot of assurances," I say as I stand to leave. "You might just make a good politician after all."

Jack is under the spell of an old power, and for the first time since I've suspected it, I understand something of its attraction. On the ride back with William, in the still moments when my thoughts are disengaged, I catch myself thinking of that work that Smith spoke of. At a glance, it seems like dominion work – gathering up the loose things, bringing order of chaos. If the people of Michigan and the world beyond us feel they need a king to do that best, then why deny it to them? Maybe Smith really is the only grown-up left on the planet. That would make him the oldest alive now. Not that age makes a good leader, but there would be no denying he's the most experienced of us. Such thoughts have the appearance of wisdom and lend some luster to his offer to join him. But when I weigh Josiah's words against Smith's, I can't escape the sense that I've been offered work in a new tower of Babel.

I run these thoughts by William, and he concurs.

"As soon as he brought it up, I felt it too," he says, "but then I thought of Josiah with a bullet through his head, and that was it. Smith is a tyrant looking for a land to conquer, no matter how he dresses it up."

I feel foolish at William's assessment.

"You figured it quicker than I did."

"I'm the sheriff, remember? Actually, it took a while. I haven't stopped thinking about Smith since last winter."

"You think he's that bad?"

"I think he's human. Josiah's ideas about being on roads, that we're all moving down one or another and the roads go to particular places, these things ring true for me. The more I read, the more I keep my eyes open, I know what he means. There's no sitting."

"Climb or slide."

"Climb or slide."

I am surprised that William has gotten his own glimpses into the head of Josiah Mench. I had fancied myself an inner circle of one, but I don't begrudge him the intimacy for long. I know by now that Josiah is for the world, whatever parts of it he rubs against.

I soon learn that Smith has gotten good intelligence on Josiah's teaching activities. Because his house is more or less behind my own, I know when he has guests. And as it's customary to nose our way into any stranger's business, I usually drop in and introduce myself. The visits are increasing in frequency and in volume.

Josiah is parked next to the stove. Maya sits on his right. Across from them is seated one, two, sometimes three or four strangers. Bibles are open on laps. The students may be filling the margins or jotting into notebooks. There is a typical rhythm too. Maya speaks a short proposition. As she leans in to receive the next, the visitors jot. This goes on for an hour, sometimes longer, before the questions

222

begin. The topics range from the broad, like civil government and commerce and education, to the particular – what we do with our hands, what we read, family life, food.

It is a typical scene from the first days, but lately visitors come by the wagon-load. And some of the faces are familiar now. Those who've come and sat under Josiah's teaching bring back their neighbors, and these return bringing more, and so on.

Josiah himself confesses a fruition of knowledge and insight that he did not have before the shooting. He wonders if the bullet has activated parts of his brain that had been dormant; and he wonders if, like Davey Alvoord's unusual ability with numbers, the gift comes at a cost of other faculties. He never walks or smells or speaks above a whisper again in this world. He is not convinced of this trade-off theory – it is all speculation – nor does he think much on it. He simply sees his new insight as a thing to be pursued, shared as quickly as he can get the words out and to whoever will listen.

"I feel it as a sweet burden," he says to me one night after a group has left. "It is an exquisite thing, but heavy."

He reads widely and the authors tend to be centuries old, so he says things like that now. Sweet burden. Exquisite. He says it through Maya, of course. I've put my ear to his lips and carried on labored conversations that way, but Maya always hovers in the corners like a mother bereft of her young. I let her do the talking if she's around, and she usually is.

"It hurts to keep it" – still speaking of his burden – "but as quick as I let it go, there's more."

"The Gospel *is* great news," I point out.

"Of course, but I had no idea of it until these last years."

"What was it to you before?"

"It was simple, and perfect. And it was sufficient for the child I was."

"I don't understand. If it was perfect, how did you…how did it become – "

"You gave it to me, and you don't understand it?"

"I gave it to you?"

"Boji Tower. In the elevator shaft, you gave me the gospel."

"And it…worked?"

"It is the power of God unto salvation…of course it worked."

Here Maya steps away to tend to Zora's crying and leaves us in one of the long quiet spells that come so easily in Josiah's presence. I think back on that day in the tower. What did I say?

When Maya comes back, I see that Josiah has been looking at me. She leans in and takes the words from his lips.

"You didn't know what you were saying…In the tower…You kept fumbling and apologizing. But the gospel was as clear to me that day as if Christ had preached it…I didn't believe in God in the pit, and by the time they pulled us out I did."

"I said that God had to lift us out of our own trouble, and the Cross was the means."

"That's right. That's what you said."

"I'm paraphrasing."

"I know."

"I don't remember you changing after that, not much anyway. You learned to read."

"I was a live seed. The change was on the inside. . . It took the long heat and pressure to break me open. And now – the Word…"

"The word?"

"I had no idea…"

"What?"

"The Word lives…and it's the gospel of God on every page." He takes a breath and lets his eyes close for a moment. He opens them slowly and says, "His creation, His history…redemption of each of us. I thought once that the gospel was believe on Christ and be saved. And it is that…" Again the eyes close, and Josiah keeps talking. "But it's just the start. It's also true…to say the oak… the oak is in the…in the acorn…"

"Josiah, you're not – "

"Believe on Christ and be saved." He opens his eyes now, but he doesn't hear me. He sees beyond the walls, and he is alone in the room, just him and his God. Maya has to shift to reach his lips.

"It's enough….not a childish thing to think that something…so simple has so much…power…a wonder…a necessary wonder."

He is slowing down, and Maya is collecting the words into full phrases before speaking them.

"But that truth wants to move out into everything... Every part of us...every square foot of the earth...everything we are...and all we do and build...and the Word, Liam...the Word..."

Josiah's body has been slipping deeper into his chair and his eyes have rolled back. Maya takes his hand and feels the pulse in the long, thin wrist. She smiles at me nervously.

"This happens sometimes at the end of a long day."

"Is he ok?"

"He says he just tires out. I don't know. He won't slow down. He won't listen. There's a work burning him up inside and he won't slow down till it's done."

"Can I help you move him?" I ask.

"No. He'll sleep right there."

"Then I'll go now."

"Liam," says Maya as I'm putting on my coat.

"Yes?"

A knowing smile says I need to look for significance in the words that come.

"Thanks for being nice." And it doesn't take me long to remember that day by the 7-11.

"Sure."

"And thanks for coming for me and Marcellus. You and Josiah, I mean."

"You're one of us. You and Marcellus. Zora. We'll always come for you."

And these words will be the closest I ever come to playing the part of a prophet.

Chapter 38

It is about this time that Josiah begins preaching sermons on Sundays. I still have my notes from the very first. I wrote this:

"Cold, but sun shining. Luke, Chandler finished the pews. Room smells of cut pine. Chapel holds about 50. New Alaiedon is here, a big group from Dansville at the back, some I don't know in front row. Will talk to them after. Marcellus shut stove damper during hymn sing. Smoke filled the rafters. Hilarious. Jo preaching from Gen 1. Maya looks nervous..."

In the outline that follows, I have these as main points: *Creation, Image, Dominion.* As I write them now I am reminded that even in the early days these three words in close proximity have emerged as the theme of the life of Josiah Mench.

In the weeks that follow, he works through the book of Genesis in big steps, taking two, sometimes three chapters at a stride. Josiah wants to preach through the Bible. At this pace, preaching 50 weeks of the year, he will preach on Revelation 22 about twelve years from now. He relates this to us on a gusty, sleety Sunday morning in February and says it with a matter-of-fact briefness, as though he were announcing the hymns for the day. I realize that in Josiah's thinking, it is much the same. Of course we'll sing O Christ the Lamb of God and My Faith Looks Up To Thee, for the text today is on Abraham's testing. And of course the preacher will preach the whole word of God, from its beginning to its end. God is ending the long famine, and the people are hungry.

Preaching is only a part of his work. During a long thaw in March, Libby and I take letters from Josiah to seven new settlements in or near New Alaiedon. We accomplish the circuit in two days, spending the night in an empty camper at the western edge of Holt. The letters invite them to a kind of seminar that Josiah has entitled *The Covenant Life: Government of Self, Family, Church, State.* It is the first of several teaching events that Spring and Summer.

The newcomers have, like pioneers of old, come on hopes of a new beginning. As in those old times, the hope comprises whisperings, some true, some tall. There's a boy, so they've heard, who heals the sick. He preaches the Bible like he believes what it says.

He practically rose from the dead. He did rise from the dead. He speaks through a prophet as God did through Moses, as Moses did through Aaron. He lives in a place where the neighbors love each other. Whatever their collected vision of Josiah and his promised land might consist of, they all know that New Alaiedon is something unusual. New Alaiedon is a bright bloom rising up from a wasted field.

It is a powerful hope they bring.

Jack has taken the Johnson house to my east. For a time, we continued to share this one after Libby and I had married. I insisted. We didn't see much of each other anyway, so he tolerated the awkwardness longer than he might have otherwise. Since the time of the shooting, Jack has shifted his affections from here to Lansing in degrees. He stayed close for the months after, even aided some in Josiah's convalescence. But slowly, the draw of power had its way, and he began taking holidays in the city – a few days at a stretch, then a week, then the whole month of August. He claimed that the basement rooms of the capitol stayed cool as autumn the whole year round.

I thought I would lose him to Smith and his plans for statehood, but he'd always kept an address here. When he told me he'd be moving, I assumed the breach was complete. When he said it would be just a few hundred yards down the road, I held the few hopes I had left even tighter. I feel it's been a good time for the two of us – not quite a healed breach, but a truce of sorts.

I am on the sickle mower behind Bella and Champ. We're taking the alfalfa down for the second cutting. It is early July. The field lies between my house and Jack's, and I can see him there in the drive packing up his horse. I have just light enough in the day to finish this acre, switch out the mower for the rake, and get it into windrows. We all sense a dry stretch, and have grown inclined to work with the signs, even when it is nothing more than a collective hunch.

That's the thinking that keeps me from braking the team and walking the 200 yards to Jack's drive, and so I am ashamed when I make a turn and see him there at the row's end waiting for me.

"Hey, I was just about to…" I lie, and make a long fuss over stopping the mower. I walk to the roadside where he's hitched the big Walker to a no-passing sign.

"Headin out," he says.

"The city?"

"Yeah."

"How long this time?"

"Few weeks maybe."

We begin ambling up the road in that direction.

"Can you water my vegetables?" he asks.

"The twins can do it."

He stops in the road and squats. He reaches down and pulls up a handful of dandelion greens growing from cracks in the centerline.

"I shouldn't be talking to you," he says. "Not about this, but…" He shakes his head, and then rolls the greens into a cigar-shaped wad.

"About what?"

He bites off one half and gives the other to me. It is a familiar gesture and ties us to better days. We both chew for a few seconds before he says, "Josiah."

"What about him?"

"He's causing some trouble."

"What trouble?"

In the last year, Jack's physique has grown into a compact version of our dad's, a knottier, wider version. I notice this as he bends for more dandelion.

"You can guess what trouble, can't you?"

"I can guess it's something Smith doesn't like."

"It's got nothing to do with Smith, everything to do with the world. He's putting thoughts into people's heads. Jo, I mean. Crazy thoughts. And that's not what we need right now."

"Who's we?"

"Survivors." He waves his hand in a circle and glances around. "The world."

"What do we need?"

"We need order, Liam. We need to get back what the dying took from us. Order and government and…things! Electricity and cars. Don't you want that back?"

"We have order right here if you'd take time to notice."

"But not everyone else does. I've been through most of the state, and it's not like here. It's not like what you and Jo think it is. This place is different than just about any other I've seen. They live like animals out there, and not that far off either."

"What do you think Smith is doing about that?"

"He's doin things. He knows about it, for one. He's learning and taking names and setting up ways that we can communicate and share things."

"And then what?"

"What do you mean?"

"And then what does he do? After he's learned everything and has a list of names."

"Then he…he governs. He leads."

"Right.."

"What?"

"You're talking about . . . authority."

"Maybe. I mean, yes, authority. What else would I be talking about?"

"Authority doesn't come out of thin air. It comes from God or it's taken by force. Which kind is Smith using?"

"It's the right thing, to have a leader."

"And whose law will he use to lead?"

"We'll make new laws."

"Now it's we? Are you gonna consult us on that? Ask New Alaiedon or any other town how they want to be led?"

Jack turns away again. This time he does not hide his frustration, but spits and stands arms akimbo, facing my half-mown hayfield.

"Like it or not, we need leadership," he says proudly.

He is imitating. He's heard the words spoken that way.

"Strong leadership now more than anything will lead us out of this disaster. It's like Washington, and we needed him then. And like

229

Churchill when England needed someone. We need a leader now more than ever."

"What do you think this strong leadership is gonna be used for?"

"For our own good."

"It's for Smith's good, not for yours or mine."

"You're wrong. You don't see it all. You're hidden away in this little…this shelter of a place, that's why."

"And Smith sees it all?"

"He sees a way out of this."

"So does Josiah."

"Josiah's ways are foolish and old fashioned."

"He sees more than you know."

"He sees too much and he needs to watch out."

He shoulders past me, takes hard strides back to his horse.

"What's that supposed to mean?"

I am shouting at his back.

"I knew I shouldn't talk to you," he says over his shoulder.

I catch his arm as he's untying the lead and turn him to me.

"What's Smith planning?"

Jack yanks himself from my grip and climbs onto the horse.

"Tell Jo that Smith is gonna come talk to him. Tell him that he needs to be…flexible. There's more going on around us than his little kingdom. It's bigger than you think is all."

"Jack?"

I put my hand on the pommel. He won't look down at me, but he doesn't move the horse either.

"Why are you here?" I ask. "In New Alaiedon, I mean."

"I live here."

"No, you don't. You stay here, but you don't live here."

"Just tryin to make straight paths for folks, Liam. Just like you're doin."

"Like in Catastropolis?"

He looks at me hard and quick, but tries to cover his surprise with a cough.

"Cata what?".

"Catastropolis. You wrote about it in a letter last year, said Smith had sent you there to do what you just said – make straight paths. Just made me think of it is all. Wondering how it went."

"Cassopolis. It went fine."

"You talked about rebels."

"Did I?"

"Rebellious is what you said."

"I remember. Yeah, they were that. Tried to hoard their wheat crop when kids were going hungry in Dowagiac."

"So you took it from em?"

"What else could we do? They were starving. Skin and bones. It was like a concentration camp, and these – *asses* in Cassopolis wanted to sell it. Had plenty for themselves and wouldn't share, so…we…helped em do the right thing."

"And you went ahead of Smith to keep an eye on things, to make straight paths for him."

"Turns out I have a gift for it."

"That's why you're still here, isn't it? To keep an eye us?"

Jack puts the horse into a walk.

"Or maybe it's just Josiah you're supposed to watch."

He ignores me. I see his knees flex and the horse begins to trot. I am jogging to keep up, but at the very edge of running.

"What happened to those kids in Cassapolis, Jack?"

But he is done with me. He breaks into an easy canter that I try to match, but I am running uphill in work boots.

"What did Smith do to em?"

I yell at the shrinking horse and rider.

"Tell Josiah not to cross him," Jack yells back.

As I watch him descend the backside of our hill and fall out of view, I tell myself I am not seeing my brother leave. I tell myself that I watched him do that last year on his overloaded sulky, but that I have yet to see him return.

That night I find Josiah and replay the conversation with Jack. He shrugs at it is all.

"What can I do?" he says. "Smith has only the authority God gives him, and he can't even use that to kill me right."

231

Josiah is not afraid. But as Maya speaks these words to me, I do think I see a blush of worry on her cheek.

As late summer turns to autumn, thoughts of Smith are once again buried in the rush of activity that precedes cold weather. We pick up the rhythms and duties of the season – harvest, canning, firewood, butchering – like the tune and words of an old song. And the work eats up the days in batches, taking weeks at a swallow. There is only the Sabbath rest to anchor us to the full year's plodding pace.

It is winter by the calendar but snowless when Jack does finally return. But where he'd at least been an occasional figure at the edge of things before, now he keeps to himself in his own house or fields for all but that work requiring many hands. Even then he is withdrawn and slow to meet our eyes. If he is still acting as spy, it is a poor one.

I give it no thought. I have written him off as lost. And that's why I'm surprised when he shows up at my back door, pressing his pale face to the glass and scaring Olive, just as Josiah had done to me years before on the night his dad died.

He is tormented, and I see right off that he's come to unload some burden, so I sit him next to the fire and have Libby take the others to the upstairs rooms. But instead of unloading, he directs our talking to seasonal worries – he is afraid the hay was too wet when we gathered it; last year's snow load on his barn roof broke two tresses, and he forgot to fix them when he had the chance; he didn't put up enough beans for the winter.

I reassure him that the hay was fine and offer to help him tomorrow with the tresses once I get the smoke house fired up. Becka put up too many beans, just like last year. He takes these with a nod, then seems at a loss for a new topic, as though we'd used up the supply quicker than he'd planned. He now faces directly the reason he's come but is reluctant to pick it up.

"Just say what you came here for, Jack."

"It's heavy."

"All the more reason."

"It's hard to start is all."

"Just start, and see if I follow."

Jack pushes his chair back, away from the fire and takes his boots off. I push mine back too so we are shoulder to shoulder. The sun is low in the trees to the west, and the dark will come quick as a drawn shade. I go to light the gas lamp that sits on a shelf behind us, but Jack stops me and says to let it go dark.

A half hour later, when the sun is gone, and the only light in the room is the orange glow behind the glass door of the stove, he begins.

"I found Ricky," he says.

I wait for more, but he doesn't speak. And as I turn to ask where he found him, I can see by the glow of the fire his shoulders rise and fall and lines of shining tears on his face. Through sobs he says, "You shoulda killed him, Lee. You shoulda killed him dead."

Chapter 39

The story comes out of Jack in bundles, like letters without dates, and we work together to put it back into the linear.

Last summer, after Jack had tried to persuade the Cassopolis group to share their wheat crop with the kids in Dowagiac, Smith himself had come with a small army and commandeered most of it at gunpoint. That's what Jack had meant when he warned me about Josiah crossing him. He didn't yet know about Ricky.

"I didn't think about Cassapolis starving, but they were gonna hurt that winter. I saw it all through my anger. Stupid. But I was thinking more clearly by the time we got to Dowagiac so when I found out Smith was selling it to them, I asked him about it. How we'd taken it from Cassopolis because they wanted to sell instead of share it. He was ready for that, though. Gave a little speech, how we needed to protect the dignity of everyone, especially those we're helping. And I bought it all."

This year the groups in both towns had worked out an agreement on a crop swap – corn for wheat. When Smith's informant in

Dowagiac reported it, he was furious, but instead of sending Jack, he sent one of his new lieutenants, a boy who'd shown some initiative in getting the most from the Frances Park farms. It seems Ricky had found a calling.

"And I was hoping Smith would punish him," I say, "even if it was just a gesture. Gave him a job instead."

"He did start there as a punishment, at least until Smith could figure out what to do with him or let things blow over. But Ricky split a guard's skull with a shovel and just stepped right into the job. Guards got all the food they wanted, and there wasn't anyone to argue with him. By the time Smith found out about it, Ricky was running the place, and doing it so well that Smith looked the other way about the guard."

"I thought it was a farm."

"A work farm. A prison farm."

"For criminals?"

"For anyone Smith can't find a better place for. Anyway, he figured Cassopolis was just the job for Ricky. At first I wondered why he was so interested in the place. It was a long way from Lansing, but then it hit me. There was something about the way they'd set things up there that when this adult walked into town to save them they didn't fall down at his feet like the others had. They didn't need him, and that was unacceptable. Same reason he hates Josiah. So he showed them how much they needed him. But this year, when they tried to cut him out of it entirely, he sent Ricky.

"A week or two after, I was working late in the west-end rooms. There's a long wall of windows that let in the sun. I like to work there at the end of the day. I was in a cubicle when Ricky came in with one of his soldiers and sat down on the other side of the partition to smoke. This kid hadn't gone with Ricky and he was asking about his trip to Catastropolis. Had heard some things.

"Ricky told him how he knew when the winter wheat was being delivered, how they'd waited that morning at a bend in the road for the wagons going north. How they'd grabbed em all up like nothing, that it only took one shot. Hit the first driver in the belly and the others surrendered as soon as his screaming started up. They put em all – six or eight boys – into a shed and locked it. But when they got back to the wagons, Ricky decided he never wanted to have to make another trip to Catastropolis so he goes back to the shed and has his boys pile brush and deadfall wood all around it. The gut-shot kid was still yelling and moaning, and when the other boys on the inside figured out what Ricky was up to, they all started in, screaming and banging on the walls trying to break their way out, but there's no window on it. They shriek and plead, but Ricky is only excited more by that. I can hear it in his voice as he tells the story, and I can hear the kid next to him snickering and asking what next, what next.

"They find some old gas in a garage nearby and douse the pile. Ricky put a lighter to it. Stale gas burns wood just fine. Ricky describes how the whole shed rocked with the kids inside trying to get out. And their screams…One of them finds an axe and breaks the hinges on the door, but Ricky had thought of that and piled the wood even higher on that side. And when they managed to swing the door in, out they came through that flame, choking, their clothes burning. They burst through it like wild animals. But as they came out and hit the ground, the rest of Ricky's boys had their fun and shot them up like they were shooting distempered cats set loose from a barrel.

"I told Smith what I heard. He was shocked, and I was glad to see that. But when I saw Ricky a few days later, sitting in the atrium with his friends, messing around like they were kids on a playground, I knew that Smith wasn't gonna do anything about it. And I knew I had to leave."

We sit in the dark and let Jack's words and images dissipate over the next few minutes like clearing smoke.

"He'll come for him," says Jack.

He is present with me again and sits upright in the chair, lighter with the burden lifted.

"But I don't think he'll send Ricky. We all know him on sight. So maybe Smith comes himself. Or maybe he's got others like Ricky who'll do that sort of thing."

Jack slips his boots on and ties them. He leans back again.

235

"My guess is he'll be quiet about it. No army coming in to wipe us out. He thinks New Alaiedon's a cult. Josiah's cult. Kill the leader and we all scatter."

As it turns out, Jack is right about some things and wrong about others. Smith does come quietly, but not for Josiah — not directly at least. And he's not worried about Ricky being seen. He sends him at night.

Chapter 40

For the weeks following we set a guard on Josiah around the clock. The job often falls to me. On Saturdays, Josiah makes his only request of us — we fold the wheelchair and set it and him in one of the small farm wagons, and let Bella tow him up to the chapel. On this Saturday in late December, the ground is bare and hard, The breeze under a low, gray sky is warm for the season and carries moisture. We all feel snow on the way.

Josiah is preaching from Leviticus, and the text for that week is chapters 9 and 10. This is where the Lord accepts an offering from Aaron and then strikes dead his two priest sons, Nadab and Abihu, for tinkering with the temple worship. It is a frightful passage for Josiah, who sees himself as a kind of priest.

He sits in his usual spot at the back of the room, his chair parked under a high table that holds an open Bible just under his nose. I am at a window on the opposite wall, facing northeast. The trail leading down through the woods to the big hay field west of our houses is now a road, cut last spring to let wagons up. I am there transfixed, watching the dark ground go speckled and then white in an hour's time. The air is thick with wet flakes the size of quarters.

Twice during this slow entertainment, Josiah bangs on the table to call me over. Both times I put my ear to his lips and hear him ask me to pray. First for him, that God would accept his sermon. And then for us, that God would let us hear it and not strike any of us dead.

There are only two times that I hear Josiah speak above a whisper. One is at his death bed. The other is this night.

The sun has set, and the reflections of the candles in the room have blotted out my view of the falling snow. The work I've brought has long been finished – new edges on the hatchets and bit axes, final touches to a poem I wrote for Libby's birthday. I am somewhere deep in a Patrick O'Brian novel when I hear Josiah bang again. When I reach him, he is slumped low in his chair. His eyes are closed, and I think he's dropped into one of his fits. But when I go to take his pulse, his eyes snap open. He doesn't see me. He closes them again and begins whispering. I listen, but these are not words for me. He is talking so low and fast that I can only make out the occasional word – mercy, God, Maya, father – the rest is a garbled static.

The whispering attenuates to silence, but his lips don't slow. He is praying frantically. Now and again his eyes open for a second or two, focus somewhere high in the room, outside of it maybe, then close. It is not the gentle swing from wakefulness to sleep, but a clenching action, as if he is opening and shutting the lids with all the muscles in his head. He seems both drawn to and repulsed by something in his visions.

When I reach out a hand to bring him back, his lips stop suddenly and his eyes open. His throat convulses and he spits out a single word in a croak of monumental effort.

"Zora."

Now his eyes do focus on me, and he pulls my ear to his lips. "Go," he says. "Something's wrong."

"Leave you?"

"Lay me down…I have to fight now…God's hand against him."

Before I can ask another question, I hear him whispering familiar words. Psalm 59. I lay him face down on the floor. He is light as a child but still has all his height. He spreads his hands out in supplication, but then grabs me by the ankle.

"Finish," he says to me.

I hear the word clearly, but I can't help asking, "What did you say?"

"Finish it. He thinks he's safe."

I lay his coat over him and walk to the door. As I open it to step out, I look back at him. He looks terrible in his helplessness, but I find myself thinking that I would not want to be an enemy of Josiah Mench tonight.

I step into Josiah's house through the back sliding door. A gas light still burns in the kitchen, and I can see that nothing is out of place here. I yell Maya's name, but the house is quiet. I yell for Marcellus. Nothing. I search the rooms and find them all empty.

At the front door, the inside mat is wet. Someone who'd walked in snow has been here within the last hour. In front of the house I confirm it. Three sets of tracks lead off the front porch, but beyond the steps the falling snow is erasing them.

I look up to Jack's house. There is a light on in the family room. He and Nate are there reading or playing board games by the stove. The walk across my field and up to the house will take several minutes. I'll have to wait while he puts his things on, gets his gun, walks back with me to my house to put on the skis. The snow is falling and filling the tracks as I stand and think.

I decide to go alone.

A quarter mile east of my house, the track of a single horse between sleigh runners angles across a yard and onto the road. I follow it up Stillman to Dobie. The horse stays on the road. There is not snow enough to take a sleigh through fields. It turns onto Sandhill and from there keeps a straight course. The full moon is obscured by cloud, but the snow-covered ground reflects the scant light. As I cross Okemos road two miles up, I can just make out a dark shape in the field of white.

My body is tuned for this. We hunt year round, and driving a wounded whitetail for miles is easiest on skis. I realize I am gaining on the horse when it turns left into an old Christmas tree farm. I have childhood memories of the place – hayrides and hot chocolate, Dad cutting the tall, skinny douglas firs that Mom liked – but it is a pine forest now, the walking rows are closed up and suited only for rabbit.

At the edge of the pines is a long straight drive. Just this side of it is an old farm field. Between it runs a drainage ditch skirted on both sides in a tangle of growth. I turn into the field. The thin layer of snow gives little cushion over the rough ground, but I find a deer trail that runs straight south. I use the woody ditch as cover and ski the half-mile length of the field, into a stand of hardwood.

I am directly east of the house. The ditch is cut into the woods too but is shallower there and dry. I take off my skis and lie in the hollow. The house is modern, brick, expensive once. Now it is just too much space to heat and has sat unoccupied these seven years.

Until tonight. Through tall, narrow windows that overlook a crumbling pool and patio, I see the flicker of fireplace light. In the same room a table holds a cluster of candles. Now and then – at intervals of a minute or two – a shadowed form eclipses the light. Otherwise there is nothing to see from my vantage.

I decide to move closer, get a look through one of the east windows. But as I lift myself, I am held there by a weight on my back.

It is a boot.

It is Ricky's.

"How'd you…?"

But Ricky can only laugh and spit out, "Get up."

Chapter 41

I can see just fine now. My wrists are behind me, tied to a kitchen chair. Across the table from me sits Smith. Ricky is to my right. The house seems to have gone untouched. Its distance from the road has protected it. The area we sit in now – high-ceilinged, uncluttered and neat – is open to the kitchen and a living area. But for the dust that hangs stubbornly in the dim light, it could be a picture of good living in the time before.

"Where are they?" I ask.

"They're fine," says Smith. "Nearby."

"That's kidnapping," I say. "You stole them."

"Punishable by death, I hear."

"It is."

"Josiah's not here to prosecute this time."

"I wouldn't be so sure of that."

I imagine him stretched out on that cold chapel floor, praying something fiery on the heads of these two. Smith looks puzzled but waves it away.

"I have to say, Mr. Taylor. You had us worried. The snow was not in our plans. It's a good thing this place had a sleigh. What are the odds?"

"Odds were good. It was a Christmas tree farm."

"Well then."

"Worried how?"

"We thought you might lose our trail."

"You mean you – "

"Yeah!" barks Ricky. "Watched you the whole way."

"We have a message for him," says Smith. "For Mr. Mench. The message is stop."

"Stop what?"

"Stop spreading it. His heresy."

"Or what?"

"Or we strike him where he's most vulnerable. Just like we did tonight. And you can remind Josiah that it was just one this time. I have a whole legion of Ricky's I can call on."

"You're sending them back?"

"Of course," he says. "I'm not a monster."

"All of them? Back with me?"

"Take my message. Make it clear. They can both return with you, unharmed."

"Both?"

"The girl and her son. Both of them. I assure you, it's no trick."

At these words I realize two advantages. Smith doesn't know that Ricky took the boy. My guess is that Marcellus jumped ship at the first low branch, and Ricky doesn't want to make his boss angry.

240

The other is that neither one knows that Zora is Ricky's child. I need time to consider.

"You said they're fine?"

"Yes."

"Let me see them."

Smith looks me over coolly, and without taking his eyes off me nods to Ricky.

I run through the contingencies but see too many variables. What will Ricky do with the knowledge? Will he care? Keep the child for himself? I can't imagine that, but Ricky keeps surprising me. And what will Smith do? My last thought before Ricky comes in leading Maya with Zora in her arms is Josiah telling me to finish it tonight. I have no clear way before me, but I do see that one hunch shines brighter than the rest.

Maya throws herself at me, squeezing Zora between us. "You came," she said.

The next words are exchanged quickly.

"Told you I would."

"You did."

"You trust me?"

"Mm."

"You trust me, right?"

She pulls away and looks at me perceptively.

"Is Jo praying?"

"Yes."

"Then I trust you."

I look past her to the table and to Smith.

"What about Marcellus?"

Smith pivots his head slowly left and right as he says, "Who is…Marcellus?"

"He's Maya's," I say. "Ricky took Maya, Zora, and Marcellus tonight. Where is he?"

"I never took no kid," says Ricky as he points to Zora. "Just that one."

"He's lying," says Maya. "Marcellus was with us. He jumped out at the cemetery."

241

"You stupid b—"

"Shut it!" Smith pounds the table. Then he speaks with a slow, steely evenness.

"It was a simple job. Get the girl and her kid."

"Don't ever tell me to shut—"

"Don't ever forget who you work for. And don't forget that I still hold your keys. Without me you're nothing."

As if to echo that, Ricky says nothing, but from where I stand I can see a clenched fist holding a leg of his chair. Smith gathers his attention again and turns it on me.

"So there you have it. The boy is probably home safe by now."

"And Ricky's ok with Zora leaving?"

I ask it as matter-of-factly as I can.

Smith glances at Ricky, but now it is Ricky's turn to wonder at me. He is about to speak when Smith interrupts.

"It's not his decision. He's—"

"Why would I care if the kid goes?"

"It's not your decision."

"He asked if I cared. I said I didn't care."

"Go to the garage."

"What?"

"Go to the garage and water the horse. We're leaving tonight."

Ricky doesn't move. He turns his head to Smith who meets his stare. I see Ricky's other hand reach for the leg on the right side. He wraps his fingers around it and squeezes.

But now Smith does something remarkable. He leans back very slowly and uncrosses his arms. Then he slides down in his chair to a point where his eyes are just lower than Ricky's. Smith is tall, and it takes quite a slouch to get there. His expression is flat, his voice even.

"Just do your job, Ricky. I'll do mine. The horse needs water. Take her to the creek and I'll get the wagon ready."

Ricky's hands let go of the chair and meet in his lap. He rubs them as if he is squatted over a fire.

"Fine," he says. He stands quickly and the chair catches on the tile slamming over. The sound frightens Zora who begins to cry.

"You're leaving?"

I put the question to both of them. I want to keep Ricky in the room.

"That's right," says Smith.

"You gonna take us back?"

Smith laughs at that. Ricky shakes his head and starts toward the kitchen.

"There's no food for the baby," I say.

Ricky keeps walking, and Maya yells.

"Hey!"

He stops and looks back.

"What?"

"He said we have no food for the baby."

"Why should I give a shit about his kid? He tried to blow my brains out! What's the matter with you?"

"He's not Josiah's kid," says Maya.

Ricky is shadowed in the darker kitchen and stands silent, but Smith lets out a hiss of disgust, and then he laughs.

"You screw that up too? You really are one stupid—"

"I said don't call me that!"

Ricky steps toward now him with a fist pulled back, but before he can start it forward, Smith puts a boot in his gut and he folds over, gasping.

"Get out," Smith says to us. "Start walkin."

Maya sets Zora down and begins working the knots on my wrist. But Smith is out of patience. He steps around the table, puts his boot to my chest and shoves me back. The chair and I slam to the floor.

"I said get out."

With Maya's help I stand. The chair is still a part of me. We shuffle to the back door that opens onto the pool deck. But before we step out, I turn. Again, I think of Josiah in the chapel, then I play the card that will either finish it or bring his family to harm.

Ricky is up to a sitting position now, but his face is set against something he fights. I shout to make sure I punch through whatever evil is building up.

"Ricky!"

He turns a stony glare at me.

243

"Zora is not Josiah's daughter. She's yours."

As he takes in my words, his limbs seem to go loose. He looks to Smith, back to us. His mouth opens, closes. He looks at his hands. Then he puts his free one on the floor and pushes himself up, standing with a ponderous strength. He stumbles once, and when he is square on his feet, he raises the gun at the three of us.

"Come here...all of you. We...I...I gotta...figure this out."

Maya's hold on Zora is fierce. Her feet are rooted. I have to lean against her to move them both toward the table. As I do this, I see Smith's hand slip slowly to a pocket.

As I slide back into the room, I whisper to Maya.

"Hit the floor when I say."

Ricky's gun is on us, but his head is swiveling between us and Smith. Smith times it well, and in a movement as quick as a jab he raises the little pistol above the table and fires.

I yell *down* and pull Maya to the floor. A hole opens up on the shoulder of Ricky's shooting arm, and his gun drops. Smith is still firing, but the table is between them now, and Ricky is under it. Smith shoves the gun under and shoots blindly. Bullets skip off the tile, crack into the windows near us. Smith grabs the edge of the table and flips it, thinking to expose Ricky, but as the table lifts, Ricky stands with his own gun leveled.

He fires once. There is a dark, misty puff at the back of Smith's head and the white countertops behind are instantly speckled. He falls straight down into a heap..

Ricky is breathless, turns to Maya and says, "Come here."

She doesn't move.

"I said come here. Bring Zora."

"You can't have her. You'll have to kill us both first."

I lean toward her.

"Maya, Jo's prayin. Don't stop trusting me now."

I put my shoulder against her back and push. She goes halfway to him but stops.

"Give me a promise first," she says to Ricky.

"I don't owe you nothin," he says.

"I throw myself off the first bridge we cross and take Zora with me – and you know I can do it. Give this to me."

Ricky sets his teeth and says, "Let's hear it."

"He lives," says Maya, pointing to me.

"He'll follow."

"No. He'll promise you he won't."

"Get in the sleigh."

"Why? What are you doing?"

"I'm just gonna tie him up. Get in the sleigh."

"I don't know where it is," says Maya, looking past Ricky to me.

Ricky pushes Maya and Zora toward a door at the back of the kitchen, but I don't wait to see what he has in mind for me. I take two big steps – me and the chair – toward one of the broken windows and launch myself through it.

Chapter 42

As I hit the glass, I hear a shot and feel a burning across my thigh. The lawn at the side of the house slopes down. I roll with it and come to my feet. The chair is still with me, but broken now. It gives in places and lets me run. Another two shots whistle by to my left, and then I am at the wood line and can hear Ricky swearing and pushing the broken glass from its frame.

I run to what looks like the thickest part of the wood, and I hear Ricky shout again. He is out of the house, shouting my name into the darkness. As I move deeper in, his voice fades. Either he's not following, or the woods are swallowing the sound. I don't want to slow, but I won't run either; the fears of being shot and going eye-first onto a branch are fighting it out. I am shuffling almost sideways through the trees and then I am tackled hard from behind.

A voice from on top of me is shushing me quiet. It is Jack's. He already has a knife out and is working at the ropes on my wrists.

"How'd you find me?" I whisper.

Jack points up to a black lump attached to the nearest tree. It blinks at me. It is Marcellus.

"Good boy."

"You ran right to us. What happened?"

"Never mind. If Ricky doesn't come for me, he'll leave right now with Maya and Zora. He thinks I'm hobbled."

We find my skis, and work back to the road. I am right about Ricky leaving. There are already fresh tracks going west up Sandhill. I don't know whether or not he thinks he's safe, but he must think he's got a jump on us, and he's trying to stretch it out. He is trotting the horse, and making good speed. The snow has stopped, but the long road ahead is empty of all but the track lines.

"Let's hope they slow," I say.

"He's run that mare hard."

We follow the tracks for two miles to where they turn north onto Hagadorn. This stretch of road is hilly, and but for their tracks, there is no sign of them for the next quarter mile.

"They're moving faster than we are," says Jack. "And you're bleeding."

My jeans have a six-inch rip across my thigh, and inside, a strip of skin the same length and as wide as my thumb is gouged out.

"Can't feel it," I say.

We ski at the pace of a long hunt, one that we can maintain all night. The tracks cross Jolly road, and a mile farther Mt. Hope. At Service Road, the tracks turn west. We are entering the campus of Michigan State University. It is the first time I've been here since the Dying. Covered in a few inches of snow, the broad space, with its huge dorms and buildings, looks much the same, but the vacancy here is as evident as in any moldering neighborhood.

We follow them north, up Bogue, and have just come through a roundabout. We are at the east side of the business school when we hear from up ahead the familiar sound of a horse neighing. Here we leave our skis and sneak along the building to its north-east corner where a car has long ago rammed into it. An old growth of weed and grass have subsumed it so that it seems a part of the ground. As I peer

246

through both back windows to get a look at the river, I see two clothed skeletons enfolded in the backseat. Another in the front has collapsed and broken in two, occupying driver and passenger side both.

Ahead of us, the Red Cedar crosses under the road, cutting through groves of high, straight maple and beech trees. The autumn has been wet and the river is high. To our left, a couple hundred yards downriver and on the opposite bank, the horse has been unharnessed and led to the water. Ricky sits on a boulder nearby watching Maya and Zora huddled in the sleigh higher up the slope on the flat sidewalk. Ricky has taken seriously Maya's threat to jump. She is bound by her wrists to one of the front seats.

"What now?" asks Jack.

"I don't know. I wish you'd brought a rifle."

"I came to break you out, that's all."

"I know."

"We could get closer."

"How?"

Jack looks east, upriver.

"Float down. He's facing away from the water. One of us floats to pistol shot, stands up, and..."

"Water's too fast."

"It's sort of fast."

"You'd freeze before we got home."

"I was thinking you'd do it."

I think through our assets.

"He doesn't know you're here."

"So?"

"So if he saw me by myself, he'd just think it's me. He wouldn't be surprised. He said I'd follow him."

"Ok. What do we do with that?"

"I don't know, but it might be something."

"He's down low from us. If one of us went back a little, came up the road on the far side, staying low, he could cross the bridge without him seeing."

"Then the other one could come down to the water."

"Distract him."

"While the other one gets close and – "

"Blam."

"And you're the sharpshooter."

Jack doesn't answer, so I repeat my words.

"Right," he says finally.

Jack moves quietly back along the building and crosses the street. There is a shoulder that slopes away allowing him to move in a crouch unseen from the river on the other side. But at the bridge the ground rises level with the street. There, he lays down and crosses on his elbows. I too am down low, and at the mid-point of his progress I lose sight of him.

I have looked away from Ricky for the time it's taken Jack to get that far, and when I look back I see that he's leading the horse to the sleigh. I move around the car, through the bike racks and around a wild tangle of saplings. The trees here are pulling all the open spaces back toward them, back into forest.

I crouch behind one of the thick trees closer to the water and watch Ricky back the mare between the poles of the sleigh. She won't cooperate. She lifts her head, then swings it. Her hooves shift and stomp at the concrete walk.

"Whoa!" Ricky's voice echoes along the open space and water. "Hell's wrong with you?"

He is trying to connect line to bridle cheek, but the mare won't submit. She is spooked.

Ricky is on the opposite side of the sleigh facing me. He doesn't see Jack crossing the road and ducking behind a huge evergreen shrub, but neither does the horse. It is not Jack that spooks her.

Suddenly she kicks at the poles, the left then the right. Ricky has only gotten one strapped in, and when she breaks into a gallop the sleigh lurches with her, crabbing along the walkway until the horse veers off and down the slope. The sleigh rides on one runner, tilting. Maya is screaming, hanging tightly to the high side as though willing the lifted runner to the ground. The slope levels toward the water, but the sleigh is still canted, the left runner cutting hard into the snow.

I see that Jack wants to move closer. Ricky is looking toward the runaway sleigh in amazement as Jack darts to another clump of shrub. But now Ricky has turned and is looking north for whatever frightened off his horse. He is looking in Jack's direction, but I fear he is still out of pistol shot. If he sees him now, things could go any which way.

I will give Jack an opening. I step out from the tree and shout Ricky's name.

He swings around, the pistol leveled at me.

"This doesn't have to go any farther," I say. "Let them go."

He looks at me as if I'm speaking Mandarin.

"They're mine. Go to hell."

Jack moves from the shrubs to a tree, then to a low sign that looks from here like a headstone. Ricky thumbs back the hammer on the revolver.

"I'll send you there myself."

I am behind the tree before two shots slap into the bark. When I peak around again, I see Ricky with the cylinder open, dropping into it more rounds. There is pain on his face. *Now*, I think, *go now*. But Jack only watches. I try to occupy Ricky so he can move closer. I sprint to the nearest tree, but I've forgotten about my leg. It's stiffened since I took off the skis.

Ricky fires once. The bullet creases my coat across the shoulders.

"Got you in the leg, huh?" he yells over. "I wondered. Saw your blood trail in the snow. This is fun! Do this all day!"

I jump out from the tree like I'm going to sprint again, then jump back. He doesn't fire. I want to keep him turned my way. I do it again, and this time he shoots high. The bullet passes above me with a low hiss through the heavy air.

I peek around the other side of the tree to get a glimpse of Jack. He has moved and is standing in the open, his gun drawn.

"Come on out!" shouts Ricky. "I'm getting bored here."

"You better get your horse!" I shout back.

"You came this far. You're not gonna stop followin. I should probly just kill ya."

I wait for the shot from Jack's gun.

"Your mare's half-way to Lansing by now!"

Again, I peer quickly from behind the tree. Ricky is looking downriver for the sleigh, but then his head turns slightly north. He is scanning the landscape of tree and building. It is a wondering look that will lead him to Jack who stands twenty paces behind him. It is a deadly range for Jack's ability. He needs to shoot now. Ricky's gun is warm now, and when he does see Jack, he won't pause.

Ricky shifts his feet again. His eyes are intent on the many shapes and shadows of masonry, ivy, and wood. He has the patient look of a hunting cat. He shifts farther, and his peripheral vision picks up something solid in the white space of the snowy slope. His head turns quickly, and he raises the gun at Jack.

"I'm a better shot than you," says Jack.

I step out from the tree now.

"Shoot him, Jack!"

"Shoot me, Jack. You better."

Jack seems to take closer aim. His shoulders tighten, and his head lowers. I wait for the shot, but even from where I stand across the river, I can see him swallow hard. I can see him hesitating.

It is all Ricky needs. He switches the revolver to his right hand, raises the arm with his left and takes aim.

I hear the shots as one report, but removed as I am, I can see both guns fire in the same frame of vision. Ricky's, then Jack's, almost overlaid. Both shooters stagger back a step, Jack falls, Ricky comes forward again and drops to a knee. He has switched gun hands again and inspects himself but keeps his aim on Jack.

Jack is on his back, one knee bent up and swinging slowly back and forth. His hand is on his belly or low on his chest. His gun lies next to him in the snow.

Now Ricky stands. His free hand is deep inside his coat. I never find out where he is shot or how bad the wound is, but he seems to be holding the side of his chest as though the bullet has only creased him there. He walks to Jack and stands over him. Some words are said that I never hear. I see Jack's hand move once toward the gun, and then Ricky shoots.

250

I am out from behind the tree, at the water's edge. I don't remember walking there or if I've come out before or after the shot. I don't remember going to my knees. The water, just a few feet below me, is black and deep. It moves fast. Jack and I canoed this river with Dad once. It didn't move that fast then. A diffused, gray light is rising as the dawn comes.

I've yelled something but I don't know what. I know this because I recall Ricky spinning around at my voice. He grins and walks down to his side of the river. We are facing each other across the swift, dark water.

"Josiah will come," I say.

"What?"

"Josiah will come for them."

"The cripple?" he asks. "Let him come. You can all come after me. You see what happens. Smith thought he could use me like a tool. He got his. And Jack…well, Jack didn't have what it took to live in either world, yours or mine. So I ain't worried about the cripple. You thought I forgot, didn't you?"

"Forgot?"

"About Marcus. That you owe me for him."

The image of the rotten foot and the bloodless incision rises up dark and hazy, like something conjured.

"Blood for blood," I say.

"You do remember."

"You've got your blood now. Let them go."

"Now you're forgettin again. Man, you're a disappointment. You tried to kill me. And tryin's good enough. Josiah himself said that much."

"You think you're safe."

"Who will he send now? Seems like he's runnin out of help. Yeah, I guess I do feel pretty safe."

"Just let them go."

"First find. She was mine long before she was Mench's."

I look downriver. The horse and sleigh, Maya and Zora are nowhere in sight, and they're on the wrong side of the river.

251

"Don't worry," says Ricky. "That old mare won't go far. Likes her warm stall too much. So why don't we just do this. Too much talk."

Ricky shifts to his shooting hand. He winces as he raises it with his wounded shoulder.

I look back at Jack's body on the slope, and I feel the heaviness of our separation. It's built up around me over the last two years, but now it is gathered and sits squarely over my back as a grief that holds me down. The adrenalin to drive my fight or flight is a useless vapor under it.

Ricky fires. A bullet thumps into the dirt between my knees. My hands are on them, turned upward. I think of Josiah. Is he still there on the chapel floor bringing his petitions to God?

He fires again. I feel the slug slip between elbow and ribs. I might be hit, but I feel only the tug at my clothes. I look up at Jack again. I am drawn to him. I want to swim across and speak last words to him. I stare long enough that my vision begins to go out of focus and then it wanders and is fixed in the middle distance. But then a movement draws my eye farther back at the edges of the scene, and my vision focuses there. Something black has crossed one of the many white gaps between objects. Deer maybe. There is another movement like it, straight north, deeper in the campus.

Ricky shoots again. I feel a burning pain on my cheek and ear, like someone's laid a hot piece of iron there. I wince at it, and through watery eyes see the dark movements emerge from the scene. Four or five long, lithe shapes are bounding in and out of the trees now, leaping over the patches of high weed and shrub. Two more catch my vision farther west. They are wheeling around the corner of vine-covered building. They are dogs, big and long-legged, and dark.

I wipe my eyes, blink, wipe again and can see them clearly now. I see them, and they are not dogs. Seven years, I think. If I get home again, I can tell Josiah that it's taken seven years for them to come down from the Mighty Mac.

Ricky has trouble holding the gun. He switches to his left hand now but takes too much time to steady his aim, and before he can pull the trigger again, we both hear the deep drawing breath and the soft thump of the pads. He turns around, and like Jack, he hesitates, as

252

though he first needs to take in the reality of what he sees. His arm brings the gun up again, but the wolves' easy motion masks their speed and before he can shoot, two sets of jaws close silently on both of Ricky's arms. He lunges backward for the water as a third, the killer, goes for his throat.

And now the air is full of sound, the growl and whine of the wolves rising to a frenzy. Within it there is an airy, wheezing note of terror from Ricky's open neck, and before the killing noises have stopped, two more from the pack join in where they can find flesh to gain a purchase and to tug their prey back to flatter ground where they can work together.

I'll not tell the rest. It is a matter for the shadows, and it is a vision I've long since tried to blot out.

Chapter 43

When I was young, my mother would contrive ways to mark the year's high days with the hope that tradition might take root. Each Lenten season, it seemed, she'd find a devotional book or a new way of reading the Bible. At Christmas she would trot out some new activity or odd food to eat, but whatever the attempt, it always seemed to lack grip. Nothing ever continued beyond a year or two, and our Easter or Christmas would revert to unadorned affairs. If she were with us today, my mother would be proud, for we keep not one but two traditions.

A year after Jack's death, Josiah arranges for all of us – his family, which has grown to five, and mine which is now six with Nate and the twins – to hitch up the same dun mare and make the same trip to the Red Cedar. At the south side of the river where God had set his boundary and said to Ricky and to the wolves, no farther, we listen as Maya reads the Christmas story. Herod thinks he is safe in his position (Josiah reminds us that the worms get him at the height of his pride), and from him the child Jesus – and his whole church, subsequently – is delivered.

For twelve years, Josiah leads the pilgrimage to this place. Then, on one hot July day he is visited by a fever that never leaves him. The old wounds on front and back of his now gray head go livid, as though some latent reaction has come to life, and for the next two weeks he descends into imbecility.

The Lord is kind in this. Josiah is spared the madness that we've seen in fevered brains. More than that, for two full days in the midst of the decline, his voice is restored. He doesn't know those gathered around him, and he is detached from the circumstances, but he delights us in lively descriptions of whatever image or recollection presents itself to his mind's eye. As his voice dims again, so does his dreaming vision, and he finishes his last days in a sleep.

He leaves us on a Monday, just minutes after the dawn. Of his death, Maya reports nothing remarkable, just a long expelled breath and stillness. She says it was as though he'd just stepped out their front door. Such was the threshold between this world and the next in Josiah's theology – no barriers at all, just a shift in perspective, like Jesus eating fish then stepping through a wall, the greater subsuming the lesser.

The tradition of the pilgrimage to the Red Cedar has persisted, and since that first trip, I have not heard the Christmas story without a profound connection to God's providence over me. It was never again a vague sentiment, but always a flesh-and-blood tale for me and mine. Yes, there is still weeping for Jack and for Josiah, but from it has come an ever-surmounting joy over God's hand in things.

The other tradition rises from the same spring of gratitude. The first work of planting begins next week, and the signs for a bountiful year are plenty. I finish this manuscript in the late morning hours, and tonight my neighbors will meet in Josiah's chapel, as we do every year at this time, to pray for the growing season and to feast on the best of last year's harvest.

There will be music. My granddaughters share Libby's gifts in the forms of violin and dulcimer. Indeed, that whole generation seems unusually proficient in the making of joyful noise. There will be food too, of course – the choicest cuts from the smokehouses have been saved; the hard cider is at maturity and said to be unusually dry; and each kitchen will attempt to outdo the next in pastry or confection. And at this celebration I shall add to the revelry the news that at least one part of New Alaiedon's history has been set down and preserved.

These traditions, I think, mark well the favorable boundaries God has set around us. By them we remind ourselves that he protects his own by telling the bullet where to strike and the wolf where to hunt. We tell each other that he provides for his own by making the seed to grow and the rain to fall. Within the circuit of his care we are called to godly work. These are the things to remember. As Josiah would say at the end of a sermon, "These are the ancient stones, not to be moved."

I, Charles Liam Taylor, have read the above history, and but for minor errors and edits am satisfied with it. I have arranged to have the oldest of Luke McHugh's daughters draw up three copies, one for New Alaiedon's archives – the old broom closet at the back of the lending library in the township hall – one for the library itself, and one for Maya Mench to keep for her own posterity. The original will pass down to the eldest surviving sons of my own clan.

The ways of heaven and hell, of blessing and curse stand before us yet, and I fear that if the story of our beginnings is forgotten, then the way of Smith will find us; our nature seems shaped to it. So let us not forget, but instead go on in the undimmed light of God's word, letting it strike us plain, as Josiah taught us to do.

Printed in Great Britain
by Amazon